Promise of a New Beginning

Sweet with Heat: Weston Bradens

Addison Cole

ISBN: 1-948868-19-9
ISBN: 978-1-948868-19-8

PROMISE OF A NEW BEGINNING

Cover Design: Elizabeth Mackey Designs
Cover Photography: Lindee Robinson Photography

WORLD LITERARY PRESS
PRINTED IN THE UNITED STATES OF AMERICA

A Note to Readers

When I met Jack Remington, I knew he needed a very strong, secure woman who would allow him to honor his feelings about his past, and who would love and adore him for the strong, generous man he was. Savannah Braden is that special woman. I hope you love them as much as I do.

About Sweet with Heat Books

Addison Cole is the sweet-romance pen name of *New York Times* bestselling author Melissa Foster, and Sweet with Heat titles are the sweet editions of Melissa's award-winning steamy romance collection, Love in Bloom. Sweet with Heat novels convey all of the passion you'd expect to find between two people in love without any graphic scenes or harsh language (with the exception of an occasional "damn" or "hell"). If you're looking for a more explicit romance, pick up the steamy edition of this title, *Bursting with Love*, written by Melissa.

Within the Sweet with Heat series you'll find fiercely loyal heroes and smart, empowered women on their search for true love. They're flawed, funny, and easy to relate to. Characters from each series appear in future Sweet with Heat books. All Sweet with Heat books may be read as stand-alone novels or as part of the larger series.

Sign up for Addison's Sweet with Heat newsletter to be notified of the next release:
www.Addisoncole.com/Newsletter

For more information on Sweet with Heat titles visit
www.AddisonCole.com

Chapter One

THE ENGINE OF the small bush plane echoed in Savannah Braden's ears as they flew past the edge of a colorful forest and began their rapid descent into the Colorado Mountains. September didn't get much prettier than the bursts of red, orange, yellow, and green foliage that were quickly coming into focus. The plane veered to the right and then cut left at a fast speed, shifting Savannah and the other five passengers in their seats. Savannah clung to the armrest and looked out the window as the dirt landing strip came into view. *The too-short landing strip.* She'd been flying her whole life, and never had she seen such a short landing strip. *Great. I'm going to die before I even get to clear my head.* She hadn't seen the pilot's face before takeoff, and now all she could make out was the back of his wavy brown hair, thick headphones over his ears, and a black T-shirt stretched tight over burly shoulders. She wondered what the man who was going to kill her looked like—and why the heck he thought he could land on a freaking Band-Aid–sized landing strip.

The couple in the seats across from her appeared far too calm in their hemp clothing and scuffed boots. They'd introduced themselves as Elizabeth and Lou Merriman, and they were traveling with their six-year-old son, Aiden. They seemed pleasant enough, but Savannah couldn't help staring at the reddish-brown dreadlocks that hung past their shoulders, as if it weren't hair at all but thick, clumpy strands of the same prickly rope her father used back home on his ranch in Weston, Colorado.

"Do you mind?"

"Oh, sorry," Savannah said, pulling her clenched fingers from the armrest that separated her from the younger, sullen man next to her with his tuque pulled down low and his shoulders rounded forward. He hadn't said two words to her the whole flight, and she wondered if he was escaping civility and had sworn off the opposite sex, too.

Savannah's emotions were fried after finding her on-again off-again celebrity boyfriend, Connor Dean, in bed with another woman—again. Her eyes stung as she remembered the evening their relationship had come to a stormy end. *A final end.* On the recommendation of an article she'd read about how to reclaim one's life after a breakup, she'd taken Friday off from work to go on this stupid four-day survival retreat that the article touted as *The best way to regain your confidence and reprioritize your life!* The timing had been perfect. There was no way she was ever going back to Connor, and in order to accomplish that, she had to get out of Manhattan. Connor was just charming enough to make her forget that she deserved more than a guy who still acted like a high school jock, always looking for the next good lay.

The plane descended rapidly, and Savannah pulled her seat belt tighter across her hips and closed her eyes. She felt her stomach flip and twist as the engines rumbled in agony. Then the wheels of the plane made contact with the dirt and the brakes screeched, sending her forward, then slamming her back against the seat.

"Ugh!" Savannah's eyes flew open. Everyone looked at her: the granola couple and their young son, and of course attitude boy sitting next to her. Everyone except Josie, the young woman who sat across the aisle behind Elizabeth and Lou. She had her eyes clenched shut and was white-knuckling the armrest. *I should have sat next to her.*

"Sorry," Savannah said with a cringe.

Savannah looked out the window, and the landing strip was a good fifty feet behind them, but at least they were alive.

Maybe this was a mistake.

The engine silenced, and the other passengers stood and stretched. Elizabeth and Lou collected Aiden and smiled like they hadn't just seen their lives pass before their eyes. *What is wrong with them?*

Josie squealed, "We made it!"

The guy with the tuque shook his head, and Savannah prayed she wouldn't pass out from her racing heart.

The pilot craned his neck as he glanced back over his shoulder and removed his headphones. Savannah caught a quick glimpse of the most handsome, rugged face and piercing eyes she'd ever seen before he turned back around and she was left staring at the back of his thick head of hair again.

A thrill rushed through her.

Maybe this wasn't a mistake after all.

In the next breath, she realized he was the man she'd seen in the airport when she was racing to catch the plane and had fallen on her butt, sending her bags flying across the corridor. He'd been cold and standoffish—and far too handsome.

I'm screwed.

PILOT AND SURVIVAL guide Jack Remington sat in the cockpit of the small bush plane with a knot in his gut. He'd been so conflicted about where his life was headed that the last thing he needed was for his body to suddenly remember what a woman was. For two years, he hadn't looked at a single woman—had never felt a twinge of interest since his wife, Linda, died in a car accident. Then, today of all days, when he was running late and already pissed after having driven past the scene of her accident, he saw that gorgeous woman with auburn hair fall in the airport. He'd wanted to walk right by her, and when she rose to her feet, he just about did. But when he'd gotten close enough to really see her, he noticed a competitive streak in her eyes, and behind that determination, he'd seen something soft and lovely. He gritted his teeth. *I don't need soft and lovely.* He pushed the image of her away and allowed his anger to turn inward again. Once he felt the familiar fire in his chest, he opened the door.

The first thing he did when he stepped off the plane was touch the earth. *His earth.* Jack considered every blade of grass, every tree, every bush, and every stream on this particular mountain to be his personal possession. Not in the legal sense, but in his heart. It was this land that had helped him to heal after Linda's death. Well, that was a lie. He hadn't yet healed. But at least he was capable of functioning again—sort of. He still couldn't sleep inside the chalet in Bedford, New York, that he and Linda had shared. He returned to the house only once or twice a month to make sure partying teenagers or vandals had not broken in. And on those nights, he slept on the back deck and showered in the outdoor shower. He'd spent most of the last two years in the safety and solitude of his rustic cabin—the cabin even his family didn't know about—set on two hundred acres in the Colorado mountains.

Last night, however, Jack had stayed at the chalet because of the early flight this morning, and before leaving the house, he'd sat out front with his motorcycle engine roaring beneath him, reminding him that he was still alive. When he'd reached the bottom of his steep driveway, instead of turning left as he always had, he looked right toward the site of Linda's accident. *Eighty-seven paces. Less than three seconds from our driveway.* Flashes of painful memories had attacked, and he'd gritted his teeth against the gnawing in his gut. *It should have been me.*

In one breath he wanted to leave behind the guilt and the anger of having lost her and move forward. He missed seeing his brothers, sister, and parents. He missed hearing their voices, sharing the details of their lives, and he even missed their loud family dinners. In the next breath he pushed the idea of finding a path back to them into the dark recesses of his mind and allowed the familiar anger and guilt to wrap its claws around him and seed in his mind, tightening each one of his powerful muscles, before he revved his engine and sped away. Jack didn't know the first thing about moving on, and no matter how much he might want to, he wasn't sure he ever would.

He turned and surveyed this weekend's group of yuppies-turned-survivalists with their nervous smiles and eyes that danced with possibilities. He'd been running survival training retreats as a means of remaining at least a little connected to civilization, and though Jack had plenty of money, the extra income made him feel like he was a productive member of society. He looked over his new students, silently mustering the energy to be civil and patient.

Lou and Elizabeth Merriman stood behind their young son, Aiden, each with one hand on his shoulder. *A granola family.* He knew from their registration form that they lived a green lifestyle, Elizabeth homeschooled little towheaded Aiden, and they were vegans. They were there to make an impression on their young son. He'd had enough granola families attend his survival camps to know that they all thought they had the answers to life and health, when the reality was that they had no answers at all. It wasn't the answers about life he was concerned with. Jack had yet to meet anyone who could give him the answers that really mattered—the answers about death and how to deal with it.

He shifted his gaze to their left. Pratt Smith, a brooding, brown-haired artist and Josie Bales, a dark-haired beauty who taught second grade for a living. Josie played with the ends of her hair. The two twentysomethings who were traveling separately—he, for kicks, and she, to find herself—were trying to pretend they weren't sizing each other up as potential hookups. *Great.* Jack didn't have anything against young couples getting together, but he sure wished they'd do it on their own time. His job was to bring them out into the woods, show them basic survival skills, and send them home feeling like they were Bear Grylls. The last thing he wanted to deal with was a couple sneaking into the woods seeking privacy and doing something stupid like getting lost or being eaten by a bear. And he didn't need the painful reminder of how good it felt to be in love shoved in his face every time he looked at them. Love had been off his plate since Linda died, and he wasn't looking for a second helping.

Now, where in the blazes was the woman who'd called and signed up three days ago? The pushy one who wouldn't take no for an answer when he'd said registration had already closed. He saw boots land on the ground on the other side of the plane. She was taking her own sweet time, and they had work to do. *She'd better not be a Manhattan prima donna.* He'd had enough of those whiny women to last a lifetime, and he never understood why they enrolled in the weekend courses anyway. He forced the thought away. The students paid for a guide, not a critic.

He planted his boot-clad feet in the dirt and opened his arms. "Welcome to survivor camp. You'll notice that there is no formal name for my program, and that's because emergencies don't come packaged neat and tidy with cute little names. We're preparing for survival. I've spoken to each of—"

"I'm sorry. The landing was a little nerve-rack—"

The woman from the airport made her way around the plane, cutting him off midsentence. As she flashed a broad smile at the others, he remembered her name. Savannah. *Savannah Braden.*

She glanced at Jack, and their eyes caught. Her smile faded; her green eyes narrowed. She was taller, curvier, and even more beautiful than he'd realized when he'd run into her at the airport.

Jack clenched his jaw. He cleared his throat and looked away, then continued.

"I'm Jack Remington, and I live on this land." His eyes drifted toward Savannah and he paused, then looked away and began again. "I served eight years as a Special Forces officer with the United States Army. I can get you in and out of here alive if you listen and work together. Let's keep the land clean and the attitudes friendly."

His eyes swept over Savannah in one quick breath—a breath

that carried hope rather than the breath that had carried the pain of loss when he'd left his home earlier that morning. She was tall and slim with auburn hair and a killer body. *Too darn pretty.* It took all his focus not to stare, and out of his peripheral vision, he watched her brush dirt from her jeans. He allowed his eyes to follow her hands as they stroked her lean thighs, and when she glanced up, he dropped his eyes to the ground. *Cowgirl boots?* He shifted his gaze back to the rest of the group, silently chiding himself for looking at her in the first place. How on earth was he going to keep himself from looking at that gorgeous woman? *I must be losing my mind.*

"Let's get your bags. Then we're going to hike up the mountain to base camp. If you need to go to the bathroom, the forest is your toilet." He ran his eyes across the group, stopping short of Savannah to avoid getting lost in her again.

"Cool," Aiden said.

"I think so." Jack smiled at the wide-eyed boy. "I assume you all met on the plane? Got to know one another?"

"Yes, we introduced ourselves." Lou pushed a wayward dreadlock from his shoulder. "Well, most of us, anyway." He shot a look at Pratt.

Pratt stood with his hands in his jeans pockets, looking away from the group. *Great. Another prick.* Even as the words ran through his mind, he knew he shouldn't be too quick to judge. Some people would consider Jack a jerk, too, and they'd be right. Some broken men were jerks, and that's just the way it was. He made a mental note to try to talk to Pratt, but for now, he had to nip this crap in the bud.

He narrowed his gaze and spoke in his favorite cold voice— the one he usually reserved for beautiful women. He didn't have time for them any more than he had time for a kid with a bad attitude.

"See those woods behind me?" He turned sideways, as if clearing a path for Pratt's eyes to follow—which they didn't. "There are bears, snakes, poisonous plants, and all sorts of scary stuff out there. You may find yourself in need of someone's help, and if you're a di—unkind—to the group, no one's going to rescue you." He crossed his arms. "I suggest you introduce yourself."

Elizabeth and Lou exchanged a guarded glance. Then they each put a hand on Aiden's shoulder.

Jack hadn't caught his poor choice of words quickly enough. He knew he was being harsh, but bad attitudes caused accidents, and there was no room for accidents in his camp.

Pratt clenched his jaw and held Jack's stare. His tall, lanky body was no match for six-four, two-hundred-thirty-pound Jack Remington, but the hurt and anger in Pratt's eyes looked familiar, and Jack knew he wasn't contemplating anything physical. A spear of guilt ran through him. There was no turning back now. He'd taken a hard line, and backing down would leave him in a position of lesser authority.

Savannah touched Pratt's shoulder. She narrowed her beautiful green eyes and set them on Jack. Her smile remained on her lips, but behind the facade, he saw a challenge. His pulse sped up.

"Why don't we just call him John for now?" she suggested in a firm, nonnegotiable tone.

What the heck are you doing and why? As he pondered her motives, he couldn't help but notice the way her jeans clung to her lean legs and curved over her hips, then dipped in at the waist. And the blasted tank top she wore was now spotted with perspiration and clinging to her chest.

Look away. Look. Away.

His eyes would not listen to his mind, and he stared right back. "This is my show and I run it my way. He's part of the team or he's out," Jack said.

Savannah took a step forward and pulled her shoulders back. "What are you going to do? Fly us all back to the airport and return our money?"

He met the challenge in her eyes with his own heated stare. "Yes."

SAVANNAH'S CHEST CONSTRICTED, and a fist tightened in her stomach as jerky Jack Remington stared her down with his black-as-night eyes. He looked like Chris Hemsworth and acted like Alec Baldwin. A wild combination of sweet and bad boy that sent a flutter of sensual excitement through her. She was not going to look away. She'd gone up against meaner wolves than him in the courtroom. She crossed her arms and planted her legs like her brother Rex might do. She'd mastered the Braden stance for the courtroom and on the rare occasion of going head-to-head with some lowlife on the subway. She could do it just as well as her brothers, even if her legs were feeling a tad rubbery at the moment.

Remington didn't budge. His face was a stone mask of clenched muscles and strength. Savannah felt the worried gaze of the others upon her. She was just about to give in when Pratt stepped forward.

"Pratt, okay? I'm Pratt Smith. Twenty-eight, an artist, and I'm here to…heck…I don't know. Do something different for a few days. Now can we get on with it?" He looked away from the group.

Jack's stare had not wavered from Savannah's, and she knew that if she was the first to look away, just like in court, he'd win. She remained steadfast, though it was difficult not to allow her eyes to drift to the muscles that bulged in his arms.

Pratt picked up his backpack and headed for the woods. Jack grabbed Pratt's arm and held tight, finally disengaging from his eye lock with Savannah.

"No one hits that trail ahead of me," Jack said.

Savannah fumed. It was one thing to gain control of a situation and another to be a jerk all the time. Obviously, Pratt was going through something emotional. Why couldn't ice-hearted Jack see that? Jack wasn't her problem to fix, and by the sound of him, he needed a lot of fixing. *I'm here to fix myself. That's enough of a challenge.*

"We have safety instructions to go over, itineraries, and guidelines. Settle down, and let's get started." For the next hour, Jack explained the danger of the mountains—including everything from wild animals and poisonous plants to treacherous cliffs and harsh weather. "You will each carry your gear and your tents. If you can't carry them, you won't have them to use. If you don't like the food, then you'll drop a few pounds while you're here. Memorize the laws of three. A person can live only three minutes without air, three days without water, and three weeks without food. Got that?" He didn't wait for an answer. "Now, for the rules. Rule number one: Never put anything in your mouth without clearing it with me first. Rule number two..."

As he explained the guidelines, trail safety, trail hygiene, and other details Savannah was sure were important, she couldn't concentrate. She couldn't help but scrutinize their leader. He spoke with a deep, commanding voice—one that made her wonder what it might sound like in a dark bedroom. No matter who or what he looked at, whether it was one of the others in the group or a plant he was pointing out, his gaze was so intense that it made Savannah shiver. Attached to his belt was a long leather sheath with a black knife handle sticking out of the top. *Danger.* That's what came to mind when Savannah looked at Jack Remington..Even as she drank in every inch of his rock-hard body, he never shifted his eyes in her direction. In fact, he hadn't looked at her since the one quick inspection he'd given her when she'd first come around the plane. Savannah was used to men taking a second glance at her. At five nine, she was hard to miss, but to not even garner a second glance? That rubbed her in all the wrong ways.

"How far are we walking today?" she asked.

Jack answered while looking at Aiden. "Three miles, and the only one that's allowed to get tired is Aiden, and if he does, as we discussed"—Jack lifted his eyes to Lou and Lou nodded—"his mother or father will have to carry him." He put a large hand on Aiden's shoulder. "You hear that, buddy? If you get tired, your parents will have to carry you, and that's a hard job, getting up this mountain, so can you be strong?"

Aiden nodded.

Jack's cheeks lifted, and his smile brightened his eyes and softened his harsh edges. "Of course you can."

Maybe you do have a softer side.

He addressed Elizabeth and Lou. "There's no cell service up here. We talked about this, and you know the risks. It's your job to keep track of Aiden at all times, not mine or anyone else's. Got it?"

So much for the softer side. You really are a jerk.

Ten minutes later, they were making their way through the dense woods. Though they entered through what looked like a trail, the flattened landscape had faded fast, and Savannah had no idea how Jack could possibly know where they were headed. They were in the midst of two hundred thousand acres with no cell phone service with a guy who didn't know empathy from apathy. How on earth would she heal herself when being led by someone like him? She reminded herself that one of the main reasons she'd chosen this particular camp was that there would be no cellular service. If Connor couldn't reach her, he couldn't try to lure her back. *Whether Jack's a jerk or not, I'm going to succeed, and when I get home, I'll be stronger for it.*

She'd never been particularly lucky in love, and after watching four out of five of her brothers find their forever loves, she longed for more. If her brothers knew how Connor had treated her, they wouldn't care that she was a thirty-plus-year-old woman who could take care of herself. They would go after him without an ounce of hesitation—then they'd console her. It was after the consoling that worried her, when they'd look at her with pity in their eyes, not understanding how their bullheaded, smart-mouthed sister could ever allow a man to treat her that way. That was why she never told them. *It's complicated.* That had been her stance on her relationship with Connor.

Other attorneys had gone so far as to call her Bulldog Braden because she was relentless in the pursuit of right and wrong. *So why can't I be that relentless when it comes to my heart?* This trip was supposed to help her climb back into the armor she'd once worn and never allow herself to be treated that way again. She eyed Jack Remington as he pushed through thick branches and stomped over fallen trees. His muscles glistened against the afternoon sun. *So what if he's hot? He's probably a*

Chapter Two

THE SUN BEGAN to drift toward the trees as the afternoon slowly turned to evening. The first day out, or what Jack liked to call the Day of Impact, would give him a clear indication of where each student stood, both mentally and physically. So far, they all seemed to be faring well, including Aiden. Jack glanced behind him at the boy, who held on to his father's hand like a security blanket. He was a cute little guy with bright blue eyes and white-blond hair. His gut twisted, and a familiar lump formed in his throat as he thought about the unused nursery in his chalet. The night of the storm came rushing back like shards of glass being driven into his heart. He never should have let Linda leave the house, but he'd been so wrapped up in his work that he couldn't—*wouldn't*—pull away.

A shriek pulled him from the memory. He whipped around with his large knife in hand, knees bent. Josie huddled against Savannah's side, her arms pulled in close, fear in her eyes.

"She thought she saw a snake," Savannah said as she brushed Josie's black hair from her shoulders. Josie's skin was milky white, and her eyes were a vibrant blue, giving her the appearance of a porcelain doll...in jeans and clunky hiking boots.

For a moment, Jack didn't move. *A snake? You freaked out over a snake?* Elizabeth and Lou stepped in front of Aiden, as if that might protect him from the snake. Jack looked down at the knife in his hand. *Or protect him from me?* Pratt stood off to the side with a smirk on his thin lips, shaking his head. Jack stole a glance at Savannah, who didn't look shaken up or amused. She had one hand on Josie's back and the other on her cheek.

"It's okay," Savannah assured her.

The kindness in Savannah's voice spiked a memory in Jack. *It's okay. I'll go.* Linda's voice crept through his mind. He turned back around and ran his hand through his hair. *Love you*, Linda had said before walking out the door. He hadn't even answered her. He'd made a noise. A grunt. That familiar love-you-too noise that couples make when they're too busy to give their spouse the time they deserve. Two long years and not once did a woman's voice ever bring back that moment. What was it about Savannah Braden that had his mind twisting in ways it never had and his body noticing the beauty of a woman again for the first time?

He turned back around to the group and shoved his knife back into its sheath.

"We're in the woods. What part of that don't you understand?" Jack knew he was fuming at himself in the memory, but he couldn't stop the hurt from coming out as anger. "Was I not clear back there? Snakes live here. We are the interlopers. We are the villains, not them. If you shriek, that tells me there's a bigger danger—a bear, a coyote, a madman—something that we really do need to worry about. A snake will slither away." As he turned back to continue the hike, he noticed that the smirk had left Pratt's lips, replaced with a furrowed brow. His eyes shifted across the woods. He wanted to know what expression Savannah wore, but now not only did he have to avoid eye contact, it was apparent that he needed to avoid verbal contact as well.

"You don't have to be such a jerk. She's young. She got scared. Cut her a break."

He took one step and stopped at the sound of Savannah's aggressive accusation. He let out a breath and turned back around, meeting Josie's eyes instead of the challenge in Savannah's. He calmed his voice enough to speak instead of yell. "Let's try to keep the screaming to a minimum."

JACK IGNORED SAVANNAH all afternoon. When she'd challenged his answers, he'd shaken his head, and when she'd asked questions, he hadn't looked at her when he answered. Now Savannah sat on a log at what would be their base camp, struggling to put together the poles to her tent, and there was no way she'd ask him for help. What was she doing here anyway? She grew up on a ranch with a house, working toilets and showers, and horses to ride up mountains. She had no camping experience, and she hadn't had time to research how to construct the darn tent before leaving for the trip. When she'd purchased it, she had been so busy worrying if leaving town was the right thing to do that she'd completely zoned out and hadn't registered a word of the salesman's lengthy instructions. She hadn't had time to do much of anything before making the impetuous, stupid decision to go to survival camp. Why hadn't she listened to Max, her brother Treat's new wife? She should have gone to one of the many retreats they owned instead of coming into the wild to live like a Neanderthal alongside this mountain madman. When Jack had spun around with that enormous knife in his hand, all she could do was remain silent and still. Her mind had screamed, *Run!* but her legs had been rooted in place. And the way his eyes had changed in an instant—as if the slightly crazy woodsman had turned into a wounded puppy and then morphed right back into the angry man—had rattled her.

Elizabeth, Lou, and Aiden had their tent fully constructed. Pratt helped Josie with her stakes, and Savannah wrestled with getting the poles through the stupid little rings of vinyl. Each time she got one in, another would slip out before she could secure the two pieces together. She plopped down on a fallen tree and let out a loud breath, then took it all apart and started over. *I could be in a five-star resort right now in Hawaii, or Nassau, or anywhere else other than these stinking woods. Maybe I should call someone to come pick me up. Treat would charter a plane to rescue me.* Savannah and her brothers had significant trust funds, though none of them flaunted their wealth. But at a time like this, an extravagant expenditure seemed like an acceptable thing to consider. She shoved one pole through the loop and finally secured the other to it, pinching her finger in the process.

"Darn it," she snapped and put the hurt finger in her mouth.

Jack looked over with a pinched and annoyed look on his face, then turned and walked away.

Jerk. Wasn't he supposed to be teaching them? How was this teaching? She'd show him if it took all night. She struggled with the next set of poles, determined to get the tent set up without any help.

She heard Josie tell Pratt, "We should help Savannah."

Pratt headed in her direction.

"I got it. I'm fine," she snapped. Savannah was capable of doing anything they were. She was just having trouble focusing. She glanced at Jack standing with his back to the group, his hands on his hips while he looked out over the ravine below, and narrowed her eyes. *It's you.* She'd lost her edge when she was with Connor, and Jack's attitude wasn't helping. It was time she got it back.

In the courtroom, she'd know her next move by watching the jury's reactions to her opponent. She scanned the other tents, noting their construction. She didn't need instructions. She needed only to focus. In the next few minutes, she was able to visually match the construct of the other tents. She was done being the helpless woman. *I'm reclaiming my mojo, so watch out, Jack Remington. There's nothing I can't do.*

Jack turned to address the group. The sun illuminated his wide shoulders, and the way the land fell away behind him, his six-four frame looked larger than life.

Why do you have to be such a jerk? She gritted her teeth, wondering if she'd be the only Braden unable to find love. *Men suck. Not that I'm looking.* She was done with them, but it would be reassuring to know that nice men still existed.

Jack's deep voice boomed through the campsite. "Grab your canteens, and if you want to wash up for the night, bring your towels. We're only going down to the stream once tonight." Jack's eyes darted all over the darn campsite except within ten feet of her.

She fell in step beside Elizabeth, wishing she'd worn her hiking boots. Back home, she could walk for days in her cowgirl boots, but this mountain was a whole different story. *What was I thinking?*

"How's Aiden holding up?" she asked.

"He's got more energy than me and Lou put together. He's doing great, but he's completely enamored with Jack." She nodded to the two, walking up ahead side by side. Aiden's head was cocked to the side as he looked up at Jack. He was rattling off questions in rapid succession. Jack answered each one as he led them to the stream. Savannah noticed the softer tone he used with Aiden and that every so often—usually when he looked at Aiden—he rubbed a long white scar on the back of his left arm.

"He's not exactly the nicest guy, is he?" Savannah said.

Elizabeth leaned in closer to Savannah and brought her hand up and shielded her mouth, like she was sharing a secret. "You know about his wife, right?"

"Wife?" She had noticed his lack of a wedding ring.

Elizabeth lowered her voice, and her brown eyes filled with empathy. "She died, and that's why he moved to the mountains. From what I've heard, he was devastated. Couldn't function. Came out here to…I don't know what…but his instincts took over and he's never really gone back, except for holidays with his family and an occasional night at the house he and his wife shared."

"That's terrible." She looked at Jack and her heart ached for him. No wonder he was so full of venom. "I thought he was in the military."

"He was. He finished his tour the year she died. I think he was planning on reupping, but…instead he kind of left the real world behind," Elizabeth said.

They walked in silence while Savannah chewed on this new and startling information. It explained so much and yet at the same time explained nothing at all. She thought of her father, Hal Braden, and how after her mother died, he'd carried on without faltering. Of course, he'd had to. He was left with six children to raise. To this day, he still claimed to speak with her from beyond the grave. She knew he would never let the memory of her mother go, and she wondered if Jack would be haunted by his wife forever, too. She watched him descend the steep hill, wondering if that was where his anger stemmed from or if he was a mean-spirited person by nature.

The wide body of water looked nothing like a stream, but rather like a slow-moving river. At the bottom of the hill, Jack bent down and ran his fingers in the water.

Savannah unscrewed the top of her canteen, walked to the water's edge, and crouched to fill her canteen. Jack grabbed her arm before she could dip it beneath the surface.

"What?" she snapped. She looked at the water, expecting to see a snake or some other danger lurking beneath the surface. Instead, she saw fresh running water. She shot a look at Jack, whose massive hand was still wrapped around her forearm.

"Whoa, city girl. This isn't a faucet. We don't fill our canteens from the stream," he said in a harsh tone. "What was rule number one that I said back at the plane?" He paused, waiting for an answer.

Aiden's hand shot up in the air.

"You don't need to raise your hand, buddy," he said.

He spoke to her angrily, then softened every time he spoke to Aiden. *How do you do that?*

"Don't put anything in your mouth without clearing it with me first," Aiden repeated verbatim.

Savannah tried to wrench her arm free, but Jack held firm.

"Right, and why is that?" Jack asked.

"Bacteria," Josie answered.

He turned and glared at Savannah. She wasn't sure if it was

the intensity of his stare or the fact that she now knew his sad history, but instead of seeing anger or determination in his eyes, she saw agony, raw and exposed.

"Aiden, tell Miss Braden what we need to do next."

Jack held her stare, and heck if she didn't feel a familiar stirring in her belly. She looked at his hand, wrapped so tightly around her arm, then back at his eyes, which weren't black at all, but midnight blue. *A sexy shade of midnight blue.*

"Boil it in the pot, then put it in our canteen," Aiden said.

"Good job, Aiden," Lou said.

Jack continued staring at Savannah for a beat too long, and this time she didn't try to yank her arm from his grasp. She gently freed it, then rubbed the red skin. The feel of his grip was still fresh, the skin still warm.

"That's right," Jack said, his eyes still locked on Savannah. "We boil it." He walked downstream and crouched while he filled the pot with water, leaving Savannah to stare at him and wonder if she'd imagined the heat that had filled the space between them.

Chapter Three

THE FIRE CRACKLED and sparked as they purified the water by the stream. Jack leaned against a large pine tree, his arms folded over his chest, feet crossed at the ankles. This was his favorite time of the Day of Impact, when the students began to feel the pain of the walk settling in to their normally coddled bodies. The fire heated their already warm cheeks, and they began to relax. He knew they weren't thinking about the fact that they still had to climb back up the hill they'd come down, and they were so euphoric over learning to boil water in order to purify it that they weren't aware of their mounting hunger. He kept food to a minimum on the Day of Impact so they would begin to see the world around them for what it was rather than as a disposable environment where they could toss trash and take things for granted.

He caught sight of Savannah and Josie sitting by the water with their pants rolled up and their shoes off. Savannah dipped her toes in the water, then wet the washcloths she'd brought with her and rose to her feet. She moved the washcloth in slow circular motions over her wrist, then up to her elbow before rinsing it again and continuing up her lean and tanned arms. Josie said something, and Savannah laughed. Her laugh was feminine, and her entire face lit up with her smile. She washed around her tank top, gently running the cloth over her shoulder and armpit. Jack could almost feel his hand around the wet cloth as it swam over her soft skin and lithe muscles. Savannah flipped her hair over her shoulder with a quick snap of her chin, and their eyes caught. He felt the edge of his mouth lift into a smile and quickly clenched his jaw into a tight line. Her smile disappeared. Jack swallowed hard, feeling his Adam's apple drag along his throat.

Darn it.

He stalked off, silently cursing himself for losing sight of what he was doing. Now he looked like a lech, and that was the last thing he was. But she was so freaking beautiful. If he were to admit the truth to himself, she was *more* beautiful than any woman he'd ever seen. He'd always been attracted to blondes like Linda—petite and quiet. Savannah had fiery auburn hair, she was mouthy, and even as he walked away, he could see her long, sexy legs.

Her laughter carried through the air, and as he listened to the unique melody of it, his gut twisted. *What am I doing, and why is Savannah Braden invading my thoughts?*

Chapter Four

SAVANNAH HAD BEEN lying in her tent for at least an hour, trying to warm up. She never could sleep with clothes on, but it was too cold not to. Even with two pairs of socks and her sweatshirt over her long-sleeved shirt, she was still freezing, and the stupid ground was so hard that she knew she'd never fall asleep. She stuck her head out of her tent and listened to see if anyone else was awake. Jack had said that he was going to be awake until the fire went out, but she hoped he'd be in his tent. The moon hung high in the dark sky, casting an eerie shadow over the campsite and reminding her of haunted tales she'd heard as a child. She wasn't afraid of the dark or of being alone. Savannah had spent hours alone in the barn at night when she was growing up, and as she crept from her tent and went to sit by the dwindling fire, she felt a burst of energy driven by the freedom that came from the crisp night air. It was a different type of freedom than riding her father's horses as they galloped along the fields, or when she won a big case. Each deep breath of this mountain's air felt as if it were cleansing her soul.

Savannah rubbed her hands together above the hot embers, took a deep breath, then blew it out slowly. *This is why I'm here.* She could barely see past the orange circle of the fire. Real life seemed very far away. She loved living in Manhattan, but being in the mountains reminded her of how much she missed fresh, clean air and the smell of evergreens. Other than when she'd visited her father a few months earlier, she hadn't seen a real forest bursting with brush and prickly bushes in ages. She even missed the feel of a lush green lawn beneath her feet. She looked down at the dirt beneath her feet and realized it had also been forever since her bare feet had touched the ground. Not a sandy beach or cold pavement, but real dirt and dried fallen leaves. Listening to the noises of woodsy creatures as they scurried beneath the leaves of the forest floor and crickets chirping out their songs, she slipped off her socks and pressed her bare feet into the cold dirt. A moan of appreciation slipped from her lips as the sweetness of the forgotten feeling came tiptoeing back. It had been too long since Savannah left work—and men— behind. This was what she needed to clear her mind and heal her heart. A little serenity could go a long way.

Twenty minutes later, the embers had burned to quarter-sized sparks of red, and Savannah had to pee. She wiped her feet and slipped them back into her socks before retrieving her boots. She fished around for her flashlight, but in the silence of the night, every sound seemed amplified. The last thing she needed was to wake Jack and be growled at—and how could he go to sleep and leave the fire burning? She grabbed a package of wet wipes and the cell phone she wasn't supposed to have with her and stuck it in her pocket. The flashlight app would be perfect to light her way.

Jack had been adamant about not bringing electronic instruments on the trip. The registration email had specified no cell phones, no iPods, and no radios. *It's not like I'm going to use the phone, but the flashlight? Everyone needs a flashlight in the middle of the woods, and I packed a battery powered one, but...Why am I explaining myself to...myself?* She touched each tree as she passed, and when she was far enough from the camp that she was sure no one would wake up and see her squatting behind the bushes, she reached into her pocket for her phone. She heard a noise to her left and froze. She held her breath, listening intently for another sound. Her pulse raced and she remembered what Jack had said when Josie had screamed. *A bear? Oh no!* She contemplated her options: Run back to the campsite? Scream? Turn on her flashlight app and look around?

A low growl tangled her thoughts into a tight web of fear. *Oh no, no, no!* She took a step backward and smacked into what felt like a brick wall. Her scream was stifled by a powerful hand, and when she swung her elbow backward, her captor caught that, too.

"Do. Not. Make. A. Sound." Jack's voice was a deep whisper, but it was his hot breath on her ear and his hard body pressed against hers that made her pulse ratchet up another notch.

She turned toward his voice, breathing in the earthy smell of his hand. Her eyes were open so wide, they stung.

"Stay still," he whispered in such a strong voice that it vibrated against her ear. "There's a bobcat to your left."

She stifled a whimper. *Bobcat?*

"No matter what I do, you cannot make a sound. I'm taking my hand away. Don't make noise."

He lowered his hand, and without it pushing against her face, her trembling turned to full-on shaking. Jack held tight to her right arm as he shifted his body between Savannah and the bobcat. Savannah grabbed hold of the back of his shirt. Her eyes finally adjusted to the dark enough to see what looked like an enormous powerful cat on the side of the hill, its shoulders pushed up below its ears, perched to attack.

Jack slid his knife from its holder on his hip and whispered, "Don't move a muscle."

Another low, rumbly growl replaced the silence.

Savannah was too scared to breathe, much less move. He reached behind him and pried her fingers from his back. His eyes never left the cat.

Her hands flew to her mouth. She hoped he wasn't going to hurt it, and at the same time, she prayed he would kill it before it killed them. How the heck was he so calm when she could barely remain erect?

In one swift move, Jack lunged toward the cat with the knife leading the way. He made a loud, deep growling sound followed by a hiss. Savannah gasped a breath. She covered her ears and huddled behind him. The bobcat turned and ran up the hill, leaving another scary growl in its wake.

Savannah breathed so hard, she thought she might pass out. Jack turned and slid his knife into its sheath.

"It was a small one. You okay?" His eyebrows drew together. And as he stepped closer and reached an arm out, Savannah practically fell against him.

Tears fell instantly, and she hated herself for being such a wimp. This was not who she wanted to be in front of the guy who already thought she was too much of a city girl. Or a guy who made her stomach flip and her heart ache. She felt his body grow rigid against her, but she was too scared to break away. She couldn't stop trembling. *Or freaking crying.* Darn it. She never cried, and here she was falling apart like an idiot.

SOMETIMES JACK REMINGTON forgot what it was like *not* to live in the wild. And, he realized as Savannah's body shook and hiccupped with sobs against his chest, he'd also forgotten that sometimes women got scared. *Even the tough ones.* He put his arms around Savannah even though he knew he shouldn't, and he told himself not to think about how soft and warm her body felt against him or how long it had been since he'd held a woman. When she nuzzled against his neck, he couldn't help but smell the coconut aroma of her shampoo, and when his hand naturally moved up her back, pressing her against his chest, the feel of her thundering heart loosened the leash on the sexual urges he'd so masterfully repressed. He grit his teeth and closed his eyes, trying to keep himself from touching her thick hair, but the urge was too powerful not to reach beneath those heavy, soft locks and place his hand on the back of her neck, feeling the gentle ridge of the top of her spine against his palm.

Savannah lifted her head from his shoulder, and when she looked up at him with those gorgeous damp eyes and he saw the fear that filled them, he didn't think, could barely breathe. He simply lowered his mouth to hers and kissed her, wanting to take that fear from her body and breathe new, safe air into her lungs. She kissed him tentatively at first, and then as passionately as he kissed her. His tongue swept the roof of her mouth, along her teeth, learning every groove and reveling in every stroke of her delicious tongue. His body hungered for more, and as her hands slipped beneath his shirt and her fingers crawled along his waist to the center of his back, then moved slowly over the scars that peppered his skin, Jack flinched. He'd spent years hiding behind the cause of them, and now, as much as he didn't want to hide anymore, he was nervous as could be.

She pressed her hips into his, and it was all he could do to stifle a groan like a teenager.

When they finally drew apart, reality came rushing at him like a barrage of fractured thoughts. Savannah didn't need a broken man like him, and he sure as heck didn't need to try to fill the hole in his heart the size of Mount Everest—a hole he'd just gotten used to ignoring.

"I shouldn't have done that. I'm sorry." He hated how cold he sounded, but he knew it was for the best. Jack took a step backward, trying to rationalize the ache in his gut to doing the right thing—even if it felt so wrong that he wanted to punch a tree.

Savannah stepped backward, shaking her head. "Why?"

"This isn't what you're here for, and it's sure as heck not what I'm here for," he snapped.

"But maybe it's what we both needed," she said.

How many times had Linda said something similar to him? *Stop working and come to bed. You need me tonight.* Jack clenched his jaw against the anger that mounted within him. He'd messed up, and the hope in Savannah's eyes nearly sent his lips right back to hers. He had to shut her down or he'd never forgive himself.

"Savannah, stop," he said. "It was a kiss. You were scared, and I got carried away. Chalk it up to the heat of the moment. Aftershock." He reached for her arm in spite of himself and she pulled away.

"Aftershock?" she spat. "I saw the way you looked at me down by the water and again right before you kissed me, and what I saw wasn't a man who was carried away."

Damn. What the heck did she want from him? He wasn't a fling kind of guy, and a woman like Savannah probably had men lined up around the corner. He wasn't ready to deal with the surge of emotion that scared the tar out of him when they'd kissed, and he wasn't sure if he'd ever be ready again.

"I'm sorry," was all he could muster.

Savannah narrowed her eyes like the angry bobcat that had just run off. "What were you doing out here anyway?" she asked. "Spying on me?" She cocked her head and looked at him out of the corner of her eye.

Jack wasn't about to tell her that he spent most nights lying awake, too anxious to sleep, swimming in and out of fitful sleep, or that he often spent several hours sitting beneath the stars, replaying that fateful night of the accident in his mind like a bad rerun.

He dropped his eyes, thinking about how tonight he'd been on the verge of tears out of sheer frustration when he'd spotted Savannah walking into the woods, her eyes wide, her slim fingers trailing from tree to tree, and how seeing her had quelled his tears. Just as meeting her had given life to stirrings he hadn't felt in years. He'd almost been glad to spot the bobcat because it gave him a reason to be closer to her.

"Jack?" she said just above a whisper. "Is this about your wife?"

How the heck do you know? Anger twisted in his gut. "No, this is not about my wife." He pushed past her. "It was a stupid mistake, okay?"

She grabbed his arm. "Hey, wait a second, please."

He spun around. He felt his chest heaving, his nostrils flaring. He looked down at Savannah. The eight inches between them seemed like a foot. She looked fragile and scared, but not half as scared as he felt at that moment as his anger shifted and swirled through his stomach to his chest and burned a path to his heart.

"Sorry. I didn't…"

He closed the distance between them and put his hands on her arms. She was so soft and so sexy, even now, scared and trembling. Every nerve in his body cried out for her touch, and his heart—his blasted heart—wanted to kiss that fear away, and so did he. He was so turned on, it took all his focus not to lean forward and taste her lips again.

"Jack," she whispered. She reached up to touch his cheek, and he held tightly to her arms, forcing them back down. "It's okay," she said.

"No, it's not okay." He needed to ease the guilt of wanting Savannah.

"We all have hurt in our lives, Jack," she said.

He felt her muscles flex beneath his palms as she reached her fingertips up and touched his arm, so tender and loving, even while he had her arms confined against her will.

"You don't know about hurt like I do," he said.

"Maybe not like you do, but I do know how much it hurts to lose someone you love and how, no matter what you do, you can't let that love go. I know that it eats you up inside, and you feel like the person's right there with you but you just can't reach them," she said.

He pushed away. "How? Wha—"

Savannah shrugged. "I've watched my father grieve for my mother my whole life, and I've grieved for her, too," she admitted.

Jack let out an angry breath and growled, "You know what you saw, not what he felt."

32

THE HURT AND anger in Jack's voice sliced through Savannah's heart like a knife. Her father was an expert at masking the pain of missing her mother, but the longing was evident in everything he did and said. Jack's pain was raw, visceral, as if his wife's death left a gaping wound and every breath carried a painful reminder that she was gone. She'd felt how his body had gone rigid when they'd kissed, as if he were scared of the kiss itself, and how his rock-hard body had competing impulses. There was no denying his instant arousal when their hips had come together.

"Your version of hurt is stubbing your toe on the streets of Manhattan," he said.

Savannah narrowed her eyes. "You can be a real jerk, you know that? Watching my father grieve—and never knowing my mother—sucked. And pain comes in all forms"—*like finding your boyfriend in bed with another woman or having to prove yourself every day in a chauvinistic industry*—"none of which are fun." She took a step forward and looked up at him. The bottom of his chin was peppered with stubble except for an area about an inch long and a quarter inch wide, where a thin white scar had laid claim. Even though she wanted to call him out again for acting like a jerk, her heart wondered if it was his pain speaking. She wanted to touch that scar, heal the pain, and reveal the real Jack Remington. Instead, she said, "Thank you for saving me from the bobcat."

Savannah focused on the ground before her as she made her way back to the camp—her need to pee forgotten—Jack's kiss still fresh on her lips, his harsh words battling with the pain she'd seen in his eyes, and her confused heart thundering someplace in between.

Chapter Five

SATURDAY MORNING, AIDEN was up with the sun, chattering in his high-pitched voice. Savannah lay in her tent, thinking about the evening before and wishing she could transport home like they could on Star Trek. She closed her eyes and took a deep breath. No matter how much she loathed the idea of pretending nothing had happened, or admitting that it had, she had to join the group and face Jack. She touched her lips, remembering the way her body shivered while he kissed her—partly from the fear of seeing the bobcat, but mostly from how good it felt to be wrapped in his big, strong arms with his hot mouth devouring hers. *Stop it. No men, remember?* She couldn't even stick to her resolutions for forty-eight hours. That had to be some sort of a record.

She still had to pee, too, which meant that not only would she have to face Jack, but she'd have to go back in the woods alone and possibly run into the bobcat again. Last night her fear had morphed into some sort of sexual hunger, and she'd been so wrapped up in their kiss that she'd forgotten to ask him if that bobcat might come back. *One thing is for sure. No more peeing in the woods alone at night.* She gathered her confidence, changed her clothes, and stepped out of her tent.

"Savannah, I waked up early!" Aiden shouted.

Savannah winced. She needed an announcement about her whereabouts like she needed a hole in her head. One quick scan of the site told her that Jack was not around.

"Good morning, Aiden. How'd you sleep?" she asked.

It always amazed her how much energy children had in the mornings.

"Good. We heard a big cat last night and I was scared, but Dad said it was just a bobcat, and I'm not afraid of bobcats. It's not like they're lions or tigers. My dad could scare away a bobcat. Mom told me all about them this m—"

Elizabeth put her hand on Aiden's shoulder. In her jeans and tie-dyed shirt, she looked comfortable and relaxed. She wore a bandanna around her hair, secured beneath her dreadlocks.

"Sweetie, let's let Savannah breathe a little. She just woke up, okay?" Elizabeth said to Aiden.

"Okay, Mom. Can we go to the water?"

"I'll take you, buddy." Lou crossed the campsite from where he'd been stacking wood for the evening's fire.

"Have fun. Jack said he'd be back in half an hour," Elizabeth said. Lou kissed Elizabeth, and she pulled him into a deeper kiss. When Lou and Aiden disappeared over the crest of the hill, Elizabeth said, "With a little one, I gotta get my fill of Lou every chance I get." She winked at Savannah.

Pratt popped out of his tent, followed by Josie. Savannah's jaw dropped. *After one night?* It dawned on her that she might have been doing the same thing if Jack hadn't backed off.

"We'll go with you, Lou." Pratt reached behind him for Josie's hand.

"Let me grab towels," Josie said, and she headed to her tent.

"Nature calls. Be right back." Savannah slipped into the woods and inspected her surroundings carefully before she chose a spot to take care of her bathroom needs. When she returned to the camp, Elizabeth was waiting for her.

"I want to go down to the stream, but I didn't want to leave you alone. Do you want to come with me?" Elizabeth asked.

Savannah wasn't used to not showering. She really wanted to get into the water to bathe and wash her hair with the organic shampoo she'd found at the Natural Store. She couldn't do that around the others.

"No. It's okay. I'll go in a little while," she answered. She knew Jack wouldn't allow her to go alone, but once Pratt and Lou were back, she could ask Elizabeth to go with her.

Twenty minutes later, Savannah had finished organizing her belongings in the tent, and as she was backing out, she heard Jack's heavy footsteps approach. Butterflies took flight in her stomach. She rolled her eyes, angry with herself for feeling anything after the way he had treated her and wishing she hadn't enjoyed that kiss so much. *Okay, Savannah, just get it over with.* She took a deep breath and climbed from her tent.

Feigning a smile, she said, "Good morning." As if she hadn't experienced the greatest kiss of her life the night before.

Jack walked past the tents to the fire pit, not once looking at Savannah.

"Morning," he grumbled as he began building a small fire.

Savannah tried to discern if she was witnessing Jack's typical morning grogginess, or if he was sincerely going to grumble at her and pretend they hadn't kissed. *I didn't peg you as a pretender, too. Darn it. I hate pretending.*

"The others went down to the water," she said.

He continued silently building the fire.

"You're not going to speak to me?" she asked.

"I said, *morning*," he answered.

Savannah saw the others making their way back up the hill. She went to his side and said in a rushed whisper, "So we're pretending last night didn't happen?"

Jack's hands stopped midair. He turned his head slowly, and Savannah's breath caught when she saw his dark, sexy eyes, but the hard set of his jaw negated the desire she thought she'd seen.

"Probably for the best," he said.

Savannah knew he was right. She wasn't even looking for a relationship. In fact, she was running from one. So why did her heart feel like he'd squeezed it until it was ready to burst?

"Okay." She didn't recognize her frail voice. "I'm going down to the water to wash up."

He narrowed his eyes. "You can't go alone."

He had a right to be upset over her breaking the rules, but there was no way she wasn't going to wash up, and now she didn't want to be around anyone. And with what was going on between them—or not going on—she knew he would let her go.

"It's daylight. I'll be fine. Besides, I didn't go when the others invited me, so I can't ask them to go again." Savannah gathered her towels and her toiletry bag and went down to the water, passing the others along the way.

"It's beautiful down there," Elizabeth said as she passed. "Want me to come?"

"No thanks. I'm good." *And too confused to want company.* "I won't be gone long."

"Josie got water for coffee. I'll save you some," Elizabeth offered.

"Perfect, thanks."

AFTER MAKING COFFEE and rolled oats for the group for breakfast, Jack checked his watch for the fourth time. Savannah hadn't been gone even twenty minutes, but it felt like an hour. He knew the dangers of someone getting separated from the group, and he'd never before ignored his own rules. Now he was breaking every one of them. If he hadn't kissed her—and if she hadn't kissed him back with more passion than he'd ever felt— he wouldn't have let her go to the stream alone. If she hadn't made his body thrum with desire, he would be down at the water's edge so she wasn't alone. The whole situation was messed up.

"I'll be back in a few minutes. No one leaves the site," Jack said to the others. "Today we're doing field instruction, so rest up while you can. You're going to need it." He headed toward the stream, reminding himself that Savannah was just another survival camp student. In a few days, he'd never see her again.

The sun beamed through the trees, warming the last of the morning chill. As he neared the bottom of the hill, he heard Savannah's voice and he stopped to listen. She was singing something he couldn't make out, but he enjoyed the melody as it filtered through the air. He tried to make out the words, but all he could hold on to was the sweet tone of her voice—and he realized that Savannah was anything but *just another student*.

He took a few steps closer, and the water came into view. Jack scanned the banks for Savannah, but didn't see her. He followed the sound of her voice through the woods to his right. When she came into view, he stopped cold. The sun glistened off of the water and illuminated Savannah's naked body. *Her perfect naked body.* Her breasts swayed with each scrub of her hands through her hair. Jack couldn't deny his body's reaction as he drank in her incredibly sexy curves and the narrow sweep of her hips. She sank into the water up to her shoulders and arched her neck, rinsing the lather from her hair. His hands instinctively flexed, the memory of the soft hairs on the back of her neck still alive on his palm. She disappeared under the water and then broke through the surface again, shaking the excess water from her tresses. Jack's mouth went dry. It was like watching an X-rated movie, only Savannah wasn't acting. She turned back toward the shore and scanned the edge of the water before walking too darn slowly to the water's edge and leisurely picking up her towel and wrapping it around her body. *Holy cow, she is sexy.* He could barely breathe—*again*—and he definitely couldn't think, which is why, when she dried herself off and lifted one foot to step into her panties, he lost his footing and slid down the hill on his butt, bumping right into a large, prickly bush.

Savannah shot a look in his direction. She pulled up her panties and her hands flew across her chest. "Jack? What…are you spying on me?" She scowled and spun around, frantically picking up the rest of her clothes.

Jack scrambled to his feet and rushed to her side. His mind was still in an intoxicated Savannah fog. "I wasn't spying. I swear…"

She spun around, clutching her clothes in front of her body. Her eyebrows were drawn together, and her beautiful lips were pinched tight. How was he going to explain this, and *why* were his eyes still locked on the milky skin of the side of her breast as it poked out beneath her arm?

"Then what were you doing?"

Thinking quick, he said, "You're not supposed to leave

camp by yourself. Don't you remember the bobcat?" He knew
he should turn away, back up, move apart from where she was,
but all he could do was stand there and argue with her.

"You knew I was coming here and you didn't stop me. Why
would I know it was a problem?"

"Darn it, Savannah."

"Turn around," she spat.

He forced himself to turn away, fisting his hands. *Why did I
have to look?* If it had been Elizabeth or Josie, he would have
covered his eyes and called out from the hill. But come on, he
was only human, and he hadn't been with—or even wanted to
be with—a woman in two years. How on earth was he supposed
to react?

"First you kiss me, then you say you regret kissing me, and
then you spy on me?"

The venom in her voice hurt more than the accusation.

"Real class act, Jack Remington. Is that your MO? Lure
women to your mountain, and then reel them in and play with
their minds?"

"Savannah." His chest filled with anger and he spun around.
"Who told you to get naked—"

She finished buttoning her jeans but made no move to hide
her bare chest.

"For the love of…" He turned back around. "Sorry. I
thought you were dressed."

"Well, I'm not, and I'm not going to do what you tell me.
I'll dress when I'm good and ready, and I'll bathe when I want.
And, Jack Remington"—he felt her hand on the back of his
neck, and heat rushed through him—"I'll kiss whomever I
please, whenever I please." Her hot breath on his ear only
heightened his arousal and rooted his feet to the earth while

Savannah stalked off toward the camp with all her possessions in her arms.

One glance of the dimples at the base of her spine, just above her low-waisted jeans, made his entire body shudder.

Chapter Six

"WHAT'S GOING ON with you and Jack?" Elizabeth asked Savannah.

Savannah nearly choked. "What do you mean?" They'd been hiking for two hours, and every time Jack stopped to identify a plant or an animal print, he made a point of not looking at Savannah, but when her back was turned, she could feel his eyes burning a path to her. She didn't think anyone else had noticed. When she'd heard him slip down the hill at the stream, at first she'd thought it was another bobcat. A second later, when she saw him sliding on his behind, a momentary flash of relief swept through her, but it hadn't lasted long. She quickly realized that he must have been watching her bathe. The angrier she got, the more flustered he'd become, and when Jack was flustered, his eyes filled with uncertainty—quite a difference from the piercing stares he usually doled out—and his sharp edges softened with that uncertainty. As quickly as Savannah had become angry, it had turned to amusement and flattery.

"I don't know. He left the camp in the direction of the stream this morning, and ten minutes later you came stomping back even though you didn't seem mad, and now he won't even look at you. I might be married, but I've still got that female

Spidey sense." Elizabeth arched a brow.

"He did come down to the stream when I was washing up, and I was embarrassed, but nothing happened between us. I don't know why he doesn't look at me. He's a weird guy," she said.

Elizabeth flashed a wide, bright smile that reached her brown eyes. "I think thou doth protest too much," she teased.

Savannah laughed.

They'd stopped again beneath a cluster of pine trees. Jack put one finger to his lips and put his other hand out in front of the group to stop them from walking any farther. Then he picked up a long stick.

"Josie, you might want to hang on to Pratt. We've found ourselves a little snake." He shot a look at Josie, who huddled against Pratt's side.

"A snake? I wanna see a snake," Aiden said.

Jack held up his finger again and shushed him. "We don't want to spook him, buddy. Do you remember why?"

"Because we're the visitors. This is his home," Aiden said.

"That's right," Jack said, just above a whisper. "I'm going to lift this leaf, and you'll see the snake. I spotted his tail as we approached, but, Josie, you cannot scream. Got it?"

Josie nodded. "Got it," she said.

Pratt held her close.

Jack was so kind to Aiden and so harsh to the adults that Savannah wondered if he had children. She knew almost nothing about him, other than he was an incredible kisser, he'd lost his wife a couple of years earlier, he had been in the military, and he appeared to be just as confused about women as she was about men.

He lifted the leaf, and Pratt laughed.

"That's a garter snake," he said. "Heck, you can find those back home."

Jack stood back up to his full height, towering over Pratt. "Yeah, you're right, you can. Would you rather have seen a rattler? Something venomous? Because guess what, crackpot. You have no idea what's slithering into your tent right now, do you?" Jack shifted his gaze back to Aiden. "What's the rule for when you're in the wild?"

"Um…I know this." Aiden bit his lower lip and looked up at Elizabeth with wide eyes. "Oh, don't leave anything behind?"

"Right. Always leave things the way they were." He put the leaf back where it had been. "So we replace the leaf, and I'll even replace the stick." Jack put the stick back where he'd found it. "Pratt, take a look behind you, just to the right of the trail. What kind of print is that?"

Pratt didn't move. His lanky arms hung loosely by his sides, his hair curled out from beneath his tuque, and he looked at Jack with a challenge in his eyes.

"Go on. Take a look." The seriousness returned to Jack's voice. His shoulders rode high and tight just below his ears, as if he were ready to strike.

Josie moved away from Pratt's side, her eyes darting between the two men. She pulled at a lock of her hair, running the ends between her fingers and thumb. Pratt took a few steps up the trail, and Jack grabbed his arm.

"Hold up." He trained his eyes on Pratt and turned his back to the group, then spoke in a quieter voice. "I'm here to keep you safe, and I can't do that if you fight me. Whatever's eating you up, you gotta deal with it. Get that garbage out of your head and think about it, talk about it, then get rid of it. Trust me on this. Don't shove it so far down that it's impossible to single out. Deal with it."

Pratt shrugged out of his grasp and headed for the trail again. "Whatever, man." He took a step deeper into the woods.

"It's my trail, Pratt." The warning in Jack's deep voice caused Josie to gasp—and Pratt to stop cold.

Savannah was intrigued by Jack's behavior. On the one hand, he was right. It was his job to keep them safe, so she and the others couldn't just wander off, but on the other hand, she'd just heard him tell Pratt to deal with whatever was bothering him, and from what Savannah had seen, Jack was holding in something that was not only eating away at him, but pushing him away from everyone else at the same time—except maybe Aiden.

"Your life is in my hands. The track that was beside you was from what looked to be a bobcat, a very large one." Jack's eyes shifted to Savannah and held, just long enough to unleash the fluttering in her stomach again. "Bobcats don't usually attack people, but if you come up on them feeding, or with pups, they're a whole different creature."

"Bobcat? Will it come back?" The words left Savannah's lips before she had time to stop them.

Jack continued pinning Pratt with a cold stare and ignored Savannah's question. Pratt gritted his teeth and took a step backward, allowing Jack to once again lead the way.

Resentment swelled within her at Jack's complete disregard for her question—and her privacy when she had been down at the water. Annoyed, she turned her focus to Pratt. He was either dealing with something pretty heavy, or he was just a brooding twentysomething. She couldn't tell which. But the more she got to know Josie, the more she liked her, and she wanted to be sure Josie wasn't getting involved with someone who could bring trouble down the road. She glanced at Jack's broad back as he led them farther up the mountain. *Why is it so easy to see trouble a mile away when I'm looking at someone else and so easy to ignore when it happens to me?*

They hiked for another few hours, and when the afternoon sun fell from the sky and the clouds rolled in, they headed back toward their campsite.

"Aiden, how many poisonous plants are in this forest?" Jack asked.

"Seven," Aiden said proudly.

"Excellent. Why are you so good at remembering things?" Jack asked.

"My mom homeschools me, and she says I'm a book boy not a TV boy and that's what makes me so smart." Aiden reached for Jack's hand.

Jack furrowed his brow and looked at him, then looked back at Elizabeth and Lou. Elizabeth mouthed, *Sorry*. Jack's enormous paw engulfed Aiden's tiny hand, and Aiden looked up at Jack as they walked.

"Watch your feet, not me," Jack said.

"Okay," Aiden replied.

"Do you remember what any of the poisonous plants look like?" Jack asked them.

Savannah watched him from behind, and she swore the muscles in his shoulders had settled down an inch or two, and he moved with a little less rigidity in his limbs as he walked hand in hand with Aiden.

"Three leaves let it be," Aiden said.

Jack flashed a bright smile over his shoulder at Elizabeth and Lou. It was the first time Savannah had seen him look happy. The smile lightened his dark eyes and brightened his skin, as if he were looking into the sun. It instantly stole his serious, grumbly facade, changing his entire persona without a single word spoken. He looked approachable, likable. He looked like someone Savannah might like to get to know better.

"Three leaves, green, shiny sometimes, sometimes they have notches like cutouts and sometimes they're smooth, right?" Aiden looked up at Jack again.

Jack nodded. "Perfect."

"Someday I'm gonna live in the woods just like you, Jack. My dad said I can do that if I want to after I'm all grown up," Aiden said.

Savannah couldn't see Jack's face from her position a few feet behind him, but she noticed the way he kept glancing at Aiden, and the attentiveness struck her. The word *dangerous* didn't seem to fit him any longer. When he was with Aiden, the words *interested* and *sweet* came to mind.

Aiden described the other poisonous plants that he remembered, and then he went through a list of which plants were not poisonous. By the time they reached the camp, the temperature had dipped another ten degrees. Savannah grabbed a hoodie from her tent and then offered to get water from the stream with the help of Elizabeth and Josie. She couldn't take another minute of being treated as if she didn't exist.

"ARE WE HAVING fun yet?" Josie asked as they reached the water's edge. She pulled the hood of her sweatshirt over her jet-black hair and dunked the pot in the water.

"What's up with Pratt?" Savannah asked. She and Elizabeth sat on a boulder a few feet from the water's edge. Streaks of sun cut through the center of the trees and cast long, active shadows across the water. Savannah watched Josie flip her black hair over her shoulder as she set the pot on the ground and began pacing.

"He's complicated, I guess. Geez, I always do this. I came here to sort of find myself, you know?" Her blue eyes shifted between Savannah and Elizabeth. She pulled forward a lock of hair and ran her finger and thumb over the ends, first with the right hand, then the left, in a quick, repetitive pattern. "I always hook up with the wrong guys. Then, when things go bad— which they always do—I swear off men and end up doing the same thing over again," Josie said.

"Welcome to the club." Savannah gathered her hair over one shoulder and pulled her hood up, too.

Elizabeth took Savannah's hand. "You girls just haven't found the right men yet. You have to kiss a lot of frogs to find your prince."

"I've kissed enough frogs for both of us," Savannah said. "You and Lou seem happy and compatible, and Aiden is too cute for words, but I'm beginning to wonder if I didn't miss my window of opportunity. I'm thirty...something...and most guys are married by the time they're in their mid-thirties. Well, my brothers weren't, and one is still way too single, but he's younger than the rest of us. I think in general, by the time you hit your mid-thirties, you're either unattached for a reason, which is usually not good, or you've already been married and divorced, and that's not always great, either."

"So I only have five more years to find the man I'll fall in love with forever? What if I never do?" Josie sat on the other side of Elizabeth, leaned her elbows on her knees, and rested her face in her hands. She stared at the ground, the corners of her mouth turned down.

"What about Jack?" Elizabeth asked.

"You keep acting like there's something there. There's not; trust me," Savannah said.

Elizabeth shook her head. "I still have the feeling there's something between you two. He's going to way too much trouble not to look at you."

"She's right," Josie said. "When we were getting ready to leave the campsite this morning, I saw him sneaking glances at you every time you looked away."

Last night, Savannah had felt something between them—a long, hard something—but for someone else to notice the connection meant that she wasn't just making it up in her lonely little head.

"I'm here to get over a bad relationship, not to jump into a complicated one," Savannah said.

"That's exactly what I'm saying," Josie said emphatically. "I don't know how I ended up in bed with Pratt. He's a nice guy, you know. He's just a little lost right now. Did you know that he's an artist? He's a sculptor. He has a degree in engineering, but he's passionate about sculpting."

"A moody artist. His personality fits him perfectly," Savannah said.

"I don't think he's just moody. I think he really feels stuck. His parents are all over him to stop messing around with art and get a real job. I mean, he lives on his own, he has a studio, but he's barely making it by each day, so they're pushing him to give up," Josie explained. "He came here to get away from them and to try to make a decision on his own."

"What kind of parents would do that to their child? He's not even a child. He's a man." Elizabeth took the bandanna off and tied it around her dreadlocks, creating a thick, snaky ponytail.

"Can I touch your hair?" Savannah asked.

"Of course. Go ahead." Elizabeth turned around.

Savannah ran her hands over the dreadlocks. "I thought they'd feel prickly or overly dry, but they don't. They're like soft ropes of hair." Touching them brought her back to Jack, who looked like he was made of hard edges and rough plateaus, but he was soft, his muscles strong yet tender. Remembering the way he'd cupped his palm around the back of her neck sent a chill up her spine.

She couldn't think about Jack. It only made his ignoring her that much harder. She turned her focus back to Elizabeth. "My father would never do things that way. He'd give me an opinion but leave the decision up to me in the end," Savannah said.

Josie jumped to her feet. "What I can't figure out is what Pratt might be like if his parents weren't doing this to him."

"You've only known him a day. Give it time," Elizabeth said. "Maybe he's a really sweet guy."

Savannah thought of Jack. "Or maybe he's too broken to ever heal."

"Thanks, Savannah," Josie teased.

Savannah rose to her feet. "Don't mind me. I'm just in my own little world today. We should probably bring the water back up or Les Stroud will come looking for us."

Josie picked up the pot of water and they began their walk back up the hill. "So you guys don't think I'm a slut?"

She said it so quietly that Savannah almost missed the question. She put her arm over Josie's shoulder. "You're no more of a slut than I am. You're young and free. Why not enjoy it? As long as no one is getting hurt, why shouldn't you enjoy each other? Even if it's only for a few days."

"Thanks, Savannah." She looked at Elizabeth and grabbed that lock of hair and began fiddling with it again. "Elizabeth?" she asked tentatively.

Elizabeth turned to face her with a wide smile. "I'm all for sharing yourself with whoever you feel will bring you pleasure, until you find the one whose pleasure you could never live without. I get a feeling about these things, and I don't think either of those two men are broken beyond repair." She held Savannah's gaze.

"Are you Jack's personal dating consultant or something?" Savannah asked.

"No," Elizabeth said. "I just see something between you guys. I don't know why, but..." She shrugged. When the campsite came into view, Elizabeth grabbed their arms and stopped walking. She lifted her chin toward Jack and Aiden, sitting side by side. Lou and Pratt sat across from them by the fire, each manipulating a length of rope. It looked like Jack was teaching them how to tie a knot.

"Those do not look like broken men to me," Elizabeth said.

Jack put his arm around Aiden and pulled him close. His deep voice boomed into the evening. "Great job! You'll be a master survivalist soon."

Aiden wrapped his arms around Jack's waist and hugged him. Savannah wasn't surprised to see Jack's body stiffen. His arm hung in the air above the boy, as if the hug were a giant leap from his arm on the boy's shoulder. He lowered it slowly toward Aiden's back, as if he were almost afraid to hug him, and in the next moment, he pulled the little boy close. The sweetness of the moment in the dimming sunlight brought Savannah's hand to her heart. Jack rested his head on the top of Aiden's hair and caught all three women staring at him.

Chapter Seven

JACK HAD BEEN dreading the night since he'd woken up that morning. He knew that the minute he lay down he'd be barraged with memories of kissing Savannah, and those images would be chased by Linda's trusting and disappointed face. He'd never cheated on her when she was alive—and now, two years after her death, he was nearly paralyzed with guilt over a single kiss. A kiss that had him thinking about plenty of other dirty things besides Savannah's lips. He couldn't push past the thought that he had carelessly crushed his wedding vows. Thinking of Linda brought his mind to Aiden and how good it felt to spend time with a child.

He sat on the boulder beside the camp with his knees pulled up, his hands steepled together in front of his mouth, and his chin resting on the pads of his thumbs. He wondered what he would be like if he had a normal life. *Normal.* Jack wasn't sure he even knew what normal looked like anymore. Was normal two adults with dreadlocks and an awesome son? Or was it a single career woman hiding out in the woods to heal whatever ache she had at the moment? Or was normal two kids searching for answers? Maybe there was no normal. *Will I ever find my normal again—whatever that is—and have the family I always wanted?*

Jack lay back on the rock and looked up at the stars, thinking of his brothers and sister. He was the eldest of six. Before Linda died, he'd seen his four younger brothers and his sister often. Now he was lucky to see them once a year. He closed his eyes and listened to the sound of Elizabeth and Lou singing to Aiden, and their voices silencing when, he was sure, Aiden had finally closed his eyes and fallen asleep. A few minutes later, the metallic scratch of the zipper on Pratt and Josie's tent broke through the silence. Josie's hushed giggles brought a smile to Jack's lips despite his internal conflict. He wondered what it would be like to camp with a woman who truly enjoyed the outdoors. Linda never had, and now, as he lay beneath the stars, he wondered if Savannah ever would. He draped his arm over his eyes to block out the moonlight and wondered if he might fall asleep right there with the cold, hard rock at his back.

He didn't hear her footsteps as she walked by, and he didn't feel a brush of wind or hear the *swish-swish* of her pants legs. It was her scent that brought Jack's arm away from his eyes and pushed him up onto his elbow. She stood with her back to him at the edge of the woods. He could barely make out her silhouette in the darkness, but he didn't think he'd ever forget the alluring curves he'd seen earlier that morning. He didn't want to be accused of spying again, but wasn't he? No, he hadn't been looking for her. She'd appeared unexpectedly. *Had she? Or was I waiting for her? Hoping she'd appear?* Or perhaps she'd been hoping he'd find her.

If he closed his eyes and acted like he was asleep, he couldn't be accused of spying, but there was no way he was going to allow her to go into the woods alone after what happened the previous night. Should he call her name? Pretend he was just walking around. *When did taking students to the woods become so complicated?*

He'd never considered himself a hider, but isn't that just what he'd been doing for two years? Hiding from the world? Hiding from himself? Jack pushed himself off the rock. *What the heck have I got to lose. Here goes.*

"Savannah?"

Savannah whipped her head around. "Jack?" She leaned forward, squinting into the darkness.

He closed the distance between them. "Are you going bobcat hunting?" *That was a lame joke.*

"Ha-ha. I wanted to go to the bathroom, but then I remembered…"

"I'll take you, but let's not push our luck by going to the same place that bobcat was before. Come on." He put his hand on her lower back, and just that slight graze of her body against him made his stomach feel funny, like he was going downhill on a roller coaster. He pushed his hands into the pockets of his jeans. It was safer that way.

Savannah stopped walking.

"What's wrong?" he asked.

"You confuse the heck out of me, that's what," Savannah said. They were standing about twenty feet from the edge of the camp. The little moonlight that had been visible by the boulder was now blocked by the taller trees.

Jack stepped closer to her, bringing her face into focus. "If it's any consolation, you do the same to me." If there was one thing Jack knew about himself, it was that between his height and his brawn, the inflection of his voice determined how people reacted to him. He knew how to come across stern and aggressive. It had become a way of life in recent years. And he used to know how to allow his sensual, flirtatious side to turn on with each breath. But that part of him had been hidden for so long, Jack wasn't sure it still existed at all. Tonight, for the first time in forever, he wanted that harsh edge to slip away. The recognition of that desire alerted the guilt and self-loathing that he'd harbored for two years and had been trying to ignore for the past twenty-four hours. *I shouldn't want her.*

"Great. Now that that's established, why is it that every time I'm alone, you show up?" Savannah crossed her arms.

"Do you ever not think like an attorney?" She tweaked every nerve in his body, and in the three minutes they'd been standing there, his pulse had already kicked up to the point where he was breathing heavily.

"Do you ever talk nicely to women?"

He looked away and smiled. She was tough…and he liked it. "I'm not a very nice man," he said.

Savannah arched a brow. "You know what I think?"

She took a step closer to him, and the stirring in Jack's stomach traveled south, bringing rise to the heat that had erupted between them the night before.

She put her cheek a breath away from his and whispered, "I think you need to walk me into the woods."

His sexual urges begged to be fed, and as he contemplated doing just that, she leaned in again and said, "I have to pee."

Chapter Eight

SAVANNAH COULDN'T PINPOINT the exact moment when Jack went from being a surly jerk to someone she wanted to figure out, but she was pretty sure it was when she'd seen him holding Aiden's hand on the trail earlier that afternoon—and maybe the thought had been driven home when he'd put his arm around Aiden by the fire that evening. In those small actions, she'd seen his angry armor chipping away, exposing a taste of emotion that seemed to scare him as much as it seemed to soften him. And even though she was on the rebound from Connor, she couldn't stop Elizabeth's words from playing in her mind over the last few hours. *I'm all for sharing yourself with whoever you feel will bring you pleasure, until you find the one whose pleasure you could never live without.* The more she observed Jack, the more open she became. She thought of her older brother Rex and how he'd always been gruff around women—until he'd fallen in love with Jade Johnson, the daughter of her father's nemesis—the man Hal Braden had been feuding with for the past forty years. The relationship between Rex and Jade had been contentious at first, and from what Rex had described, they'd both fought it every step of the way. She'd never seen Rex happier, more content, and less guarded than he'd been since falling in love with Jade.

Savannah smiled at the surprise in Jack's eyes. She supposed it had been cruel to tease him the way she had, but as she'd seen with her brother, she thought perhaps there was a kinder, gentler man who lay beneath the anger. She wasn't Jade Johnson, and there was no family feud to contend with. The only thing holding her back from wrapping her hands around his beautiful, hard body and kissing him until she cracked that armor away was the memory of what it felt like to be hurt by Connor. Savannah had to believe that just because Connor hurt her didn't mean all men would.

Jack cleared his throat. "Right." They crossed the campsite and entered the forest on the other side. Savannah was aware of every breath as she walked just behind Jack, a little embarrassed that she had to pee at all, much less that she needed a babysitter while she went.

"See that rock over there?" Jack pointed to a large boulder. "I'm going to scope it out. Stay put."

"I'm not a dog, you know." Why did he have to speak so rudely?

He took a step forward and stopped, then turned to face her. He opened his mouth to speak, then looked to the side, as if he'd changed his mind. "I'm sorry," he said a little less grumpily. "Please wait here."

Feeling vindicated, Savannah grinned. "Okay." She watched as he disappeared around the boulder with one hand on the leather sheath hanging from his belt. Then he came around the other side and motioned her over.

"Need anything else?"

He was still so curt that her nerves tightened. She held up her biodegradable wet wipes and wiggled them before his eyes.

"I'll wait over there."

Savannah felt her cheeks flush.

After she was done, she found him with his back to her. In an effort to crack the walls he had constructed around himself, she tiptoed to him and wrapped her hands over his eyes.

"Guess who?" she teased. She didn't feel his cheeks lift in a smile or his back jump with a stifled laugh. Instead, she felt the tiny muscles at the edge of his cheekbones contract as he clenched his jaw. Savannah dropped her hands, her hopes at levity deflated. "Sorry."

He turned to face her again with the same irritated look he'd given her enough times since they'd arrived that it was already etched in her mind.

"Why are you doing this?" he growled, grabbing her wrists.

His eyes had gone almost black, and the word *danger* floated through Savannah's mind again. She wondered if she had misjudged him after all. Maybe he didn't have that softer side. Maybe she'd imagined it.

"Why, Savannah? I'm an angry bastard," he said in a harsh whisper.

She could barely breathe. His eyes were still black as night, but as she looked closer, she realized she hadn't misjudged him. It was restraint that she read in his clenching jaw, the muscles straining in his neck, but it was desire, thick and lustful, in his eyes.

"I don't know," she managed. Her legs weakened and her pulse sped up at the flames igniting between them. "Maybe...I..."

"I'm broken, Savannah. I may not be fixable. You're better off going back to your high-rise cement city and using your sexy charms on one of the men there." His nostrils flared with each heavy breath, and Savannah could tell that he was at his breaking point.

"I'm here now." Savannah touched his ripped abs with her fingertips. She felt him shudder beneath her touch, and she looked at her hand in surprise. He released her wrists, and she placed her palm over his hammering heart and stepped closer. He smelled like the earth and sheer masculinity, and as he stared down at her, she reached up and touched his cheek. It felt just as she'd thought it might as she was lying in her tent earlier in the evening, remembering every line of his striking features. Her finger trailed the edge of his clenched jaw, lightly touching the muscles as they rose and eased repeatedly, and Savannah couldn't keep herself from stepping on her tiptoes and planting a soft kiss on the center of his chin, then running her finger over the swell of his lower lip.

He growled a dangerous indiscernible warning that only further stimulated her desires before whispering, "Savannah."

His plea landed in her ears as an invitation. Without any conscious thought, she lifted up on her toes again and ran her tongue along the lip she'd just touched.

"Jack," she whispered, hoping he heard the invitation in her voice, too.

His eyes opened wide and then narrowed again, and in the next second, he hauled her against him, taking her in a deep, passionate kiss, just as he'd done before. He devoured her as if he'd been starving for only her. His tongue moved forcefully through her mouth as he took a fistful of her hair and angled her mouth beneath his, opening it wider to him. The pleasure and pain was so intense that she moaned, earning an apprecia-tive, greedy sound from him. His teeth found her neck, and his strong, sensual hands began roaming.

His eyes opened and "*Savannah*" came out full of desire.

His mouth covered hers like he'd been waiting for her his whole life. Savannah drew air from his lungs, clawing hastily at his shirt, pulling it from the confines of his jeans and pushing her hands beneath, grabbing the hot bare flesh of his scarred back. She lifted his shirt and bent to kiss his chest. She felt him breathing harder, his muscles flexing with restraint, as he lifted her face, taking her in another rough kiss.

"We should stop," he said between feverish kisses.

"No," she panted out.

His hands were rough and sure as they stripped off her shirt and she stumbled backward toward the boulder. He pressed her against the cold, hard rock, and then he put space between them to pull his own shirt over his head. The shock of cold air against her already heated flesh had her reaching for him again. His chest was dense and powerful as he held her close, kissing her neck. He touched the button of her jeans and drew back, piercing her with a hot stare—a fierce lion ready to take his lioness. She reached down and unbuttoned her jeans, then stepped from them, shivering with desire as much as from the cold. She'd never been that bold with a man before, but Jack was just that—*all man*—and she wanted every bit of him.

He trailed his eyes down her body, swallowing hard, his Adam's apple jumping in his thick neck. His eyes landed on the little skin-colored patch on her lower abdomen.

"Birth control patch," she whispered quickly.

He kissed her again. "*Man*, I didn't even think about protection. It's been so long."

Jack unbuttoned his jeans, then drew the zipper down slowly, holding her against the rock with nothing more than his hungry stare and a silent promise of animalistic sex. He stepped from his pants, and Savannah raked her eyes over his incredible body, the ache of need simmering to a boil, and knowing as his powerful hands clutched her rib cage that he was tortured with the same burning need.

As they explored each other's bodies, they both went a little wild, and Savannah opened *all* of herself to his rough, hungry hands. She wasn't new to sex, but with Jack she was insatiable. She didn't know or care why she'd allowed Jack Remington to touch her bottom in ways she'd never imagined wanting a man to, but she knew she needed *more*, and no part of her wanted to hold back.

TOUCHING SAVANNAH WAS nothing like Jack had imagined it would be. He'd been with only a handful of women before marrying Linda, and their sex life had been fulfilling. He'd never felt like he was missing out on anything. But when he touched Savannah, the animal in him came out, and his desires went way past making love every Wednesday and Saturday night. The nagging guilt in the back of his head silenced the moment he'd put his lips to hers. And everything afterward was fueled by pure visceral need. He'd never have touched Linda in the ways he'd just touched Savannah. He'd always thought it was too dirty. Wrong. But with Savannah, it was neither of those things, and as her body trembled in his grasp, he knew he wasn't going to stop there. He was powerless against the desires she'd unleashed. In one quick move, he lifted her off the rock, clenched fistfuls of her hair, and took her in another penetrating kiss. Every part of her was delectable. The need to possess her was so strong that he didn't realize how forceful he was being, and as her back hit the rock, she whimpered.

He drew back, releasing her hair. "I'm sorry. I'm—"

Her eyes were at half-mast as a grin formed on her lips. "It was a good hurt," she whispered.

He kissed her hard and fast, his mind playing tricks on him. He wanted her. He needed her. But this was *Savannah*. Smart, sexy, sensual Savannah Braden, the woman who challenged everything he believed about himself. He didn't want to screw it up. A groan came from deep in his chest. It had been so long since he'd been intimate with a woman, he may not last the first time they made love. Truth mattered to Jack, and wasn't it better if he were honest now than disappointing her later? He didn't care if she thought it made him less of a man as he said, "Savannah, I haven't been with a woman for two years. I don't even know how long I'll last."

She held him as he tried to pull away.

"It's okay," she said.

The need in her eyes rivaled his. "If I don't, I'll make it up to you." He kissed her tenderly and whispered, "Promise."

As their bodies came together. Savannah curled her fingers around his shoulders with a loud gasp.

"I'll stop," he said quickly.

"Please don't," she said with a heated stare.

The forest noises fell away, replaced with the sounds of their breaths coming fast and hard, and eventually, easing to a single sated rhythm. Jack was consumed with new sensations, feelings he hadn't experience in forever. It was a miracle that he felt anything other than anger or guilt—and this was so vastly opposite, so *beautiful*, he was overcome with emotions as his heart opened to her.

Chapter Nine

SAVANNAH WAITED FOR embarrassment to find her as she pulled her sweatshirt over her head. She shot a glance at him, leaning naked against the boulder, his eyes trained on the ground, and she wanted so much more of him. Everything about him was complex. He was a striking combination of hard masculinity and, Savannah was sure, a big, loving heart buried deep inside. A man without a heart wouldn't look like he did after doing what they'd just done. A man without a heart would be gloating.

She leaned against the boulder beside him. "Are you okay?"

He nodded, and when he looked up at her, his expression pained.

Savannah's heart stopped. "What's wrong?" *Oh no. You regret it.*

"Nothing and everything all at the same time," he said softly.

"I'm not sure what that means."

"Savannah." He reached his arm around her and pulled her close. "I haven't been with a woman since my wife died, and before her, well, there weren't many. But never—*ever*—have I been so rough, and I just want to be sure I didn't hurt you."

And there it was. His soft heart. "Jack, you didn't hurt me. I've never felt this close to anyone before. I really don't know why I went so wild, either, but"—she shrugged—"I couldn't get enough of you. No matter how much you touched me, it wasn't enough. It's still not enough," she admitted.

He nodded. "It scares the heck out of me."

She didn't know how to react to that. *Me too?* That would be a lie. It didn't scare her. In fact, she wanted to do more. She moved in front of him and stood between his legs.

"You didn't promise to marry me. We shared our bodies. We shared emotions. Why does it scare you?" She saw the answer in his eyes as he furrowed his brow and swallowed hard again. *Guilt.*

He shook his head, and his dark eyes glistened with tears. "It's late, and it's hard to explain. Let's get towels and go wash up. We can talk some other time."

The way he shut her down stung, and as they finished dressing, Savannah wondered if she'd made a mistake. He came to her side and looked at her with such pain in his eyes she regretted feeling so put off. Complex didn't even start to explain Jack.

"Savannah, I'm not good at any of this," Jack admitted. "Right now I want to reach up and touch your cheek. I want to brush your hair from your shoulder and feel you in my arms, but I've just touched you in every private place imaginable, and I don't know you well enough to put my dirty hands on you again. We don't even have a proper shower where I can help bathe my memory away from your body."

Her heart melted at the thought that he'd even think to do that. Where did the gruff, angry man go? "So we did things a little backward. We can get to know each other now."

She reached for his hands and he pulled them away. "I need to wash up."

"I didn't peg you as a neat freak," she teased. She pressed her body against his, drawn in by his thoughtfulness. "Let's go wash up. I have no expectations. To be honest, I'm still reeling at you talking to me instead of growling."

"I can't make any promises about how I'll be ten minutes from now or tomorrow. I definitely don't trust my own emotions right now, but I don't regret being with you."

"THIS IS ONE thing that my concrete city doesn't have enough of," Savannah said as she dipped beneath the cold water. Her teeth chattered and goose bumps covered her arms and legs.

"You're freezing." He wrapped his arms around her.

"No, just my outside is. My inside is warmer and happier than it has been in a very long time."

"You really are incredibly beautiful," Jack whispered. He'd been dying to touch her face after they'd been close, and now, as he reached up and cupped her cheek, he had to close his eyes. She fit perfectly against his palm, and when she leaned into his hand, he shivered with the memory of what they'd done in the forest.

"Thank you," Savannah said. She touched the back of his hand and pressed it to her cheek. "You're not so bad yourself."

He took the washcloth from Savannah's hand and washed her back in slow, gentle stokes as he learned each dip and curve of her body.

"Jack, are you different from who you thought you were?" Savannah asked.

"That's a strange question," he said, but he knew just what she meant.

"I know." She gathered her hair and moved it to her other shoulder so he could wash beneath it. "Out here I'm nothing like who I am back home. I'm so strong at home. I can do anything, and I never ask for help. But out here I'm, I don't know. Weak or something."

He turned her so she was facing him. "You're anything but weak. I see a strong woman who's also feminine, and the combination is...*frustrating*."

Savannah frowned. "Honesty is good, but after what we just did, maybe you could sugarcoat it a little."

He moved in closer and lifted her chin to look at him. "That was sugarcoated."

He smiled down at her, then touched his lips to hers, and despite the cold air that enveloped them, every swipe of her tongue heightened his desire. She pressed her body into him, and he wrapped her in his arms—like it was the only place she could possibly belong—and he had no idea how he'd gone without her for the last two years. When she wrapped her hands around his neck and lifted herself up, it was only natural for him to help her legs find their way around his waist. Savannah deepened the kiss, making sexy little noises that sent his urges soaring again.

Savannah held tight to his shoulders as they surrendered to their passion beneath the shadows of the moon.

IT WAS NEARLY three in the morning when they finally arrived back at the campsite, and as he kissed her good night,

Jack wondered how he would get through the next few hours without her. And in the next breath, he wondered how Savannah could find her way into his heart in such a short period of time. He'd always counted himself lucky for having met and married Linda, who he'd thought completed him in every way he could imagine. Now, with Savannah, he realized that there was so much more of him that he never knew needed completing. Could a man get this lucky twice in his life? Jack closed his eyes, waiting for the anger that had eaten away at him for years to come rushing back, but for the first time since he'd lost Linda, he was able to fall asleep without first enduring hours of misery.

Chapter Ten

SAVANNAH AWOKE WITH the sun, and though she'd slept only a couple of hours, she felt refreshed and ready to tackle the day—and Jack Remington. Boy, had he thrown her for a loop. She'd expected hot sex, but she couldn't have anticipated the dirty things she'd wanted to do with him, and by the time they'd returned to the campsite, he'd become tender toward her. The more tender he became, the more her body reacted to him.

As she dressed, she tried to calm her nerves about seeing him again, and before getting out of her tent, she took a few minutes to gather her courage and strength, wondering how he would act toward her. They'd agreed not to hide their feelings but not to flaunt them, either. Savannah knew she might have trouble with that. She was a Braden, after all, and all Bradens tended to err on the side of overly affectionate with those they cared for. *Cared for.* Savannah realized that even though she hardly knew Jack, her heart had already embraced him.

"I'll get her!" Aiden's voice carried through the thin tent walls. A few rapid footfalls later, Aiden poked his blond head into her tent. His wide eyes were full of mischief. "Hi, Savannah. We're learning to build a shelter. A *real* shelter. Are you almost ready? Jack says we can't go till you're ready."

Savannah touched his nose. "I'm as ready as I'm going to be, but is everyone else up this early?"

"Yup."

"Then I better get my butt in gear." Last night came rushing back and she felt her cheeks flush.

Aiden ran away from her tent, yelling, "She's getting her butt gear on!"

Savannah buried her face in her hands. She crawled out of her tent under the amused scrutiny of four sets of adult eyes. Jack's eyes were locked on the ground.

"I said get my butt in gear, silly boy," she said with a laugh.

Elizabeth sidled up to her. "What were you up to last night?"

She looked around to see if anyone else had heard her. "What do you mean?"

"Relax. No one else knows. I had to pee, and when I was in the woods, I heard something. At first I thought it was Josie and Pratt, but then I clearly heard the name *Jack*, and it wasn't spoken, if you know what I mean." She poked Savannah in the ribs and arched a brow. "I see you took my advice."

"Oh my gosh. Do you think anyone else heard us?" Savannah's eyes darted from Lou to Josie and finally to Pratt, none of whom were paying her any extra attention. "I'm so embarrassed."

"I just told you no one else knows. Sheesh, your head is still in the clouds isn't it? There's nothing better than that new-relationship-after-sex euphoria." Elizabeth sighed with a dreamy look in her eyes. She nodded toward Jack. "He seems more relaxed today, too. He's not nearly as cranky."

"I don't know if I'd call it a relationship." Savannah watched Jack as he filled a backpack with supplies. He *was* moving with less rigidity, and his mouth was no longer pinched. He glanced up, and Savannah noticed his furrowed brows—and how strikingly handsome he really was—only this time it wasn't his features she was assessing. As she drank in his angular nose, high cheekbones, and strong chin, it was his words that she heard. *I see a strong woman who's also feminine, and the combination is...frustrating.* His honesty was his most attractive trait, and a refreshing change for Savannah, who lived in a world of misrepresentation and deceit. Jack caught her gaze, and she held her breath. When he smiled, the deep worry lines that had traveled across his forehead disappeared, and Savannah let out the breath she'd been holding.

She made a conscious effort to keep a little distance between herself and Jack. She didn't want to make him uncomfortable, and she didn't need to look like a moon-eyed girl in front of the others. She knew that everyone would see right through any efforts she made to hide the way her stomach fluttered and her pulse skipped when she looked at him.

Despite the bright sun, the temperature beneath the cover of the trees was downright chilly. Savannah had just pulled her sweatshirt over her head when she felt Jack's hand on her lower back. It could only be Jack's enormous hand, as it covered her almost completely from hip to hip, and if she concentrated hard enough, she could still feel the heat of it against her bare skin. Now his hand slid off as quickly as it had landed. Savannah scanned the campsite. Pratt and Josie were packing their supplies, and Lou, Elizabeth, and Aiden were playing tic-tac-toe in the dirt. No one appeared to be looking for them.

"You sleep okay?" Jack asked in a serious voice.

She turned to face him, and her smile stuck half formed on her lips. That shadowed look was back.

"Yeah. What's wrong?"

Jack's eyes shifted left, then right, finally landing on Savannah's. "Nothing."

Savannah heard, *Everything.* She touched his arm, and his muscles tensed. "Jack?" she whispered. "What am I not getting here?"

He shook his head. "Nothing. It's going to be a long day. You have what you need?"

"Jack, I have everything. You gave us a very precise list. Please tell me what's going on." She looked over her shoulder, relieved to see the others were still busy. She turned back to Jack, and the fluttering in her stomach turned to a sinking feeling.

Jack clenched his jaw. "Come here." He stalked off to the edge of the woods. Savannah followed, her insides twisting with regret. *He's going to say it was all a mistake. It's over. Darn it! When did I start caring so much?*

"Savannah, what we did last night—"

She held up her hand. Hearing him say the words was going to be far too painful. Instead, she said it for him. "It was all a mistake and you want to forget it ever happened."

Jack's eyes flashed dark. He hunkered over her and touched her elbow, turning her away from the others. "What? Why on earth would you think that?"

"Isn't that what you came to tell me?"

Jack caressed her arm. "No. I wanted to tell you that what we did last night meant a lot to me. But, Savannah, if you don't want this, please tell me now. I'm not the kind of guy who wants or needs a fling. Honestly, I don't even know *how* to have one."

Savannah shook her head. She needed clarification. Her

legal mind kicked into gear, and she wanted to know precisely what he meant. In no uncertain terms.

"Exactly what are you saying?" she asked.

"This is really hard for me." He let go of her arm and ran his hand through his hair. "For two years, I never looked at another woman. Then you burst into my life all bossy and confrontational, and not only can I not take my eyes off of you but I can't stop thinking about you. It took all of my willpower not to crawl into your tent this morning. And when you came out of your tent to join the others, looking so beautiful with that smile that gets to me a little more every time I see it, I had to suppress the urge to take you in my arms and kiss you until neither of us wanted to do anything but sneak off into the woods." He looked away. "This is crazy. I sound crazy, and I know that."

When he turned back to her, his eyes searched hers, and she knew she should respond with something, anything that would make him feel less nervous, but she couldn't find her voice. She was still stuck on *I can't stop thinking about you.*

"Look," he began. "I was with one woman for ten years. I barely remember anything, much less anyone, before she came into my life. Then I lost her, and my world ended. It stopped, Savannah. Do you know what that's like?"

She shook her head.

"And then I'm finally able to function like a normal human being. I can teach people basic survival skills, fly my plane, go into town…" He began pacing. "Okay, maybe it's not *normal,* normal, but it's functioning all the same. Crazy, right? That I'd let my life stop like I did?" Jack stopped pacing and crossed his arms, then uncrossed them and continued. "Anyway, now…I'm kind of lost again."

"Because of me?" She couldn't really follow what he was saying. Was he unhappy about what happened between them or was he glad it had happened?

He stepped forward and folded her in his arms. "*Man*, Savannah. Even this." He took a step back. "Touching you in this innocent way sends my body into overdrive."

Savannah lowered her gaze to the bulge in his jeans and raised her eyebrows. *I guess that's my answer.* She looked up at him and grinned.

"Great. It's really funny," he snapped.

He ran his hand through his hair again, and Savannah warmed at the nervous habit.

"I have to go lead those people out into a dangerous forest, and while I should be thinking about shelter construction, rolling hitches, and sheepshanks, I'm thinking about your naked body pressed against mine. I can't even go down to the stream without thinking about you and getting aroused."

Savannah laughed. She knew exactly what he was feeling, because she was feeling it, too. Just looking at him made her get all quivery inside.

"Great." He shook his head. "You go ahead and laugh, but it's not that easy to hide it, you know? Not to mention that I want to kiss you so bad right now that I'm conjuring all sorts of dirty fantasies."

She used his bulging forearms for balance and lifted up on her toes, kissing him lightly on the lips. He grabbed her arms and deepened the kiss. When they drew apart, she asked, "Will that hold you over?"

"No. It won't hold me over. Now I'll be like this all day."

She loved the way the muscles in his arms twitched when he was nervous, and the way he held her possessively, as if he couldn't stand the idea of her walking away.

"Well, I can't exactly help you with that now, can I?" she teased.

Jack began pacing again.

"Why are you so twitchy?" she asked.

"I'm not twitchy," he barked.

"Horny?" she teased.

He stopped pacing and stared at her.

"I guess two years is a really long time," she said.

"I don't want to talk about it. I don't know what I want. No. I do know what I want, but..." He lifted his eyebrows flirtatiously.

"Stop." She laughed. Inside she was jumping up and down, silently cheering, *Yes! Oh, yes!* She glanced back at the camp and noticed that everyone's backpacks were sealed up tight and they were milling around, probably waiting for her and Jack so they could get started on their activities for the day. None of them were looking their way, though, so she doubted they'd seen them kiss.

"We have to go," Jack said.

"Jack, I know you have a job to do here, and I don't want to get in your way."

"You can't get in my way," he said with a cold tone.

She felt her face fall.

"I'm sorry. See? I'm frustrated and I'm going to be a jerk to you. I know I am. I don't remember how not to be." He touched her arm, then dropped his hand. "I gotta stop touching you." He shoved his hands in his pockets and then pulled them out quickly.

"Jack." She could see him working himself up into a frenzy. As an attorney, she'd seen it with her clients a million times.

When they were pulled out of the attitudes they wore like shields, the feelings they'd hidden for so long wreaked havoc with their emotions and sent them into the same frenetic state.

"I'm sorry if—" he began.

"Jack."

"I don't mean to—"

"Jack!" she said firmly.

He opened his mouth to speak, and she touched his cheek, forcing him to stop trying to talk and focus on her.

"You're not going to be a jerk to me because I won't let you." Startled at her own vehemence, she wondered why she'd been so weak with Connor when she could be so strong for Jack.

He stared down at her with a serious face. "We'll talk?"

"I'm counting on it." *And so is my body.*

Chapter Eleven

THEY BEGAN THE morning with a three-mile hike along the side of the mountain. Jack had talked for the first mile and a half about the importance of finding the right spot for building a shelter. He described what to look for in adverse weather conditions, showed them how to choose a location that appeared free of animal dens, and taught them the dangers of not being aware of their environments, warning them to look for branches in danger of falling and rotten tree trunks. When he spoke, his eyes were drawn to Savannah. She looked even more gorgeous than she had earlier that morning. Her cheeks were flushed from the steep incline they'd ascended, and her hair had gotten mussed as she ducked under branches. Jack was relieved that the guilt that had gnawed at him hadn't returned.

Jack led them back down the mountain flanked by Aiden and Pratt. Pratt had on another dark T-shirt and the same black tuque he'd worn since he arrived. Lou walked on Aiden's other side, while the women chatted behind them. He'd been counting down the hours until Savannah would be in his arms again, and as consuming as that thought was, every time he looked at Pratt he felt a need to get through to him. His brooding eyes reminded Jack so much of his younger brother

Sage that he couldn't leave him to deal with his trouble on his own.

Based on his experience with his own brothers, Jack was pretty sure there was no way that Pratt would talk about whatever was bothering him. He hoped that he might find a roundabout way to eke it out of him. He hated to see such a young man so angry all the time. It was one thing to have lost the woman you loved, but quite a different thing to just be angry at the world. He was mulling over the right approach when Aiden broke the silence.

"When I grow up, I'm gonna be a survivor man, too," Aiden said.

"You can be anything you want to be if you work hard enough at it," Lou said.

"No, I can't," Aiden said. "I can't be Superman no matter how hard I try."

"How do you know unless you try?" Lou winked at Jack.

Pratt made a *tsk* sound.

That was all Jack needed to know that Lou had hit home with something.

"I guess…" Aiden scrunched his face and thought about the question. "I guess I have to try; then I'll know."

"Good plan," Lou said.

"Pratt, tell me about what you do. Your registration form said artist." Jack hoped his comment sounded innocent.

Pratt pulled at the edge of his black T-shirt. "I sculpt," he answered.

Jack had heard his voice so rarely that each time he spoke, the deepness of it took him by surprise.

"What medium do you use?" Lou asked.

Pratt shrugged. "Mostly metals. Bronze, brass, aluminum,

iron. I also do some smaller sculpting with clay and some wood carvings."

Jack noticed the hint of excitement in his voice. "My mother is a sculptor and a painter. I've always been fascinated by her ability to create fantastic things out of her imagination. How did you get into it?"

Pratt shrugged again. "Friends, I guess. While I was at college, I studied on the lawn of the art building. That side of the campus had the most shade and the people were, I don't know…more interesting."

"Than?" Jack asked. He heard Savannah laugh and glanced behind him. She was holding on to Josie's hand and they were both doubled over with laughter. Elizabeth had a wide smile on her face, and she waved to Jack. He smiled.

"Than what?" Pratt asked.

"The art students were more interesting than who or what?" Jack asked.

"Oh, than the engineering dudes. They were dolts. Repressed. You know the type. They think they're smarter than everyone else and all that." For the first time since they'd arrived, Pratt looked at Jack with a hint of levity in his eyes. "You're not an engineer, are you?"

Jack laughed. "Not anymore."

Pratt shook his head, and his mouth lifted to a crooked smile.

Jack felt a shift in Pratt's attitude, and he was glad to see hints of a nicer guy beneath the sullen exterior. "It's okay. I studied engineering, but I went into the military after college and ended up in the Special Forces." That year, Jack had met the men who would become like brothers to him. And years later, after Linda's death, he'd erased them from his life just as he'd abandoned his own family. He'd even removed their numbers from his cell phone. "You're right about engineering school. It's pretty serious stuff. So did you graduate?"

"Yeah," Pratt said.

Jack could not reconcile the young man with the black tuque pulled down low over his forehead with the other eggheads he knew in college. Great men, but they were highly intelligent, and not one of them had a creative bone in their body. "So, why sculpting? Did you dislike the engineering field?"

Aiden pulled on Jack's pants leg. "Excuse me, Jack, but what's sculpting?"

"I'll let Pratt answer that."

"Well, it's when you take something—like a hunk of metal or clay—and you reshape it until it looks like something else. Sometimes you have to use really hot fire, which is cool, and sometimes you can just use your hand or you use tools." Pratt nodded. "Do you use Play-Doh?"

"Uh-huh," Aiden said.

"That's sculpting," Pratt said.

"Cool. So I can be a survivor man and a sculptor." Aiden beamed at his father.

Lou patted him on the head. "That's right. You can do anything and everything you want, and if you need to learn how, we'll find a teacher."

Pratt sighed. "You probably shouldn't tell him that, 'cause it's not really true."

"What's not?" Lou asked.

"That he can do anything he wants to do."

"I don't understand. Of course he can. If you work hard enough, you can accomplish just about anything. Right, Jack?"

Lou said.

Two days ago, Jack would have agreed with Pratt. His future looked like it was going to be one of a reclusive angry man with no hope for happiness. Now, as he looked back at Savannah and felt a fluttering in his chest, he felt a glimmer of hope that he might not be held hostage by that anger forever. It was the strangling guilt that he wasn't as confident about.

"I think everyone should try as hard as they possibly can at anything they do in life. It doesn't matter if you're a garbage man or the president. Hard work pays off." It had taken every ounce of Jack's energy, his spirit, and his willpower to fall back from the public life he'd once lived and come to a place of solitude in order to suppress the guilt that surrounded Linda's accident. He'd known the cost when he'd done it. As much as he wanted to disappear, it was difficult to turn his back on the people he loved. Now he wondered if he'd tried hard enough. When he told Savannah that before meeting her he'd finally been able to function like a normal human being, he was telling the truth. What he hadn't realized then, and what was becoming clearer by the minute, was that he wasn't functioning like a normal person at all. He'd been functioning as an angry, guilty man who was able to deal with only a modicum of civilian life—and functioning was stretching it. *Maybe it's time to deal with all this garbage head-on.*

"I'm not talking about the ability to do what you dream of. I'm talking about society's perceived value of what you do and the expectations of others," Pratt explained.

It sounded to Jack like he wasn't the only one waxing introspective.

"I know all about societal norms." Lou patted Aiden's head. "Some people think we're rebelling against the system by homeschooling, but we just want Aiden to have a chance to learn more than schools allow. We want him to find his own likes and dislikes, and we want to nurture them through schooling. But there are even some parents who think it's weird, so they don't offer play dates and such."

Jack looked over at Lou, noticing the content look in his eyes and the way he carried himself without any false bravado—his shoulders a little hunched, his belly a little soft. Lou wore hemp shorts and a loose cotton T-shirt. He appeared very comfortable in his own skin. Something Jack envied. "So why do it?" Jack asked.

Lou put his hand on Jack's shoulder. "Why live in the woods?"

Because I was too angry to live around people. "It makes me happy."

"Exactly. Aiden's happy when his mind is fulfilled, so we're there to help," Lou said. He mussed Aiden's hair. "What does Dad always tell you, Aiden?"

"Always do what you love. Those who don't like it don't matter and those who matter don't care," Aiden said in a bored voice, as if he'd had to say it a million times.

"I've heard that a million times," Pratt said. "I don't get it because, like, my parents are all over me to go back to corporate America and they do matter to me. There is such a thing as caring too much."

"My family doesn't love what I do, and they matter more to me than, well, just about anything else in life." The words left Jack's lips before he could think to stop them. His family had reached out to him so often during the first few weeks after Linda's death, and he'd pulled away—ignoring their efforts and their offers of help. At first it just hurt too much to see the people he loved when the one he loved most would never be with him again. As time progressed, the guilt of not seeing them wore him down and he was afraid to face them, but not a day went by that he didn't miss his family. Before Linda had died, he'd spoken to his mother every week on the phone, sometimes twice a week. She'd tell him about her gardens or her latest sculpture, and he'd enjoyed those conversations. And Siena and Dex, his twin sister and brother, had just turned twenty-six in June, and he owed them a visit.

"So, how do you handle it, Jack?" Pratt asked.

"Not well, I'm afraid, but my position is a little different. I sort of lost my mind after my—for a while," Jack answered. They were almost to the end of their hike and back at the stream, and he didn't want to talk about Linda and stir up all that anger and guilt again. He was enjoying the short reprieve. "The real question, Pratt, is how are you handling it?"

Pratt held Jack's gaze. "Not very well, either, I'm afraid. Arguing with my parents. I thought that crap would end when I left for college, but they want to control my life."

"Too many parents want to do that, and it's a real shame," Lou said. "I hope I never do that to Aiden, but who knows what'll happen ten years from now, or twenty. Live in the here and now. Maybe you both can let your family members know this is what you need to be happy. If they love you—which I'm sure they do—they'll eventually come around, but arguing to prove your point won't make it heard any louder. If anything, they'll turn a deaf ear."

Lou may have been speaking to Pratt, but as Jack listened to his advice, he realized that he'd argued with his family, demanded that they leave him alone and let him deal with Linda's death and the guilt he felt on his own terms, but not once did he have a heart-to-heart, calm and rational discussion about any of it. He'd been too angry and they'd been too hurt.

Maybe it's time to heal more than just my own broken heart.

Chapter Twelve

BACK AT THE stream, they cooked a stew of lentils, rice, carrots, and potatoes, and after eating as a group, Jack told them to take a few minutes to clear their heads and prepare for the shelter prep lesson. When he addressed the group, his eyes often drifted to Savannah, and each time they did, her stomach dipped like a fan girl seeing Tim McGraw for the first time.

Savannah and Elizabeth watched Pratt and Josie on a boulder nestled beside two large trees. Pratt lay on his back with his head in Josie's lap, and it struck Savannah how fast people connected with one another.

"They're cute, huh?" Elizabeth said.

"When I look at them, I see how free they are. Like real life doesn't exist. As if it's just the two of them without a care in the world," Savannah said.

"But you know that in a paucity of hours, they'll be back to the real world, and who knows what will happen, or if they'll ever see each other again."

Savannah's smile faded. *A paucity of hours.*

Jack joined them a moment later. "Ladies, how are you holding up?"

"This has been amazing, Jack." Elizabeth looked in the

direction of her tent. "I think Aiden is quite taken with you."

"He's a cute kid. Seems really interested in all of this. I hope he can hold on to that as he gets older," Jack said.

"We'll instill the lessons that you've taught him. Don't worry." Elizabeth touched Savannah's arm and said, "I think I'll join them."

Elizabeth turned her back to Jack and lifted her eyebrows with a wide smile toward her. In Manhattan, Savannah had one close girlfriend, Aida Strong, and she was so different from Elizabeth. Aida was a snarky and aggressive attorney, and Savannah enjoyed the time they spent catching up over drinks or dinners and passing quips back and forth when they passed each other in the hallway. Aida was a true city girl at heart, and as Savannah looked around the mountain, she knew that Aida would never have made it past the dirt landing strip, and she was glad for Elizabeth's company.

Jack crossed his arms and planted his feet in a wide stance as he watched over the group, a position she'd come to know as one of either anger or of caretaker and proud instructor. As he rubbed the back of his left arm with his right, she had the feeling he was proud of not only leading the group, but at having taught them a few things along the way.

Her heartbeat ratcheted up as she drew her eyes slowly down his profile. The way his shirt and jeans strained against his impressive, taut muscles reminded her of the way he'd been standing when they'd first landed, only now when she looked at him, the first thing she saw wasn't the harsh exterior. It was the birthmark just to the right of his left ear and the way he rubbed the thick white scar running down the back of his left arm.

Without turning to look at her, Jack said, "Some people consider it rude to ogle others."

Savannah laughed. "Like when they're bathing in the stream and that other person comes tumbling down the hill?"

He looked at her then, and she could tell he was repressing a smile. "I was keeping you safe."

"From?"

"Bobcats," he said, and finally the smile broke free. He reached for her hand. "You realize this is a four-day course, right? This is our last night together."

Savannah didn't want to think about it. "Yes."

"Just making sure," he said.

"What kind of answer is that?" Savannah opened her eyes wide. "Wait. Is this your way of saying that whatever this is between us is over when we leave?" *I thought you weren't a fling kind of guy.*

"Nope. Just making sure you're thinking about it." He picked up a rock and tossed it into the stream.

"Do you want to talk about it?" She supposed they should even if she'd rather wait one more day and enjoy their remaining time together without the stress of worrying about what comes next.

"Nope. But I would like to spend time with you tonight." He looked at the water once again.

"Me too." She could see something pulling at his mind, sending worry lines across his forehead again. "Jack, is something wrong?"

"Nope. Just thinking about stuff. Come on. I'll teach you how to build a shelter. You never know when you'll be caught outside of the concrete jungle."

Part of Savannah wanted to nail down where they were headed, but it frightened her, too. They'd have plenty of time to think about that later in the evening.

They joined the group, and Savannah couldn't shake the feeling that Jack had something big on his mind. She could only hope that it wasn't about not wanting to carry their relationship past the weekend.

Back at the fire pit, they listened to Jack explain how to make a shelter using materials indigenous to the mountain and woods.

"Key elements to remember are length, warmth, wind direction, and of course...what?" Jack looked to Aiden for the answers.

"Be away from animal dens," Aiden said. He looked at his mother and then his father with a proud smile. Elizabeth pulled him close and kissed the top of his head.

"Right. Excellent. All we really need are sticks and leaves. Later I'll show you how to use mud and vines to secure and insulate a shelter, but for now, we're focusing on the basic structure. The first thing I want you to do is to gather sticks about yay high." He held a hand up to his chest. "We're going to place them at an angle, so be sure they're not too short. Remember, no one goes alone, so grab a buddy and take off."

Aiden rushed to his side. "Jack, after we do this, will you help me pack my own survivor bag with rope and stuff?"

Jack raised an eyebrow in his mother's direction. She shrugged, then nodded.

"Sure, buddy. We'll do it as soon as we're done," Jack said.

Elizabeth appeared by Savannah's side. "Ready?"

"Sure." Savannah took one last glance over her shoulder at Jack as they headed off in search of sticks.

Finding appropriate sticks was not as easy as Savannah had thought it would be. Most were too short, some were too heavy, and others snapped like brittle bones. They grabbed the few appropriately sized sticks they could find. In her mind, she toyed with the idea of her and Jack in a homemade shelter in the woods. *We wouldn't need any insulation at all.*

"How are you holding up?" Elizabeth asked.

"Fine, why?"

"I don't know. Tonight's our last night here, and Lou said he and Jack talked with Pratt and that he had the feeling Jack needed help finding his way back to his family as much as Pratt did."

Savannah had already pushed the thought from her mind. She didn't want to think about it being her last night on the mountain with Jack. "What do you mean?" Savannah asked as she reached for a stick.

"He didn't say much. Just that when Jack talked about how he handled things with his family after his wife's death, he seemed a little stressed."

"Well, that explains why he seems a little distant today," Savannah said. "How did you know about his wife?"

Elizabeth looked away.

"Elizabeth?"

Elizabeth sighed. "You can't say anything, okay?"

"Okay. I promise," Savannah said, not knowing if she could keep the promise.

"Linda's family has been really worried about him. I know her younger sister, Elise, but we weren't really close before Linda died, so Jack and I had never met. Anyway, Jack sort of dropped off the face of the earth, and now Linda's father is not well. He's got terminal cancer."

"Oh no, that's terrible," Savannah said.

"Really sad. He's a good man, and they're really worried because the last time Jack saw him they had a blowup, and

Ralph—that's Linda's father—said things to him that he shouldn't have. Mean things. And he wants to apologize before he dies. Anyway, Lou and I registered for the trip, and when I told Elise, she asked if we'd let her know how he was doing before they, you know, pushed their way back into his life." Elizabeth shrugged.

Savannah chewed on the information for a minute before responding. "So you're here to spy on him?"

"No. We're here because Jack has the strongest reputation in the business, and we wanted to come on this type of retreat. We thought it would be good for Aiden and good for us as a family. But when Elise found out…They love him so much, and if you could see Elise's dad. He's so fragile right now, and what he wants more than anything on earth is to fix things with Jack. I mean, I was coming anyway. What was I going to do? Tell her I wouldn't let her know how he was doing?"

"No, of course not. Jack definitely has some unresolved anger and guilt. What are you going to do? Will you eventually tell Jack?" *Will I?*

"No, I don't think so. I'll let them know that he seems to be still really hurting. You saw him when we arrived. He could barely speak without anger spewing out in all directions. Since you two connected, he's softened, but you can see he's still fighting those demons, and he could be for years to come. From what Elise said, he was never an angry person before the accident. She thinks he blames himself, and if what she says is true, then talking to Ralph might alleviate a lot of that guilt." Elizabeth touched Savannah's arm.

Savannah chewed on the reality that Jack might be wrestling with his anger and guilt for years. *Years.*

"I'm sorry I didn't tell you when we first met, but I didn't know if it was my place or not. When I saw that budding interest between you two, I didn't want to ruin it with this stuff, but when you asked me just now, I didn't want to hide it from you."

"That's okay. I get it. It probably would help him to talk to her father, but that really has to be his decision. Does he know he's sick?" Savannah felt like she held this new knowledge in her hand, and it was a weighty and precarious position to be in.

"No. By the time he was diagnosed, Jack had basically disappeared from their lives but, of course, not from their hearts," Elizabeth said. "The disease has progressed really fast. It's terrible—first Linda, now her father. And Linda's accident was so tragic."

"Jack hasn't shared the details of her accident with me, and I don't know if he ever will, but I'd rather hear it from him when he's ready." She hated keeping any secrets from Jack, and even though Elizabeth had been planning this trip before she even knew Elise would want her to check on Jack, it still felt wrong not to tell him she knew Linda's family. She couldn't decide anything right then. She was too confused to think straight. "I hope they can all get the closure that they need." Savannah thought of her father and the way he maintained that he was still in contact with her dead mother. She wondered if she was setting herself up to be hurt by continuing things with Jack.

No one can compete with the ghost of a lover.

Chapter Thirteen

LATER THAT EVENING, after Aiden was safely tucked in bed, they told ghost stories around the campfire. Lou and Elizabeth sat hip to hip, Elizabeth's hand resting on Lou's thigh, her head on his shoulder. Josie and Pratt snuggled together on the other side of the fire. Savannah longed for that kind of comfort. She'd spent so many years being the brave, strong career woman that being able to let down her guard and rely on someone else seemed more appealing than sex and chocolate combined. Her previous boyfriends hadn't been interested in discussions about her feelings or snuggling just to be close to each other. Their idea of comfort was buying her a box of chocolates once a month. Maybe that was why she'd never felt completely comfortable in a relationship. She always felt like she was on guard—in her relationships and at work. When she was with Connor, she was already deemed a notch below him because he was a celebrity, so she worked extra hard to impress him and his peers, and as a lawyer, she had to be on top of her game every minute. She inhaled the charred, smoky smell of the campfire and allowed herself to dream of a life where she could relax by a campfire more often.

Savannah glanced at Jack sitting a foot away from her on the grass. His arms rested on his knees, and he was staring straight ahead, into the darkness. She had the urge to reach out and touch the curve of his back, but she knew that Jack had to maintain his professional appearance as their guide, even if she hadn't been able to keep herself from kissing him earlier that morning. Luckily, as she'd thought, no one seemed to have seen them. At least no one was treating them any differently. They didn't need to throw their relationship—or whatever it was—in anyone's face. Savannah didn't even know where they were heading, and now that she knew how worried Linda's family was about him, she wondered if she had even more to worry about. Was Jack really too broken? Was she once again ignoring big red flags? Or was the feeling that she'd been brought to his camp for a reason real? She glanced at him again, hoping he'd want to see her even after they left the mountain. She knew she would not only want to continue seeing him, but she also knew she'd love to spend evenings with him by a campfire. Just the two of them.

"I THINK WE'RE going to turn in." Elizabeth stood and reached for Lou's hand. "Jack, today was amazing, and thanks for helping Aiden pack his survivor bag. He set it beside the tent, and when we put him to bed, he said he knew everything he needed to and that he was going to survive the wilderness." She laughed. "I think you have an even bigger fan now."

"I'm glad to hear it," Jack said. "Sleep well."

"We're turning in, too," Pratt said. He pulled Josie close and kissed her forehead. "Jack and Lou, you gave me some stuff to think about today on the hike. Thank you."

"Glad it helped," Lou said with a wave. Then he climbed into his tent behind Elizabeth.

"You guys did great today," Jack said. He'd felt Savannah's presence near him all evening, and at first it had been torture to not be sitting close enough to put his leg against hers or touch her hand, but he'd also been mulling over what Lou had said about family, and that had given him something else to focus on. *Arguing to prove your point won't make it heard any louder.*

He caught Savannah looking at him with a smile on her lips but worry in her eyes.

"Hey," he said.

"Hey."

"You all right?" he asked.

"Yeah." Her smile faded. "You looked so deep in thought tonight. Are you okay?"

"I've got a lot on my mind, but yeah, I'm fine." He moved closer to her. "There is one thing I've been dying to do all afternoon." He put his hands on her cheeks and kissed her. Just the taste of her lips and the smell of her fresh skin made his body react. He had planned on one light kiss, just enough to take the edge off from thinking about her so much, but as he deepened the kiss, he couldn't pull away.

Savannah, however, could. She pulled back and whispered, "We're in the middle of the camp."

He blinked away the fog of desire. "Right." What was he doing? He leaned in closer. "I want to make out with you all night long." He leaned his forehead against hers. "But I'd really like to talk and get to know you. So it's probably better if we don't go anywhere just yet. I can't be trusted when I'm alone with you."

She ran her index finger down his chest. "I'll take that as a compliment."

"I'll get a blanket, and we can hang out here by the fire." When he returned, he spread the blanket, and Savannah joined him beneath the stars.

She snuggled against him. "I can't believe tonight's our last night together."

"It's our last night here, but it doesn't have to be our last night together." He took her face in his hands. "I can't help it, Savannah," he whispered. "I know we're in the middle of the camp, but I have to kiss you again." He pressed a soft kiss to her lips. "I'm not very good at small talk," Jack admitted. *Who am I kidding? I suck at small talk.* Ever since Linda's death, he'd been afraid of saying the wrong thing. He worried that his guilt and anger would seep into every conversation, and that was enough to drive him into silence. Luckily, Savannah filled the gap.

"I can talk for hours. My brothers roll their eyes at me, and I know it's because I say what they think, and it's not always the most appropriate thing to say aloud. We're so close, it's like we can read one another's minds." She shrugged. "I tend to call them on things they wish they could keep hidden."

Jack realized she had been doing the same thing to him. "How many brothers do you have?"

Her eyes lit up. "Five. I'm the typical adoring sister, I'm afraid."

Jack laughed. "That's cute. I think my sister is the same way toward me. I have four brothers and a sister."

"You have a big family, too. Don't you love it? Gosh, I can't imagine life without them. We're all really close, and my brothers are all like you—big and burly, very masculine."

He could tell by the excitement in her voice that she really did adore them, and it made him long to be close with his family once again.

"They're also overprotective," Savannah added. "If I had cell service, they'd probably have called me sixteen times already to make sure I was okay. Are you close to your family?"

Jack thought about lying. It would be easier than admitting that he'd driven them away. But he didn't want to begin a relationship with Savannah based on lies. "We used to be. I'm the oldest, and until two years ago, we were all very close." He smiled at the thought. "There are eleven years between me and Siena and Dex, the youngest. They're twenty-six, twins. Siena's a model. She's a firecracker. You'd like her. Dex is a gamer. Well, he calls himself a gamer, but really he's a game developer."

"That's cool, but isn't it funny that there's even a career like *gamer*? I can't even imagine what that would be like." Savannah laughed.

Savannah laughed without any worry over what he might think, or if he thought what she said was funny. Her confidence and ease were two of the things he most admired about her, but the sound of her laughter, the uninhibited joy as it left her lips, that's what brought a smile to his face.

Before escaping to the mountains, Jack used to say the same thing to Dex about his career, and Dex used to tease him about being old. *Man, I miss him.*

"Not that there's anything wrong with it," Savannah added. "It's just so different from anything I grew up with. We rarely even watched television on my dad's ranch." She sighed. "So, eleven years between you and them? Second marriage for your parents?"

Jack loved how easily she reeled off her thoughts, like they'd known each other forever. "Accident," he said with a smile. "Or maybe on purpose. Who knows with them? Sage is twenty-eight. I'm sure you know of him."

"Sage Remington is your brother? As in the artist?"

Jack nodded. "The one and only. I can hardly believe how quickly he climbed that ladder to fame. His sculptures are in museums all over the world. He's a great guy, too."

Savannah's eyes washed over his face. "I guess I should have seen a resemblance, but I never put two and two together."

"He got my mother's artistic talent. She's been sculpting and painting since before I was born. She put her family first, though, and that probably hindered how far she could go. It's hard to pour your heart and soul into art when you're already pouring it into six children and a husband. She never seemed to resent us for it, though. My mom is like a shining light. She's the happiest woman I know."

There were so many things Jack had missed in his family's lives over the past two years that, as he said their names, he was hit with the same pang of longing that he'd felt recently when he was back in New York.

"Then there's Rush and Kurt. Rush's thirty-two. He's a competitive skier, and Kurt is thirty, a writer." Rush was six two, with massive legs and powerful arms. As a competitive skier, there was not an inch of him that wasn't solid, and despite the five-year age difference, they'd always been close—until Jack left Bedford Corners for the mountains. He looked at Savannah and brushed a strand of hair from her chin. "I really miss them. How about you? Youngest, oldest?"

"I'm in the middle. Treat, Dane, and Rex are older than me and Josh and Hugh are younger."

"Why does Hugh Braden sound familiar?" Jack tried to remember where he'd heard that name.

"He should. He's one of the top race car drivers in the Unit-

ed States, handsome as Patrick Dempsey and cocky as can be."
She laughed. "I shouldn't say that. Hugh's the youngest. He can
be a little self-centered, but he's changed a lot over the last few
months. There's nothing we wouldn't do for one another."

"That's nice. That's how we always were." As he had on the
way to the airport, Jack thought about trying to find his way
back to the life he left behind and the family he loved. Savannah
struck so many chords in his heart that, as he looked at her, he
swore he felt his heart softening. At the same time, his nerves
tightened. She made him want to jump the hurdles he'd
believed were too big to even try, which scared the heck out of
him.

"You're not like that anymore?" she asked.

"They are, I guess, but…" He took her hand. "You know
what? I can't sit and talk. I'm sorry. I thought I could, but this
is making me a little anxious. Can we walk a little?"

They walked down the hill toward the stream. The sky was
clear, and the moonlight filtered through the umbrella of trees,
illuminating their path. Jack's chest constricted, thinking about
the things he wanted to tell Savannah. Before they got any
further involved, she needed to know who he was—and the
secrets he'd been hiding. He'd have to figure out a way to ease
them in.

"Tell me about your parents," Jack said.

Her eyes lit up again. "My dad is the best. He's a thoroughbred horse breeder, and he still lives on the ranch where I grew
up in Weston, Colorado. He's this big, burly cowboy. Gosh, I
love him so much."

She turned away with a dreamy look in her eye, and it made
Jack think about his father and how proud of him he'd always
been. His father fought for his country; he took care of his

family. To Jack, he was everything, until their relationship had fallen apart, and now he wondered if he'd ever feel that way again.

"Rex helps him run the ranch," Savannah explained. "Treat, my oldest brother, owns resorts all over the world, but when he and Max, his wife, first got engaged, he moved back home to help on the ranch and to be closer to Max. Now he basically runs his business from there."

Jack wanted to know everything about her, and when she spoke of her family, her whole face lit up. He didn't want to take away that spark, but he wanted to know more about her family and about the loss of her mother.

"You mentioned that you lost your mom. Would you like to share that with me, or is it too painful?" They walked along the bank of the stream, and Savannah was quiet for a beat too long. Jack realized he'd touched on a sensitive subject.

"She died when I was little."

She glanced at him, and he could tell she was trying to smile, but the tug never curled her lips up. He took her hand and brought it to his lips, pressing a warm kiss to the back of her fingers.

"I'm sorry, Savannah. You must miss her terribly. If it's too difficult to talk about, we don't have to."

"It's okay. I miss her, but I had just turned four. I didn't really know her, and I don't remember her. I only really remember what Treat and my dad have told me over the years." She took a deep breath. "So, that's my story. Why aren't you close to your family anymore?"

Jack had been trying to figure out how to tell her about the fallout after Linda's death, but no matter how he turned it in his mind, he always came back to the same conclusion. Savannah would learn that Linda's death was his fault no matter how he told the story. Nothing after that mattered. Once she knew that, he was sure she'd walk away and never look back.

"After Linda's accident, I was pretty messed up. We'd just set up a nursery and were going to try to have a baby." He tightened his grip on her hand just so he could feel something other than the guilt that was creeping up the back of his neck and clawing at his throat. "But we never had a chance. She died the weekend before we were going to start trying."

"Oh, Jack. I'm so sorry. That must have been devastating."

"I have always wanted a family, so it was really hard. My family was all over me, trying to take care of me, get me to talk to therapists, you know. They were trying to help me through it."

"That's good, right? They love you."

"It should have been, yes. But I wouldn't let them. I couldn't let them. Savannah, I'm not sure how to explain any of this. It was like someone took my soul and shredded it to pieces, then threw it into the wind, and I was left grasping for the pieces and trying to pull myself back together." The night of the accident came rushing back. The blinding storm that had doubled in power over the thirty minutes she'd been gone, the flashing lights of the ambulance and fire trucks. The smell of burning oil and rubber and the flames. *Oh man, the flames.* Jack let out a loud breath, trying to keep the memory from lodging itself into the forefront of his mind again. He finally felt like his head was on straight, and it had felt good not to live under that cloud of guilt, even if for only a day. He wanted that feeling more than anything else in his life—including Linda—and with that thought came the strangulation of guilt. *Will this ever end?*

"Jack?" Savannah touched his shoulders. "Jack, you're shaking."

He tried to push past the guilt, but it was too late. His body ached from it.

"You must really miss her."

Savannah's voice held so much compassion that he was drawn to it despite the guilt. There was something about Savannah that sliced through the guilt and pulled him through to the light on the other side. *If only I could hold on to that light instead of slipping back into the darkness.*

"I do." *But it's the guilt that eats away at me.* As much as he wanted to tell her that Linda died because of him, he couldn't bring himself to do it. He didn't ever want to see the disappointment in her eyes.

"Well, I'm sure your family understands that. Have you tried to talk to them?" she asked.

He shook his head. "I realized today that I hadn't. They tried, but I couldn't hear their offers of help. I was too angry. Too guilty." Jack released her hand and crossed his arms, rubbing the scar on his arm again. "Savannah, I told you before that I'm not the right guy for you, and the more I think about it, I'm not sure I'm the right guy for anyone."

"Why do you keep saying that? Lots of people lose loved ones and go on to have other relationships."

He heard the hurt in her voice, and the knot in his gut tightened. He didn't want to hurt her, and seeing the pain in her trusting eyes was killing him.

"I'm not like them. I've got too much crap in my head, and every time I look at you, I want something more. I want to have a normal life again. I want to be able to walk down the street without feeling like I wish I could hide, but..." He couldn't bear for her to know the truth, and when anger forced different words from his mouth to hide the truth, he was incapable of stopping them. "Look, I'm not like you. I don't even live in my house. I hide in the mountains most of the time. The idea of being in the city with all those eyes on me makes my skin crawl."

"So…what are you saying?" Savannah took a step backward, as if his words burned.

The words he'd said settled in his mind, and he realized that they hadn't been hiding the truth at all. They were the truth. He had to deal with his own issues before he could fall any harder for Savannah—or let her fall any harder for him. "This can't work, okay? It sounds like you have a really close family. You're a high-powered attorney, and I'm an ex–Special Forces guy turned recluse. I'm not sure I'll ever get past all the crap in my head to be able to move on. No matter how much I want to."

Savannah narrowed her eyes and crossed her arms. Jack pictured her doing that in a courtroom.

"How do you flip your emotions like that? Are you totally psycho, or is this a ploy?" She stepped closer, so they were only inches apart.

Jack looked away.

"Look at me, Jack. You owe me that."

He looked down at her with his jaw clenched so tight he thought his teeth might crack. He wanted to kiss her and wipe away the hurtful words he'd said and forget the truth he'd only just realized. *I hide in the mountains. I'm not sure I'll ever get past all the crap in my head to be able to move on. No matter how much I want to.*

"I might not know much about what you're going through, but I know honesty, Jack. I deal with it every day with my clients and the people who sue them. I can smell bull a mile away. This doesn't reek of bull, but I don't think it's the whole story, either."

"I'm not one of your clients, Savannah."

"No, you're not, but you're the man I just had sex with. Twice. The man I let touch me in ways I've never allowed before, and that's a heck of a lot more than a client." Her chest rose and fell with each angry breath.

"Is that all it was? A quick roll in the hay?" He clenched his fists, wishing he knew how to deal with all of this. "I didn't force you to do anything." He groaned. "Savannah, can't you see how conflicted I am? Can't you feel it?"

"Yes," she whispered. "That's the reason I'm not walking away. I'm conflicted, too, Jack. I'm not sure if you're crazy, or if you're the person I think—or hope—I see beneath all the anger."

He felt his nostrils flare and his face heat with anger at being so frustratingly confused. Why couldn't she just listen to him and heed his warnings? She was so good. He didn't deserve her.

"Do you want to know why I came here?" she asked.

He nodded once, a curt, angry nod.

"Because for the past two years, I've been dating this jerk who cheated on me. Many times over." She laughed, but Jack recognized the pain in her eyes. "I didn't even like him, Jack, but for some reason, I kept going back for more. I might be an ice queen in the legal realm, but with him? With him I was this weak, stupid girl." She swiped angrily at a tear as it dripped down her cheek and reached the corner of her mouth. "Then...then I come here trying to rebuild my confidence and prove to myself that I really can be *strong Savannah* once again and that I won't fall back into the enabler role like I was with him."

"Savannah." Jack reached for her, and she swatted his arm away.

"Then I meet you, and you're this guy with a massive chip on his shoulder, but I'm drawn to you like a magnet. And now I find out that I've done it again. I've latched on to some worthless, angry, insecure mountain man."

Jack reached for her again as she turned away. "I'm not worthless or insecure."

She wrenched her arm away. "Fine. Sorry. But this isn't about you. This is about me. I fell right back into being the enabler in some crazy relationship that can never work. I'm so done with this." Her lower lip trembled, and tears tumbled down her cheeks.

Jack reached up and brushed the tears away with the pad of his thumb, and just feeling her soft skin reminded him that she didn't deserve the anger he was pummeling her with.

"Don't you see?" he said through gritted teeth. Then he took a deep breath and let it out slowly. When he spoke again, he'd reined in his anger. "Before all this crap happened to me, I was normal. I wasn't an angry jerk. I wasn't a freaking mountain man. I was a loving husband and a hardworking man."

"Too bad you can't live in the past, Jack."

Her icy stare nearly bowled him over. "Savannah, I want this. Us. I want to see what's there. I just don't know how to get from here to there."

Savannah threw her shoulders back, as she had the first day he'd met her, when she'd stood up for Pratt right after they'd landed. "I want this, too. But I can't be that woman anymore. I can't fix you, and I can't be your battering block while you figure it out." She turned and began walking back toward the camp.

"Savannah," he called after her. Five long, fast strides later, he was beside her and walking fast to keep up with her determined pace. "Savannah, tomorrow's our last day here. Please don't leave things like this. I'm sorry. I tried to warn you and I tried to stay away from you, but I couldn't, and I don't know why. Savannah, I'm so sorry for that. I didn't mean to hurt you."

She turned to face him with tears streaming down her cheeks. "Too late."

Chapter Fourteen

MONDAY MORNING, SAVANNAH lay in her tent with puffy eyes, nursing her broken heart. She'd cried for most of the night and had beaten herself up over how much she already cared for Jack. What she felt couldn't be real—it had to be an emotional reaction from the combination of being hurt by Connor and then allowing herself to fall for Jack. No one felt that strongly about another person after just a few days. Maybe she needed to talk to Danica, her cousin Blake's wife. Danica had been a therapist prior to falling in love with Blake, who had been a new client at the time. Maybe she could help Savannah weed through whatever was making her fall for the wrong guys.

Savannah couldn't even look at Jack as they disassembled their tents and inspected the campsite to ensure that they'd left nothing behind. She was too pissed at herself. She had seen the warning signs, had even contemplated them, and she still let herself get caught up with him.

"Is everyone about ready?" Jack called across the site.

Hearing Jack's voice sound deflated, as if he were having a hard time making it through the morning too, tugged at her heart.

He continued. "As soon as Pratt and Lou are back, we'll roll out of here." Lou and Pratt had gone down by the stream to rinse out the pots from breakfast.

Jack picked up the sticks from their makeshift shelter—the one Savannah had fantasized about sharing with him—and carried them into the woods. She forced herself not to look at him. She didn't want to see his midnight-blue eyes or the stubble on his cheeks that felt so good beneath her palms. Instead, she grabbed her bags and took one last look around the campsite that she knew she'd never forget. She'd opened her heart to Jack in ways she never had before, and she got hurt. As angry as that made her, it made her stronger, which was what she'd come to the mountains for in the first place. *At least it wasn't a failure.*

"Aiden?" Elizabeth called into the woods. "Aiden?"

Savannah scanned the empty site. Her heart leaped into her throat. *Aiden!* She saw panic in Elizabeth's eyes and went to her. "When did you last see him?"

Josie took off running toward the stream and called over her shoulder, "I'll go see if he's with Pratt and Lou."

"I don't know." Elizabeth's voice trembled. "Twenty minutes? I was busy packing."

Savannah ran to Jack, hating that the angry mask he'd worn when they'd arrived had settled back on his beautiful face. "Aiden's missing."

Jack's eyes did a fast sweep of the site, then the perimeter. "Elizabeth, how long ago did you see him?"

Elizabeth was circling the site, calling Aiden's name.

"She said about twenty minutes ago," Savannah answered. "I'm going to look for him."

"No. You stay here. I'll go," he said. "He's probably down by the stream with his father."

"If he's not, then I'm going. I'm not going to sit here while that little boy is out there alone." She lowered her voice. "Remember the bobcat?"

Jack gripped her shoulders. "You're not going in the woods alone. I'm not losing you, too."

Lou and Pratt sprinted past Josie into the camp. Josie's voice came over the crest of the hill, out of breath and unable to hide the fear in her eyes. "He's not at the stream!"

Elizabeth's face was beet-red as she screamed Aiden's name.

"Where's Aiden?" Lou yelled. He grabbed Elizabeth.

"I don't...know. He was right here, and then..." Elizabeth cried.

"Where's his survivor bag?" Jack's eyes searched the site. "Elizabeth. Do you have his bag?"

She shook her head.

"I'm going to find him," Lou said, moving toward the hill.

"Hold up." Jack looked at Pratt. "Pratt, go with him. Leave a trail on the trees like I showed you so you can find your way back. Do not separate. You two go east. I'll go west."

"Josie, you stay with Elizabeth and do not let her leave this site. You hear me? If anyone finds him, you yell as loud as you can and bring him back here to the camp. If he shows up, you don't let him leave. No matter what. We meet back here in"— he checked the time on his watch—"thirty minutes. Everyone. Right here. Elizabeth, we'll find him. He can't have gone far, and since he took his bag, he's probably nearby playing survivor man."

"I'll go that way." Savannah pointed to her left.

"Savannah." Jack's chest swelled as he pulled himself to his full height.

"I'm perfectly capable of searching for him, and I'm not

going to be told what to do by you or anyone else. There's a little boy out there, and he needs as many eyes looking for him as possible." She set her jaw and met his stare. She was not going to be waylaid.

"Then you come with me." He grabbed her arm, surveying the woods. Then he dragged her ten feet to their left and, still holding her arm, stalked into the woods. "I don't know why you have to be so stubborn."

"You can let go of my arm now," she said. "How are we going to find him?"

"We're going to do what I taught you on the hike. Look for recent signs—freshly broken twigs, footprints." He stopped walking and cast a hard, hot stare at her, then released her arm.

"What was that look for?" *And why did it make me want you all over again?*

"Come on, Savannah. How can I concentrate on anything with you around? I'm a mess. Can't you see that? I hear it in my own voice." He moved farther into the forest and hollered Aiden's name, then faced her again.

"Don't you get it? I have never wanted to change for anyone before, and you make me want to change. I know I'm messed up. I never claimed I wasn't. But you make me want to have a life again."

Empathy swept through her. "A life, or your old life?" she asked softly. She scanned the ground with every step as they walked deeper into the forest.

Jack stopped again. "Is that what you think? That I want to replace my old life? That you're somehow like Linda? You're nothing like her. She was quiet, meek, petite, blond. She'd never argue over anything. I don't think we raised our voices more than twice in ten years." He moved a lock of hair from her shoulder. "What I had was love and a normal life. That's what I meant. I miss those things, and you make me want them again." He turned and resumed the search.

She was at a loss for words, confused. Did he mean he did want a relationship with her? Silence stretched between them until she finally said, "We should call for Aiden."

They both called his name, and Jack continued talking as they moved farther up the mountain.

"I thought I was happy before, completely fulfilled, and I was. Then. But when I'm with you—and the night we spent in each other's arms—it made me realize that there was more to me than I ever knew or understood, and you brought those other parts to life."

Jack called out in a deep voice, "Aiden!" Then he turned to her again. "It's you, Savannah. I want to change because of you. You opened my eyes." He turned to the other direction and hollered Aiden's name before turning back to her again. "I don't expect you to wait for me or stand by me or any of that. What you said makes sense. You're the last woman on earth I want to hurt, and you don't deserve my crazy mood swings. I'm going to try to finally deal with my own issues, and if I can find my footing again, and if you're interested, we'll go from there." He shrugged. "All I can do is my best. And if I can't do it, well, then what have I lost?"

A lump formed in Savannah's throat. "Darn it, Jack." She turned away before he could see her eyes fill with tears. Out of the corner of her eye, she caught a flash of a bunch of sticks leaning against a tree.

"Jack," she whispered. "Look."

Jack followed her eyes to the base of a large tree, where he saw the tips of sticks leaning vertically against the tree. Most of the trunk was hidden behind a large bush. They approached the tree, and both let out a sigh of relief when the makeshift shelter came into view. Jack crouched down and peered inside.

"Thank heavens," Jack said as he reached into the shelter and lifted Aiden into his arms. "Hey, buddy, that's quite a shelter."

Aiden blinked several times, like he was coming out of a foggy dream. "Jack! I survived the woods, just like you."

Jack pressed him to his body. His right hand covered the back of Aiden's head. "You sure did, little buddy. We were worried about you. Did you forget the rule about never going into the woods alone?"

Aiden looked at Savannah. "No."

"Then why did you?" Jack asked.

"Because I knew Mom couldn't go 'cause she had to pack, and Dad was at the stream. I just wanted to survive the woods," Aiden explained.

"Aiden, look at me."

Aiden shifted his big blue eyes to Jack.

"I'm proud of you for remembering what to do, but the woods are dangerous. There are bears and bobcats and all sorts of nasty things out here. You have to promise me never to go into the woods again no matter what you want to prove. Promise?"

Savannah felt tears fill her eyes at the joy of finding Aiden and the tenderness that Jack showed toward him.

"I promise. I'm sorry," Aiden said.

"We're getting ready to go on the plane, so now we have to leave the woods."

Aiden wiggled out of his arms. "Okay. Let me get my stuff." He climbed back into the shelter. When he returned, he had a handful of rope and put it in Jack's hand. "I made slip knots just like you showed me."

Jack picked Aiden up and hugged him tight. "I was worried about you," he said. He reached a hand out and touched Savannah's cheek. "Aiden, let's make a promise."

"A promise?"

"Yes, a promise. Let's promise not to hide in the woods anymore. Both of us. I promise if you promise."

Savannah could barely breathe. In one breath, he made her angry, and in the next, he filled her heart with hope. That couldn't be a healthy combination, but she was drawn to him in ways she knew would taunt her days and haunt her nights.

Chapter Fifteen

JACK OPENED THE cargo hold and began removing the luggage. The flight into New York had been relatively smooth, and it had given him time to think through the previous few days. Normally, he'd land, say farewell to his students, pick up a few supplies, and head back up to the mountains feeling like he'd unloaded a great weight from his shoulders. This afternoon, the anxiety that usually drove him to expediently say goodbye to his passengers had turned on him, and he dragged his feet. He was in no hurry to go back to the mountains—or to say goodbye to Savannah.

"Jack, we can't thank you enough," Elizabeth said as she picked up her bags. "I don't think any of us will ever forget this trip. Thank you for bringing Aiden back to us. Aiden will never forget what you taught him. Right Aiden?"

Aiden wrapped his arms around Jack's legs. "I promise not to hide in the woods. You promise, too, right?"

Jack crouched down and looked him in the eyes. "You bet I do, buddy. No more hiding." He tousled his hair and stood back up to shake Lou's hand. "Lou, you helped me out there. Thank you."

"I don't know how I could have done that, but if I did,

you're welcome." Lou embraced Jack. "Thanks for everything, man. I hope we see you again sometime."

Pratt picked up his backpack and slung it over his shoulder. "I still can't believe you're an engineer." He pulled his tuque down past his eyebrows. "You're much cooler than the guys I went to school with."

"So are you, Pratt. What did you decide to do about your parents?" Jack smiled when Josie appeared by Pratt's side.

Pratt laced his fingers with hers. "I'm going to talk to them. Really talk, not fight, and if they don't like it…" He shrugged. "Well, I guess they'll need to make a choice. See me and agree to disagree on my career choice or forget they have a son."

"Pratt," Josie chided him.

Pratt lifted the right side of his mouth in a smile. "I'm kidding. I won't let that happen." He looked at Jack. "She's a ball breaker."

"Josie, you keep him in line, you hear?"

"I'll do my best," she said. "We're just hanging out for a while, nothing serious." She lifted her eyes to Pratt, and Jack could tell there was more to them than a couple of kids *hanging out*.

"Enjoy the now, Jack," Pratt said.

"Thanks, Pratt. You too. Josie, watch out for snakes." As they walked away, Jack caught a glimpse of Savannah hugging Elizabeth, then Aiden and Lou. *I need to fix the past to enjoy the now.* He looked away, thinking of when he'd first seen Savannah and how he'd assumed she was a spoiled city girl. *Boy, was I ever wrong.* They headed into the airport terminal, leaving him and Savannah alone under the warm afternoon sun. Her cheeks were flushed as she came to his side.

"You look different than you did when you arrived," Jack

said. "Prettier."

A flush rose on Savannah's cheeks. She put her hands in the front pockets of her jeans and looked at the plane. "You know, I thought you were such a selfish jackass when you were so hard on Pratt when we first arrived."

"And now?" He was afraid of what she might say, but he couldn't take his eyes off of her. The sun glistened, highlighting the blend of yellows and greens in her beautiful eyes. Jack didn't think he'd ever forget the look in her eyes when her legs were wrapped around his waist in the stream—like she'd been dreaming of him her whole life. And even if she hadn't, he was going to keep that image in his mind as inspiration to follow through with what he'd promised.

"Now I see Jack Remington, a man, a widower, and a soft-hearted-survivor-man-slash-pilot." She licked her lower lip. "Who can be a real jackass when he gets scared."

"You had me there for a minute. I thought I'd made out like a bandit. Do you have to be brutally honest?"

"I don't know how to be anything but," Savannah said. "I'm afraid Bradens don't lie very well. My big rancher father drove morals and ethics into our little brains on a daily basis."

"I'm going to miss you, Savannah," he said. He stepped closer to her, breathing in her fresh, feminine scent, knowing it might be the last time he would be able to. His heart ached at the thought, and he swore to himself that he was going to do everything within his power to fix his life so he could be in hers. But Jack worried that a woman like Savannah would have her pick of better men than him.

"This all feels so weird. Two nights ago, I would have sworn we'd be leaving hand in hand today."

He put his hand on her cheek, and she pressed her face into

it. "You took a broken man, and in a few short days, you opened his eyes to what he was missing. You deserve so much more. You deserve a man who is whole."

Savannah moved away from his hand. "People always think they know what other people deserve, and I'm so sick of it. What does it even mean to say that I deserve someone who's not broken? Maybe I'm broken. Have you ever thought of that?"

Jack smiled, though he didn't mean to. He could tell from the way Savannah's lips pinched tightly shut that she didn't appreciate it, but she was so beautiful when she was fired up.

"You're not broken, Savannah. You're hurt. There's a big difference. You're a smart, strong woman with a solid career and probably better things to spend your time on than worrying about my baggage." He searched her eyes for understanding, but what he saw was anger and hurt. "Savannah—"

"You know what, Jack? Maybe you're right." She blinked away the dampness from her eyes and kissed him on the cheek. "I'll miss you, too." Savannah picked up her bags and walked away.

Jack's stomach twisted. She glanced back, and he raised his chin and tried to smile, unable to pull himself together enough to even manage a proper wave. She disappeared behind the terminal doors, and Jack let out the breath he'd been holding. He grabbed his gear and headed for the terminal, wondering if he was strong enough to face the life he'd abandoned.

Chapter Sixteen

SAVANNAH CLIMBED INTO a cab and gave her address to the driver. She stared out the window, thinking about how arrogant and cold Jack had been when they'd first seen each other at the airport and how she'd been turned on by everything about him. She leaned her head back against the headrest and closed her eyes. *What am I doing? I went from a man who wants every woman on earth to a man who's afraid of what wanting a woman does to him.*

Savannah pulled out her cell phone and turned it on. Messages began flooding in. What had she been thinking? She usually couldn't go a day without checking messages, much less several. She was sure her voicemail would be full, and she wasn't in the mood to deal with clients. She had another attorney covering for her, and he'd just have to cover for her a little longer. She needed a good, strong dose of sanity. She called her father.

"Savannah, how are you, darlin'?"

Hearing her father's deep voice thickened the lump in her throat, and all of a sudden she was a little girl again, climbing onto his lap when someone at school had hurt her feelings. Hal Braden was six foot six, like her eldest brother Treat, and he was the epitome of a broad-chested aging cowboy: rugged, leather-skinned, and big-hearted. He was just what she needed.

"Hi, Dad," she managed. "How are you?"

"Oh, doing fine, I suppose. We had two fillies born, and Rex has been taking good care of them. Got buyers already." Hal Braden was an affluent thoroughbred horse breeder, and although Savannah and each of her siblings had large enough trust funds that would allow for them to not work a day in their lives, he'd brought them up to work hard and to love with their whole hearts. Savannah wished she hadn't taken the latter so seriously.

She smiled at the mention of her older brother Rex. Jack reminded her so much of Rex that she wondered if she should have called him instead of her father. He might be able to enlighten her on the ways of angry men.

"Enough about me. How's my girl?" her father asked.

Forget Rex. Calling Dad was definitely the right move. She needed his familiar, caring voice to wrap around her in a virtual embrace.

"Good, Dad. I'm good." Tears welled in her eyes, and she pressed her finger and thumb to them. "I...uh...I'm just getting back in town from that survivalist training camp I told you about."

"Run by Jack Remington?"

"Oh my gosh, Dad. How'd you know?" Savannah asked.

"Treat did some research on the guy."

The Braden grapevine travels swiftly once again.

Savannah watched the busy streets of New York as they drove toward her Manhattan apartment. *Of course he did.* "I'm a big girl, Dad. I don't really need Treat tracking me down."

"He wasn't tracking you down. He was making sure you

weren't going into the mountains with a crazy man. He said anyone can put anything on the interweb. Besides, Treat's always going to be Treat."

Savannah sighed. "Internet, not interweb." As the eldest, Treat had always taken care of and protected Savannah and her siblings. She shouldn't be surprised or bothered by Treat following up on her trip, but she intended to give him a talking to just the same. She wasn't a kid anymore, and she didn't need other people deciding what was good or bad for her. Why couldn't they see that she didn't need protecting? *Only my heart does.*

"Interwhatever. This Remington guy, did he treat you all right? Your brother said he's got a strong military background, no history of reprimands, solid pilot's license."

"Dad, he was fine. Really." *Why am I so annoyed? Treat's always been overprotective.*

"All right. It's good that you made it out of the woods okay. Did you learn anything?" he asked.

She mulled over the honest answers she could give. *That I love bad boys. That I'm weaker than I thought. That I want to run back to the woods and find Jack.* Instead she gave him a safer, and still honest, answer.

"Yes, all the things I needed to know. I can now build a shelter, tie knots, and recognize plants that could kill me." *If only I could recognize the men who would be a danger to my heart before they actually did any damage.*

"Well, I'm not sure why you need all of that in New York, but I guess you know best," her father said.

Her father was always careful about supporting the things they did. Right then, she needed support of a different kind. "Dad, I'm a pretty strong person, right?"

"Other than your mother, you're the strongest woman I think I've ever known, Savannah. Is there something on your mind?"

She pictured him leaning against the kitchen counter, his long legs angled out from his body, his thick eyebrows drawn together as he waited for her to lay her problems out before him. *What am I doing?* She couldn't run to Daddy when things got tough. That alone would prove that she wasn't strong or confident.

"No, Dad. I was just checking."

"All right, but if you need me, you know where to reach me. You going to make it to Hugh's award ceremony?"

Hugh was always winning one award or another. They'd all head out to wherever the event was being held, and Hugh would flash a smile, dole out hugs, and inevitably get swept away by some leggy woman they'd never see again. She smiled. *Hugh's every woman's dream come true—the face of Patrick Dempsey on Hugh Jackman's body and with a love of all things risky.* Regardless of how much she loved Hugh, all she could think was that he probably left a trail of broken hearts in his wake just like the men she needed to avoid.

"I wouldn't miss it," she answered. "Good to talk to you, Dad."

"Vanny?"

"Yeah?"

"You can learn all the fancy skills you feel you need, but the strength and ability to survive comes from within. You just remember that, darlin'. And you're a survivor. There ain't nothing this world can hand you that you cannot endure."

The tears she'd been holding back sprang free. *I hope you're right.*

JACK'S VINTAGE INDIAN Chief motorcycle snaked swiftly up the long gravel driveway of the Bedford Corners home that he and Linda had shared. Jack leaned into the curves that used to bring him such comfort. Now, riding beneath the canopy of trees that arced overhead felt strange, and the air beneath, oddly cold.

He parked his bike in front of his cedar-sided chalet and placed his helmet on the back. After Linda had died, he'd holed up inside for days, wallowing in guilt and hiding from both of their families, until seeing her ghost in every photograph and reliving the memories they'd shared drove him into darkness and he'd escaped to the mountains. He walked past a wooden rocker as he climbed the porch steps, remembering the day he and Linda had purchased it from a man who looked like Grizzly Adams at a farmer's market on the outskirts of town. Jack unlocked the heavy wooden door. When he stepped inside, it wasn't the cooler temperature that had him rooted to the floor of the open living space. It was the emptiness that came with it. The way a room felt when it had been uninhabited for too long. Stale. Lonely. Dead. Like a garden after the vegetables and leaves had withered away and all that was left were the brittle stalks.

Jack forced himself to step inside. He blew out a breath and closed the door behind him. He looked down at the wide slats of wood beneath his feet and followed their lines to the sunken living room tucked just beyond the dining room table to his right. The stone fireplace that once crackled with warmth now stood barren before the rich blue couches. He managed a few steps in that direction and felt the kitchen looming to his left.

Linda had been a talented cook, and as he turned to look at the stainless-steel stove, he pictured her wide smile as she'd leaned over multiple pots atop the stove, her hips moving to imaginary music. He could almost feel her eyes lifting from a pot and catching his, could envision the tilt of her head and her blond hair spilling into her eyes as she blew him a kiss. His heartbeat sped up, and he turned his body fully in that direction.

Get a grip. He closed his eyes, and when he opened them, the image was gone. He pushed through the tightening in his chest and his racing heart and forced himself to move past the kitchen to the staircase.

His legs felt like lead as he took each step up the open slat-ted staircase. At the landing at the top, two bedroom doors remained closed. He hadn't been in them for months. He turned, his muscles trying to spur him into a hasty retreat, but his mind brought him back to Savannah and he fisted his hands, then spun back around with a growl.

"I'm not turning back." He lowered his eyes and stormed to the first bedroom door, grabbing the cold metal handle and turning it fast and hard, then thrusting the door open. He stormed into the master bedroom, and anger boiled in his veins. Savannah's voice sifted through his mind. *Too bad you can't live in the past, Jack.* Heat spread up his neck and cheeks. He threw open the double closet doors. His chest expanded with every breath. Two years he'd lived with the strangling guilt and self-loathing. Two long torturous years. He reached into the closet and grabbed a fistful of Linda's clothes, then yanked them from the hangers and threw them on the floor at his feet. His arms shook at the sight of them.

He reached in again, and his large hand grasped three outfits and tore them out of the closet with a loud *snap* as the hangers broke with the force of the pull. Adrenaline surged him forward, and he used both hands to rip the clothes out of the closet—and out of his life.

"*Freaking* Linda. *Freaking* storm." Handful after handful of her clothes piled around his feet. He reached deep into the back of the closet and grabbed a white garment bag. Tears filled his eyes as he stepped forward and buried his face in the white plastic garment bag that held his wife's wedding gown. His shoulders rounded forward as pain stewed in his gut, then traveled to his chest, where it swirled and gained strength before finding its release through his swollen throat, filling the room as an indiscernible, tortured wail. He gasped for breath, his chest convulsing with sobs. His biceps strained against his sleeves, shaking as he tore the plastic garment bag from its hanger and collapsed to his knees, burying his face in the cold plastic, his tears pooling against his skin.

It ends here. It has to end here.

Chapter Seventeen

TWO HOURS LATER, Jack carried several green Hefty bags full of Linda's clothes out of the house and dropped them on the front porch. He circled back up the stairs and stood in the middle of the master bedroom. The mattress lay bare as bones, stripped of its sheets and comforter; the empty dresser drawers hung open and cockeyed. The closet doors were open wide, exposing the first space he'd conquered. He wiped his face with the crook of his elbow and drew in a loud breath. His eyes burned from the tears that had already fallen, and as he left the room and approached the other door off of the hall, he thought he didn't have any tears left to shed.

He grabbed the knob and turned it slowly. His arms would not fling the door open. No matter how hard he tried, his muscles fought against his mind. The veins in his forearms snaked beneath his skin, thick and blue. He turned away, burying his hand in his hair and bending over as he groaned with frustration.

Several fast breaths later, he turned and faced the door again. He couldn't bring himself to turn the doorknob. He clenched his fists and raised his powerful leg. One fierce kick broke the door free from its hinges, splintering around the lock.

The next sent it slamming to the floor. Jack stormed into the room, his eyes locked on the crib beneath the window. He hulked across the floor and gripped the railing, fresh tears streaming down his face. He dropped his eyes to the stuffed elephant in the corner of the crib and reached for it, then brought it to his chest as he lowered himself into the rocking chair in the corner of the room, clutching the stuffed toy as the memories rushed in again. *Let's get the nursery ready just to get in the mind-set of having a baby around. I'll buy baby clothes and everything.* She'd been so excited the month they'd put together the nursery. *He'll have your eyes, Jack. And your height. I hope he has your height.* He brought the elephant to his face and pressed it against his cheek. *What if it's a girl? She'll be as beautiful as you*, he'd said to Linda. *Let's start trying Monday. It's the first of the month. A great time to start! Oh, Jack, I'm so excited.* Linda was a planner, always had been. The idea of trying to get pregnant and having a "start" date fit right into her organized and efficient lifestyle. Neither of them could have known that she wouldn't make it through the weekend. He crushed the elephant between both hands and allowed his body to feel every soulful tear, every wrench of his heart, every kick in the gut of saying goodbye to the child they'd never even had the chance to try to conceive.

A STREAK OF light sliced through the window and moved slowly across the hardwood floor of the nursery. Jack's tears had dried hours ago, but he hadn't been able to move from his perch in the rocker. His throat was dry, and his chest ached. He rose to his feet, moving slowly as he opened the closet doors. He took the baby clothes from the hangers carefully, folding each little outfit and placing it inside the crib; then he took that pile of unworn clothes and moved robotically down the stairs, feeling defeated and relieved at once. *It's time. I've hidden long enough.*

With the baby clothes packed neatly in a grocery bag, he set them on the front porch. He locked the door, then leaned against it and slid down to the floor, contemplating his next move. He'd been thinking about it all afternoon. There was only one thing he could do with Linda's clothes, and it would require reaching out and mending a fence. He needed to call Linda's sister, Elise, and give her Linda's clothes, and the idea of making the call seemed impossible.

The baby clothes could go to Goodwill, but Linda's clothes should go to her family. *I'm her family. Was. I was her family.* Jack didn't want to keep any of Linda's clothes. As much as it felt like he was ripping out a part of his soul, each time he thought of Savannah, he felt a rush of hope, and that hope stirred his heart in a different way—a better way. He no longer wanted to hold on to the past. Those few days he'd spent with Savannah had reminded him of how it felt not to be consumed with anger and guilt, and more importantly, for a few intimate moments, the loneliness that had consumed him day in and day out had fallen away. He hadn't realized how dark his life had become until Savannah, and all her stubbornness and all her beauty, barged in and lit up his world. He was ready to move forward.

Chapter Eighteen

SAVANNAH WAS GLAD to be back at work Tuesday morning. She'd stayed up most of the night before thinking about Jack. She'd tossed and turned all night, wishing she could see him—even though she knew she probably shouldn't. *Why is he consuming my every thought?* Now she threw herself into the work that had piled up while she was gone.

She hung up the phone with a client and weeded through the stack of messages on her desk. *How will I ever get through these?* She prioritized them into separate stacks: clients whose lives would turn inside out if she didn't call them back immediately, clients who only *thought* their lives would turn upside down, and people who might one day become clients. The remaining two stacks consisted of other legal documents she had to take care of and...Connor Dean. Not only had he filled her voicemail and sent her too many text messages to count, but he'd also left seven messages with her assistant, Catherine. She couldn't fathom why he was trying to get in touch with her at all. She'd already severed their working relationship and handed his files off to another attorney. His window of apology should have ended a year ago. *Darn it.* She had hoped that when she didn't return his calls, he'd get the message and leave her alone, but now it looked as though he'd continue to hound her if she didn't reiterate that it was over. As she picked up her cell to return his call, a knock sounded at her door; then the door flew open.

"Hey there, girlfriend. Lookie, lookie." Her associate, Aida Strong, came through the door carrying a large bouquet of roses. She was almost as tall as Savannah, with the same slim hips and long legs. Against Aida's fitted white skirt and blouse, the red roses looked even more vibrant.

Savannah's pulse sped up as she came around the desk. "Who sent them?" *Jack? Maybe he's not such a Neanderthal after all.*

"I didn't read the card." Aida tucked her long, straight blond hair behind her ear and set the vase on Savannah's desk. "Catherine said they just came, and I was coming in anyway, so I snagged them. They're gorgeous." She handed Savannah the envelope that came with the flowers.

Savannah read the card and then tore it in half and tossed it in the trash can. "You know what? I'm going to ask Catherine to bring them down to the mailroom staff. They'll enjoy them."

Aida arched a brow. "Connor?"

Savannah sighed. "Unfortunately. I'm going to call him right now and tell him to bug off."

Aida cringed. "I'm sorry. How was your weekend? Is that guy as handsome as he looks on the website?"

Savannah sighed. "Jack Remington is even hotter than he appears." *And even more sensual and the best kisser ever and…broken. Jack Remington is broken.*

"Yeah? Why am I getting a sex vibe here?" Aida smirked. "I knew I should have gone along as a chaperone. Tell me what I missed."

Aida and Savannah had started with the law firm within a month of each other five years earlier and had become close friends overnight. Aida was as snarky as Savannah was tough, and in the male-dominated legal entertainment business, they needed all the support they could get.

Savannah's cell phone rang, and she glanced at the screen. "It's Josh. I'll catch up with you later."

"Okay, but I'm taking these. Don't waste them on the mail-room staff." Aida took the flowers and winked on her way out the door.

Savannah answered the call. "How's my best-dressed brother?" Josh was one of New York's leading fashion designers, and as such, he was always impeccably dressed.

"I'm well, Savannah. I heard you were back in town. How was your survivor weekend? Will you be hitting the reality network next week?"

"Not a chance, although I really enjoyed it. It was nice to get away from the city, and other than a scary bobcat, it was actually pretty fun." She could almost feel Jack's body pressed against her back again, as it had been that night. She shook her head to get out from under the memory.

"A bobcat, Van?" Josh had recently gotten engaged to his childhood crush, Riley Banks, and now they were full business partners at JRB Designs. Ever since the engagement, Josh had been reaching out to Savannah more often. They both lived in Manhattan, but before Riley had come into his life, Josh had kept to himself. Savannah was glad for the change, and she enjoyed seeing him.

"Just a little one. It scared the heck out of me, but Jack scared it away. How's Riley?"

"Amazing, as always."

Savannah sat on the edge of her desk. "Why does everyone have an amazing love life but me?"

"Still bummed about Connor?" Josh asked.

"I can't even believe I stayed with him as long as I did. Why didn't you guys knock some sense into me?" Savannah stood and paced, rubbing an ache at the base of her neck. She hadn't told her brothers about Connor cheating on her, and she wasn't going to go down that road now. She'd like to forget Connor ever existed.

"Like you would have listened?"

You know me too well. "Okay, enough about *him.* What else is going on?"

"Kaylie's singing at a concert in Central Park tonight. Blake and Danica are going to be there, and Ri and I thought you might want to join us." Kaylie was Danica's sister.

"Kaylie's singing again?" Kaylie had given up her singing career when she had twins a few years earlier. Savannah toyed with the idea of going to the concert. She had nothing else planned, and the idea of sitting around her apartment thinking of Jack was torture.

"I think she's testing the waters. Blake said they were coming along to support her because this is her first big event since she had Trevor and Lexi. I think it'll be fun. We can hang and talk, maybe go for a drink."

Savannah did want to pick Danica's brain about her apparent inability to date men without baggage. "Sure, what time? I have a lot of stuff to catch up on here."

"Eight?"

"I think I can make that. I'll meet you at the bridge."

Savannah ended the call, and before she could get interrupted, she called Connor.

"Hey, Savannah. I was beginning to think you'd dropped off the face of the earth."

Despite loathing how he'd treated her and the way he'd disregarded her feelings and disrespected her, she felt a spear of lust shoot right through her at the sound of Connor's smooth, sensual voice. She cleared her throat and put her hand on her hip, steeling herself against his seductive ways.

"Nope. I'm still around, but, Connor, I'm not sure why you're still calling me. We broke up, remember?" She couldn't believe she was even wasting her breath on him.

"Come on, Savannah. That was nothing. Mimi's just a friend."

She could hear the smile in his voice, and it infuriated her. "Just a friend. That's supposed to make it better? Connor, do you even hear yourself?"

"Babe, calm down."

"Didn't you ever take Dating 101? You never tell a woman to calm down. I'm done, Connor. I've wasted enough breath on you. Please don't contact me again." She ended the call with a shaking hand. Clapping noises came from behind her, and she spun around, ready to tell someone off. Her eldest brother, Treat, filled the doorframe, dressed in a dark suit and tie, his thick black hair perfectly coiffed and a proud smile on his lips.

"Bravo." Treat wrapped his arms around Savannah. At six foot six, he towered over her.

She hugged him halfheartedly and stepped away, still agitated from talking to Connor. "What are you doing here?"

"Business meeting. I'm flying back home at six." Treat and his wife, Max, lived in Weston on the property adjacent to their father's.

"I have a bone to pick with you."

"Dad said you were a little miffed at me." He raised his eyebrows. "I'm not sure I want to be on the other end of your wrath after witnessing you taking down Connor Dean. Be gentle."

She pushed him playfully as he lowered himself into a chair. "You checked up on Jack Remington?"

Treat didn't even flinch. "Of course."

"What do you mean, *of course*? Treat, I'm thirty-four years old. I think I can take care of myself."

"I have no doubt of that," he said. Treat crossed his legs and reached one thick arm over the back of the chair beside him. "Vanny, why are you so angry?"

"Because." *Connor's a jerk, and I really like Jack and I got hurt again.* "I just don't see why you're always following up on what I'm doing. It's...invasive."

"Invasive." He met her serious gaze with his own.

"Yes and embarrassing. Demeaning."

"Demeaning? Really?"

"Treat, stop it. You know what I mean. I'm an adult, and your checking up on me makes me feel like a child." She paced in front of the windows, not even sure herself where she was going with the conversation or why she was saying these things.

"Savannah, I didn't check up on you. I checked up on him. You're my sister. My attractive, well-off sister, and there are a lot of creeps out there. I'm just protecting you." Treat stood and came to her side. "What's going on? What's changed?"

She leaned against the windowsill and covered her face with her hands. "Oh, Treat, my life is such a mess. I know you meant well, but Jack's a nice guy, really."

"Yes, I know."

She looked up at him. "You know? I thought you just

checked up on him, you know, his background, not if he's a nice guy or not."

"I did." He leaned on the windowsill beside Savannah. "It turns out that his brother Rush is a competitive skier, so I called Blake. He knows Rush well, and…" He shrugged. "Jack's a good guy. He was even awarded a Congressional Medal of Honor when he was in the Special Forces."

"Of course he was." Savannah sighed. "And Connor's the hottest actor around."

"Vanny, what's the parallel? Clue me in."

Savannah pressed her lips into a tight line and narrowed her eyes, then shook her head, but she couldn't keep her eyes from filling with tears.

"Oh, Savannah. You and Jack?" He laughed.

She swatted his arm. "It's not funny."

"No, it's not. I just should have known. You're the most bullheaded, competitive woman I know, and from what Blake said, Jack's as stubborn as a mule. Of course you were attracted to each other." He clapped his hands together. "Tell me what I can do? I assume from your pout that it was a tryst gone bad?"

"I don't know what it was, but I know that I can't get him out of my head," Savannah admitted.

He looked into Savannah's eyes with a serious face. "Then you know about his wife?" Treat spoke with the same paternal tone her father did.

She lowered her eyes. "Yeah. Just that she died. I don't know how or any of that, and I know that the last thing I need is a guy who's still living with the ghost of his dead wife. But, Treat, why can't I get him out of my head? I mean, with most guys, I'm strong. I make them work to date me. Well, maybe not Connor. Heaven only knows how screwed up I am to have let him mess with my head for so long. But you know me. I'm not a pushover, and from the minute I saw Jack, I was…." She covered her face with her hands again and shook her head with a groan. "He's this weird dichotomy of tough and tender, and it's frustrating and scary, and I don't know if I should run away or run toward him."

"You know when I met Max she was the same way." His voice softened. "She wore a coat of armor so thick, I never thought I'd break through. But in those moments when we were close, I saw hints of her softness, and I knew I had to try." Treat looked away, as if he were watching a memory unfold.

"I'm not sure it's the same as the harshness that he has. He lost his wife, and I think he feels like he doesn't deserve to be happy or something."

Treat took her hand in his. "Savannah, pain comes from all different sources. We build up walls that seem like they'll protect us, and we stay behind them, safe from the world. Or from our fears, or whatever stuff we have going through our minds. And then someone comes along that causes a tiny crack in the wall, and suddenly there's a stream of light breaking through. Pain is pain. It doesn't matter where it comes from. It all hurts. And until the right person's light shines through, there's no impetus for change." He placed his arm over her shoulder.

"So then what? We just never change?"

"Then we hide in our hole some more. But when the right person breaks through, anything is possible."

"You could make dog poop sound romantic." She rested her head against him.

"Blaming yourself for your spouse's death is a big hurt, Savannah. He probably needs time." Treat put his arm around her shoulder as she sat up.

Blaming yourself? "What do you mean, *blaming yourself?*"

"I thought you knew. According to Rush, Jack blames himself for his wife's death. Apparently, there was a storm. He'd just come back from an extended tour and was exhausted. He let her go out in the car alone, and shortly after she left, the storm picked up and…"

"And that's when the accident happened. Oh my gosh, no wonder he's haunted." Savannah remembered the anguish she'd seen in his eyes when he told her that he wasn't sure if he could move beyond his past.

"It's worse than that, Vanny. He's the one who found her."

"Oh, no, Treat. That's awful." She ached for what Jack must be living with every moment of every day.

"How much do you like this guy, Savannah?"

"I don't know. A lot," she said honestly.

"Well, then, all I can do is support whatever you want to do. It seems like he's a good man with really bad luck. So you tell me, what can I do to help you? Do you want me to talk you out of thinking about him?" He spoke with a serious tone, but Savannah recognized the tease in the way his eyes lit up.

"You know I won't listen," she admitted. "It doesn't matter. I'm not contacting him and he hasn't contacted me, so this whole thing will blow over and I'll be left nursing another broken heart. I'm getting pretty good at that."

Treat stood and pulled her into his arms. She relaxed against him, needing the security of his strength. It forced her to admit the thought she hadn't wanted to breathe life into.

"This broken heart feels a lot different from any other I've ever had."

Chapter Nineteen

JACK SAT ON the back deck of his chalet as the afternoon shifted into evening. The brisk air prickled his skin as he listened to the crickets, tree frogs, and other night sounds of the seven acres that buffered his chalet from the rest of the world, contemplating how he was going to approach his future. Every time he thought of calling Elise, his mind traveled to his brother Rush, and his gut tightened. Rush had never understood Jack's need to disengage from the life he knew and the family he loved. After Linda's death, Rush had tried to be supportive, and the more Jack fought his support, the colder Rush became. The last few times Jack had seen him, Rush had reminded him that if he hadn't been so darn wrapped up in himself, he wouldn't have let Linda go out in the storm. Jack saw red, and he'd finally called Rush for what he was. *You're a spoiled womanizer who wouldn't know how it felt to love if it kicked you in the butt, let alone how it feels to lose the one you love.* He'd been so angry that he'd taken it even further. *If I never see you again, it'll be soon enough.*

He eyed the phone on the table by the glass doors. All it would take was one phone call. Elise would come and pick up Linda's clothes, and he could be done with it and finally move forward. Jack's gut told him otherwise. He couldn't move forward with any sense of normalcy with his family chaos looming over him.

Jack rose to his feet and walked to the edge of the woods, feeling the call to walk in and disappear or fly back up to the mountains for another month. He'd been tempted to tell Savannah about the cabin in Colorado that he'd called home for the past few years, but fear had held him back. The attraction to Savannah had been so intense, so potent from the first moment he'd set eyes on her, that it had scared him to no end. He'd tried hard to deny it, but it was too strong. His resolve had cracked and he'd let Savannah in. *Way in.* But the cabin was sacred. It was his hideaway, the one place he didn't have to worry about seeing Linda's ghost, since he'd bought it after she'd passed away. Not even his family knew where it was. He wasn't ready to expose the only safety net he had. *What if I can't pull my crap together?*

Savannah's face flashed in his mind, and he felt his heart opening. A smile stretched across his face with the thought of her. He reached up and ran his finger along the curve of his lips, disbelieving that the emotion could be felt in this of all places. The place that had thrust him so deeply into guilt and anger that he'd had to run away. *Happiness.* Even the thought of it felt odd in his mind. Jack laughed, a quick, unexpected laugh, then turned back toward the chalet.

"I can't believe it," he said with another slight laugh. He headed inside, feeling a rush of strength, and picked up the phone.

For a minute Jack stared at the receiver, playing out how he might acknowledge his brother when he called. *Hey, Rush. It's me, Jack.* Or, *Rush, hey, it's Jack.* Picking up the phone to call his brother should have been a simple act. So why was his chest constricting, and his jaw clenched? Why did he feel his body slip into some sort of defensive state with every nerve strung tight? Because every time he thought of Rush, he saw his father's stoic face right behind him.

Jack set down the receiver and sank into a dining room chair. He leaned his elbows on his thighs and dropped his face to his hands. *I'm so messed up. This is insane.* Savannah's words replayed in his mind. *I've latched on to some worthless, angry, insecure mountain man.* He sat up tall and breathed in, expanding his chest and broad shoulders to their full capacity. *Worthless.* He rose to his feet, curling his hands into fists. *Insecure.* He was anything but worthless and insecure. Angry, yes. What guy wouldn't be angry? He killed his wife. But insecure? Worthless? Is that what everyone thought of him now?

He stalked down the step into the sunken living room and snagged the framed medal from the built-in bookshelves beside the fireplace and scanned it. He needed to reiterate his value in his own mind. *Congressional Medal of Honor. Above and beyond the call of duty.* He touched the glass above the word *valor.* Pride swelled within him, drawing his shoulders back. He flexed the muscles in his legs, feeling his strength, and he stood taller. He set the medal back on the bookshelves and, wearing courage like a cloak, he went back to the phone. Without any hesitation, he dialed Rush's number. His heart pounded against his chest. Each ring of Rush's phone sped up his pulse.

"Hello?"

Rush's deep, familiar voice sent a pain right through Jack's chest. He swallowed to alleviate the tightening in his throat. He opened his mouth to speak, and his mouth was so dry he couldn't form a single word.

"Hello?" Rush's tone was guarded.

"Rush," Jack managed.

Silence filled the airwaves.

"Rush, it's Jack." He grasped for the right words. Heck, he grasped for any words. "Don't hang up."

"I'm not hanging up."

The tension in Rush's voice was equal to the fear in Jack's as he pictured Rush standing, much like Jack was, with his body tense, legs rooted to the ground, biceps twitching.

"I know this is too late and I wouldn't blame you for hanging up after the things I've said to you." *We've said to each other.* "Rush, I'm done running, man." He closed his eyes, disbelieving that he'd just said the words he'd sworn he'd never say, much less want to say. After Linda died, he didn't think he'd ever want to stop running away. Savannah made him realize how wrong he'd been.

He heard Rush blow out a breath, and Jack pictured his shockingly blue eyes—which were as light as Jack's were dark—in a conflicted stare, a mixture of cold anger and warm brotherly love.

"I'm calling Elise to come get Linda's things." *Come on, Rush. Talk to me!*

"Don't." Rush's emphatic statement took Jack by surprise.

"Don't?"

"Her father's really sick. Terminal. You'll only upset her more," Rush said.

"Terminal?" Jack's voice faded to a whisper. "Ralph?" Before Linda's death, Jack and Ralph had been close. He had fond memories of talking about the military and politics with Ralph, watching football together on Thanksgiving, and sharing many intimate conversations mulling over the differences between men and women. He smiled at the memories, but the smile quickly faded as he remembered their last interaction. It had been right after Linda's accident, when Ralph had made no bones about his blaming Jack for Linda's death. Jack had known then that it was grief speaking, but Ralph's words had only confirmed what Jack believed to be true.

Jack rubbed the scar on the back of his arm.

"Jack, you've done enough damage to that family. Don't make it worse," Rush said.

His words sliced through Jack's courage like a knife, leaving him grasping for strength as he lowered himself to the chair once again.

"Rush, I gotta see him." Jack closed his eyes. He had to see him and clear the air. It wasn't just Ralph who had said cutting, hurtful things.

"The guy's on his deathbed, Jack. What good will it do?"

Rush's voice softened, and Jack was glad for the change. Maybe there was hope for them after all.

"I'm not sure, but I owe it to Linda. We were solid before she…before the accident."

"That was a long time ago, Jack. It took months for him to be able to move on, and he finally has. A lot has happened over the past two years while you've been hiding out like Saddam Hussein."

Jack stifled the urge to tell his brother to kiss off. Jack had earned his medal during the capture of Hussein, and he knew that Rush was just trying to push his buttons. He wondered if his father was right there behind him, goading him on. His father was always goading them on. *Be a man.*

Jack couldn't get sidetracked by crap going on with Rush. If Rush didn't want to let Jack back into his life, that was something he'd deal with at another time. With this new information, the fragility of life reverberated through him like a double-sided blade. Every slice tried to steal his strength and courage. Jack rose to his feet and stared out the window and into the darkness.

"No way. I owe this to Linda and I owe it to Ralph." Savannah's words ran through Jack's mind. *I see Jack Remington, man, widower, soft-hearted-survivor-man-slash-pilot. Who can be a real jerk when he gets scared.* Jack wasn't going to run scared anymore. Today he was making changes, and nothing was going to stop him. Not even his love for his brother. "I called because I wanted to try to clear the air with you, Rush. You're my brother, man, and I love you, but I get it. You still see me as some prick who ran away from his life, and I don't know how to fix that. But I can fix the stuff with Ralph, and I intend to. With or without your support."

"Selfish as ever," Rush said before hanging up the phone.

Jack lowered the receiver from his ear, clenching it so tightly that his knuckles were white. He would not be dissuaded. He went outside and snagged his backpack from his motorcycle and leafed through Savannah's registration form; then he picked up the phone and dialed her number. His forehead was damp with sweat despite the cool breeze coming through the open dining room window as seconds ticked by and her phone rang two, three, four times and finally went to voicemail. Hope soared within his heart at the sound of her recorded voice, reiterating the reason he wanted to change. *Savannah.*

"Hey, this is Jack." *Why do I sound so stern?* He made a conscious effort to soften his tone, pacing while he left the rest of his message to try to walk off residual frustration from his conversation with Rush. "Savannah, I...uh..." *Shoot. I should have prepared.* "I'd like to see you. Talk to you. Whatever you want. I don't care if we talk on the phone or...I sound like an idiot. I'm sorry. If you have any interest, please call me." He left her his number and hung up the phone feeling as nervous as a high school kid asking a girl out for the first time.

Before he lost his courage, he called information and got the number for Elise. The phone rang three times, and he mentally prepared to leave a message. *Elise, this is Jack. I—*

"Hello?"

Linda? Jack held his breath. *Her voice was identical to Linda's. Elise. It's Elise.* It had been so long since he'd spoken to her that he'd forgotten how similar they sounded.

"Elise, this is Jack. Jack Remington. Please don't hang up," he pleaded.

"Jack? Oh my gosh, Jack. Why would I hang up?"

Tears filled his eyes. "Why would you—I can think of a hundred reasons." The words tumbled out without thought. Relief stole the tension from his body. He leaned against the wall, his neck arched and his eyes locked on the ceiling. *Thank goodness.*

"Oh, Jack. I'm so glad you called. I was going to try to reach you, but I was afraid to. I didn't know if you'd be angry, or if, you know, it'd be too much of a reminder."

Elise's kindness also reminded him of Linda, and he lingered in that pleasant memory for a beat before answering.

"I heard about your dad, Elise, and I'm really sorry. I know he probably doesn't want to have anything to do with me, but I'd really like to apologize to him. In person if he'll allow it." *Come on. Give me this one break.*

"He wants that, too, Jack. He feels horrible about the things he said. He drove out to your house once a week for months, just to try to get in touch with you. He said he left letters."

Jack swallowed the thick, acidic taste of guilt. "He did. I got them, but I never opened them. I couldn't, Elise. I could barely breathe. I know that sounds dramatic and probably crazy, but for a while there, I think I was crazy. It took a long time for me to become clearheaded, and the anger ran so deep that I couldn't deal with any of it."

"We know, Jack. Remember we all knew you before Linda's accident, and people don't change overnight. We knew you were grieving."

Hearing her assess his emotions so easily and without judgment—so different from Rush's harsh reaction—drew tears from Jack. He clenched his eyes shut and pressed his finger and thumb to them, but he could not stop the flow of tears. He sucked in a quick breath in an effort to compose himself, but it didn't help.

"Oh, Jack," Elise said. "Honey, you've been angry for so long that you probably haven't grieved."

Jack sucked in another breath. "I…" His voice was swallowed by more tears. His lower jaw shook with the force of his sadness. "I'm sorry," he finally managed, though it came out as a whisper. *Could I have been so angry that I never really grieved?* He had no idea if that was possible, but he was so thankful for Elise's kindness, and the memory and feelings it evoked, that he didn't care. If he had yet to grieve, he could face that. Now he could face anything.

"Jack, please. We're past the accusations and the anger, but we're all very worried about you. Linda wouldn't have wanted you to hide away from the world for so long. You know that. She'd want you to be happy and to live a fulfilled life, Jack. Linda loved you, and that's what people who love each other hope for."

He sank to the floor. "Thank you," he said in a gravelly, shaky voice.

"You don't have to thank me, Jack. I care about you. We all do."

"Elise, I have…" He took a deep breath, trying to keep the sobs that were wrenching his chest to keep from swallowing his voice again. "I have Linda's clothes. I can't keep them."

"Linda's clothes? You've had them all this time?"

Jack nodded, then realized she couldn't see him. "Yes. Baby clothes, too." Fresh sobs burst forth, and he buried his eyes in the crook of his elbow.

"Oh, Jack," Elise whispered. "Are you home?"

"Yes."

"I'm coming over."

The line went dead, but Jack couldn't lift his arm to set the receiver on the console. He couldn't raise his head from his arms. He could barely breathe as the grief worked its way through every cell of his body. His limbs trembled, his stomach ached, and his teeth wouldn't stop chattering. Jack gave in to the helpless state, and the room filled with his cries as misery worked its way from somewhere deep within the recesses of his heart and soul and left him feeling depleted and hollow.

Chapter Twenty

SAVANNAH LEANED ON the wall of the Gapstow Bridge, scanning Central Park for Josh and Riley. There were more families than usual strolling through the park. Whether that was due to the pleasantly cool evening or the impending concert, she couldn't be sure, but it was nice to see people strolling instead of hustling at the typical frenetic pace of the city. The changing leaves reminded her of the Colorado Mountains, which brought her back to Jack. Savannah sighed, wishing she hadn't stood up for herself after all. It wasn't like he was treating her badly or trying to hurt her. He'd told her how confused he was. He was honest. *What is wrong with me?*

She saw his face in every man she passed and heard his voice when there was no one in the room. She thought about contacting him through his website but then realized that doing so would just be feeding into her weakness when it came to men. This time she wasn't going to be the woman who chased down unworthy lovers. She'd had enough of that with Connor. *But Jack's not unworthy!* There was no comparison between Connor and Jack. Connor never professed a single emotion toward Savannah, while Jack didn't hesitate to bare his soul and say exactly what he was feeling.

A hand gripped her shoulder, and she started, then spun around and found her younger brother Josh looking down at her with laughter in his eyes.

"You scared me half to death." She hugged him and realized that he was just about the same height as Jack. She felt the difference between Josh's lean, muscular frame and Jack's thick, powerful body.

"Hey, Savannah." Riley embraced her. "I feel like I haven't seen you in forever." They were a striking couple. Riley appeared youthful and happy in skinny jeans and a red spaghetti-strap blouse with her shoulder-length hair framing her face, and Josh looked handsome in khaki pants and a short-sleeved white dress shirt, which set off his dark eyes and black hair.

"I know. It does feel that way, but ever since you and Josh got together, I see more of you both than ever before, so I can't complain," Savannah said.

"We tried to call you." Josh wrapped his arm around Riley's waist. "We were going to try to meet earlier, but I guess you're screening your calls."

"Not from you I'm not." She pulled out her phone and made a *tsk* sound. "It was still on silent from my meeting. I'm sorry. Wow. I have six messages. Did you call me that many times?"

"Three," Josh said. "Let's head over to the concert."

Savannah covered her ear and listened to her messages as they headed toward Rumsey Field. When Jack's voice came through the phone, she stopped in her tracks and grabbed Josh's arm.

What? he mouthed.

Savannah held up a finger as she listened; then she put her

phone in her jeans pocket and hugged Josh as she squealed.

"Good news?" Riley asked.

Savannah's smile faded. She realized she hadn't told Josh anything about Jack, and now she wasn't sure she should. He'd think she was nuts getting excited over a man while on the rebound from Connor.

"Oh, um…" *Shoot.*

"I bet it was Ja-ack," Riley said in a singsong voice.

"Jack?" Savannah glared at Josh. "Don't tell me. Treat called you? I swear sometimes this family is so messed up." She stomped off in the direction of the field.

Josh and Riley caught up to her.

"He stopped by before he left town and said he'd just come from your office. One thing led to another. He was just worried about you," Josh explained.

"Whatever. You guys must think I'm so messed up." Heat flushed her cheeks. She shoved her hands in her pockets and kept her eyes trained on the ground.

"I was there, Savannah. Treat really was worried, but not because he thinks you're messed up." Riley spoke so fast that Savannah had to watch her mouth to make sure she didn't miss a word. "He was worried because he said that, for the first time ever, he'd seen something in your eyes that made him believe that whatever happened between you and Jack was real. And he was worried that if *you* didn't recognize it for what it was that you might always regret it. He just asked us to make sure you were okay. That's all. I promise." Riley sucked in a quick breath.

Savannah's jaw hung open. She blinked away her surprise. "He said that?"

"He did," Josh said, then kissed Riley's cheek.

"What did he see?"

"Maybe what we saw when you listened to Jack's message?" Josh said with a smile.

Savannah felt her cheeks flush. "I didn't realize I asked that out loud." *Treat could see how I felt? I'm a goner.*

They reached the field where the concert was already taking place, and Kaylie's voice boomed through the speakers. Crowds of people stood before the stage calling out to her. She looked radiant beneath the lights. Her blond hair cascaded in waves over her shoulders as she sang into the microphone, swinging her hips and working the crowd.

"I forgot how well Kaylie can sing," Riley said as they made their way along the outskirts of the crowd toward the stage in search of Danica and Blake.

Savannah heard the music and Riley's comment, but she was thinking about returning Jack's call and what the call itself meant. His message was so cute, like he had no idea what to say. *I'd like to see you. Talk to you. Whatever you want.* Her stomach fluttered. *He is thinking about me.*

"SAVANNAH! RILEY! JOSH!" Danica stood at the side of the stage, waving her arms. Her dark corkscrew curls sprang out in different directions and hung just past her shoulders, so different from her sister's shiny blond hair.

"I feel like we're having a family reunion," Savannah said as she embraced Danica and then her husband, Blake. Blake had grown up with Savannah and her siblings. As cousins, they'd spent many summers hanging out on her family's ranch together.

"Still gorgeous," Blake said to Savannah. Blake was tall, dark, and handsome, and before meeting Danica, he'd used those good looks to his advantage and lived the life of a player. Taking any woman, anytime, anywhere. But the moment he set eyes on Danica, he'd fallen for her, and he'd cleaned up his act.

"Not half as gorgeous as your wife," Savannah teased.

"Very true. And look at these two." He nodded toward Josh and Riley, who were nose to nose, whispering as they stared into each other's eyes. "Looks like they're doing a photo shoot for *Romance* magazine." He laughed. "Dude, care to give your cousin a hug? Pry yourself away from your fiancée for a second?"

"You're always so needy," Josh teased.

"Blake, you look so happy," Riley said as he wrapped her in his strong arms.

"What's not to be happy about? I've got a beautiful wife, her sister's singing soulful songs, and I'm with family. I'm a lucky guy." He put his arm around Danica.

"Savannah, Treat tells me that you went through Jack Remington's survival camp. He's got such a great rep. How was it?" Blake asked.

She couldn't keep herself from smiling. "Awesome. I learned a lot."

Josh raised his eyebrows. He masked his comment—*that's not all*—with a cough.

Savannah and Riley both punched him in the arm.

"Oh, did you meet someone there?" Blake asked. "I'd be surprised if Jack allowed that. He's a surly guy these days."

Surly and passionate. "He is surly, to most people." Savannah moved out of the way for someone to pass and repositioned herself beside Danica. "But there was a young couple who hooked up and he didn't seem to pay much attention to it. He kind of ignored that aspect and just went on with the course." *Probably because we were too busy trying to keep our feelings in check.*

"Remington? That's Rush's brother? The one who lost his wife?" Danica asked.

"Yeah," Blake answered. "He closed himself off from everyone, and I don't think Rush even knows where he lives these days. Anyway, did you meet someone special there or just a weekend fling?"

His family doesn't know where he is? "I'm not really sure yet," Savannah answered.

Kaylie began another song, and Savannah was glad for the distraction. She really wanted to bend Danica's ear. As the others turned their attention to the stage, Savannah moved closer to Danica.

"Can I pick your therapist brain for a few minutes?" Savannah asked.

"Of course. What's up?" Danica turned away from the stage and stood shoulder to shoulder with her, giving Savannah her full attention.

"I know you helped my brother Dane and his girlfriend, Lacy, deal with her fear of sharks and relationship anxieties, and I'm a little worried about my ability to choose the right men in my life. I wondered if you'd mind helping me sort of figure out why, or at least how to stop doing it."

"Well, Lacy's my sister, so I knew a lot about what she'd been through already. I don't know that much about your background other than your mother passing away when you were little and your father raising you, and he seems warm and loving, but also stern enough to have raised you all to be successful—and, I thought, confident." Danica furrowed her brow. "A lot of times we can get clues to our issues from our own thoughts. Why do you think you pick the wrong guys? And how often do you pick these guys?"

"Well, I'm thirty-four and I haven't picked the right guy yet, so that must mean I've picked a lot of bad ones, and I'm not sure why." The music had become white noise in the background of their conversation. Luckily, the others were wrapped up in the white noise and not in Savannah pouring her heart out.

"Tell me about your last three relationships," Danica said.

Savannah sighed. "Last three. Well, I dated Connor Dean, and he cheated on me several times and I kept going back to him. Then there was Paul Chaste before him. He was an attorney, and we dated for a few months, but he was just too boring. No spark, you know?"

Danica nodded.

"And before Paul I dated Matt Brewer, and we got along great, intimacy was great, but we had different goals in life. He didn't want a family and I did." Savannah shrugged.

"I'm not seeing a pattern here, Savannah. Clue me in on what I'm missing."

"What do you mean? There's a definite pattern. I can't seem to pick the right men. Am I insecure? Am I needy? Bossy? I know I'm a royal pain and stubborn sometimes. Is that the issue? I can take it, Danica. Whatever it is, just give it to me straight." Savannah crossed her arms, bracing herself for the painful truth.

Danica smiled.

"What? Is it all those things?" *It's worse than I thought.*

"No, no." Danica turned to Blake and said, "I'll be right

back."

"Everything okay?" Blake asked.

"Yeah. We're going to step away from the stage for a minute."

Great. Now we need privacy. This must be horrible.

When they were away from the others, Danica pulled Savannah down beside her on the grass. "Okay, here goes. A pattern is when you do something over and over, like Blake or Kaylie before they settled down. They went from person to person, never forming any attachments. That's a pattern, Savannah. You've dated the wrong guys. There's a huge difference, unless each of those guys possessed some quality that made it impossible to have a relationship with them."

"Well, Connor was a serial cheater. That makes it pretty impossible."

"True, and we can talk about that, but the others?" Danica held Savannah's gaze.

Savannah shook her head. "Boring and no kids. Those were deal breakers for me. But they were nice guys and they were professionals, no other glaring issues."

"So why do you think you have the issue?"

Savannah took a deep breath. "I stayed with Connor for almost two years. He cheated time and time again, and I kept going back, and now…now I'm interested in a guy who is emotionally available only some of the time. When his past bogs him down, he's blocked off by a wall so thick I can't break through."

"Can't or won't?"

"I thought this was going to be easy. You know, I tell you my trouble and you say, *Oh, Savannah, it's because you're insecure because your mother wasn't around to nurture you, or you're too stubborn for any man to love you.* Heck, I don't know." She turned away, embarrassed by her inability to even get *having an issue* right.

"Savannah, I didn't say you don't have some issues. We all do. I said I don't see a pattern with your choices in men. So, this recent guy, is he so blocked off you can't get through or you won't make the effort to get through? In other words, are you trying and he's resisting?"

"Sheesh, Danica. This is why I don't go to therapists. You ask the hard questions that I don't want to answer." Savannah was irritated but only with herself.

"Hey, you came to me. We don't have to talk." Danica pushed herself to her feet and brushed off her jeans. Savannah reached up and pulled her back down.

"That's another thing. Don't therapists have any fight in them? You'd walk away and leave me all conflicted?"

"Sometimes the only way to work things out is to reach deep inside and pull out the muck so you can see a little clearer. If I'm here to dig you out every step of the way, you'll never want or need to clear the way yourself. Wow, I really do sound like a therapist. It's been years since I closed my practice, and here I am spouting off this stuff." Danica laughed.

Savannah watched Riley whisper in Josh's ear, and again she longed for that closeness. "See, even you don't like it. But the truth is, I need you to push me." She loved Danica and she trusted her, and something told her that she needed to reach out with honesty in order to get some answers. "It's Jack Remington. He's the one I hooked up with over the weekend, and he's the one I can't stop thinking about."

"And he's the one whose wife died." Danica put her hand on Savannah's arm. "That is a tough one, but unless he's

sleeping with multiple women, there's no connection to what
you experienced with Connor, so it's still not a pattern."

"He's not. Before me, he hadn't had sex with a woman for
two years." Savannah waited for Danica's jaw to drop or for her
to laugh and say, *No really, how long has it been?* But Danica
didn't do either of those things. She nodded and drew her
eyebrows together.

"Wow, that's a lot of hurt, and if he really did become as
reclusive as Blake said, then he's probably buried it all beneath
some other emotion."

"Anger," Savannah admitted. "He is pretty gruff when you
first meet him, and he's riddled with guilt, but not always, and
when it falls away, he's tender and loving, and passionate,
and…"

"Does he have angry outbursts? Is he aggressive?" Danica
asked.

"No." Savannah shook her head. "When I first met him, he
was just walled off. And he spent a lot of time trying not to look
at me. Or talk to me. You know the type. He spoke forcefully
no matter what the topic was, one firm tone. No smiles, except
when he spoke to the little boy who was there. He actually
smiled when he spoke to him."

"He does sound a little boxed off. How'd you two come
together? What changed?"

Savannah leaned back and put her weight on her palms. She
crossed her legs at the ankles as she remembered the night she'd
seen the bobcat and how scared she'd been. "I went into the
woods at night to go to the bathroom, and there was a bobcat
that I hadn't seen. And suddenly Jack was there, rescuing me.
Before that there was all this attraction between us, a buildup of
sexual energy that was red-hot, but we both had these brick

walls up—me because of Connor and him…well, you already know why. And when he saved me from the bobcat, it was like all those walls came tumbling down, whether we wanted them to or not."

Danica leaned back beside Savannah. "Well, that all sounds very normal to me, not at all worrisome. Now, if you were really the one who pulled him out of his celibacy, then that could go one of two ways. Either there's some meaningful connection that can't help but continue to grow, or he'll deal with his issues and move on. Like you broke the dam, and it was wonderful, but he might want to explore what else washes in."

"You don't sugarcoat things, do you?" Savannah looked at Danica, and she still had a serious look in her eyes. "What?"

"Nothing. It's funny, you know? I'm with Blake, who had too many women for any one man, and here you are with the opposite problem, but the worry is the same. Savannah, I'm going to go out on a limb here and say this even though I don't really know your full history or what you've gone through in relationships. And I'm going to say this as the woman who married into your family. Not as a therapist but as a friend. I would imagine that the only thing you're up against as far as picking the wrong guys goes is that you are very successful and beautiful, and that's a threatening combination for many men. But beyond that, you're just looking for your forever love, so follow your heart. If Jack turns out not to be ready—and there's a good chance that he's not—then what have you lost?"

My heart. "A little self-respect." Her cheeks grew warm again thinking about the things she and Jack had done in the woods. "I've already done more—and different—intimate things with him than I have with any other guy, and I *wanted* to."

A smile stretched across Danica's lips. She leaned in close and whispered, "That doesn't mean there's something wrong with you. That means you're wildly attracted to him."

Danica watched Blake crossing the grass, and in her eyes Savannah saw love, want, and a hint of the intimacy between them. She wondered if the look that Treat had seen in her eyes earlier that afternoon, and Josh and Riley had seen when she'd listened to Jack's message, was similar to what she saw in Danica's. She felt her cell phone in her pocket, and she knew the answer was only a phone call away.

Chapter Twenty-One

THE KNOCK WAS so faint that Jack almost didn't hear it. He lifted his head from his arms and pushed himself from the spot on the floor where he'd been sitting since he hung up the phone with Elise. The second he opened the door, there would be no turning back. Jack tried to picture Linda's sister. The last time he'd seen her was shortly after Linda's accident. She'd been as torn up as Jack was. He took a deep breath and pulled the door open.

"Jack." Elise walked in without giving Jack time to react, and she wrapped her arms around him and pressed her face to his chest.

Jack's breath caught in his throat. She was more than a foot shorter than Jack, and she'd always worn her hair in a short pixie cut, but now her blond hair fell past her shoulders, so similar to Linda's that when his hand brushed against it, he had to swallow the sadness that rose. She drew away from him and shook her head. Her warm blue eyes held no anger or blame, and the smile on her lips offered Jack even more relief. He felt the tension in his shoulders ease.

"Hi, Elise," he managed, closing the door behind her. "Come in. Let's sit down." Elise and Linda had been as close as sisters could get. She was twenty-eight when Linda died, and Jack remembered the devastation that had lingered in her eyes afterward—and how that devastation drove his guilt deeper and deeper into his psyche. Now that despair was evident only in the shadow that flickered in her eyes and left as quickly as it had appeared. Jack thought he might be the only person who would recognize it for what it was.

They sat on the sofa, facing each other, Elise with one leg tucked under the other and her arm across the back of the couch and Jack with his elbows leaning on his thighs. His heart felt heavier than it had a few moments before, and although he didn't see blame in Elise's gaze, his internal guilt tethered his eyes to the fireplace.

"Jack, I'm so glad to see you." Elise touched his arm.

He turned his head and looked at her, praying he'd have the strength to say and do the things he needed to. He wanted to move forward, but suddenly the road between wanting and doing seemed paved with glass.

He forced a smile. "I never thought I'd see any of the Grays again, and here you are, sitting on my couch."

Elise's smile wasn't forced, and when it lit up her eyes, Jack sat up, taking note of the similarities between her and Linda. The high cheekbones, the way a dimple formed beside her cheek when the smile reached a certain point, and a simple cock of her head, which brought Linda's voice back to him, *Oh, Jackie, don't be silly.* How many times had she said that with the same look in her eyes?

Elise dropped her gaze. "I know, Jack. I look just like her. I always have, but now that my hair is longer…"

"It's remarkable. Your voice, too." He turned his body toward her so he could study her more closely. A memory snaked its way into his mind, and he had to share it. "She sat right there once with that same look on her face. We'd just decided to try to have a baby." His throat swelled, and he paused as a chill ran through him. "She said…" He narrowed his eyes to keep the tears that burned from falling. "She said, *Let's do it, Jackie.* That was all. *Let's do it, Jackie.*"

"She loved you, Jack, and she would have loved your children." Elise touched his arm. "Do you remember when you guys first got married? Remember how she made me promise to never let her turn into one of those sisters who forgets she has a life outside of her marriage?"

Jack nodded.

"She never did, Jack. She always made time for me *and* you."

A tear tumbled down his cheek. He tried to blink it away, but more tears spilled, and he dropped his eyes to the couch.

"I miss her, too, Jack." Elise wiped her own eyes.

"I'm so sorry, Elise. Not just for letting her go out that night, but for being such a jerk afterward. I loved her so much, and I missed her—miss her—so much."

"I know you do, Jack. We all do." Elise's voice was just above a whisper. When she spoke again, strength had returned to her voice. "But, Jack, everyone misses you. Your family, my family. You have a lot of life to live ahead of you, and we worry about you."

"I know." His voice cracked. "I thought I could escape the pain. I thought if I didn't see anyone, I could forget the blame and the accusations in everyone's eyes."

"Jack, no one blamed you but yourself."

Jack shook his head. "Your father blamed me, and I'm sure everyone did."

"No, Jack. What Dad said, he said out of anger and grief. Don't you remember? The last time you saw him, you two argued. I remember it like it was yesterday. It was on Linda's birthday after she'd died, and he told you to stop blaming yourself and to pull yourself together."

Jack remembered it well. The shock of rage that tore through him. The gall of anyone telling him to forget his pain—to forget Linda—and move on with his life. They didn't understand that he was unable to do that. He could not physically muster the energy to even think about forgetting or letting go of the guilt.

"Jack, look at me."

He met her empathetic gaze.

"It was you who blamed yourself, Jack. You argued until my father was red faced. Remember? Think about it, please. It's important that you see how things really happened. You got right in his face and said that you would never speak to him again if he continued to tell you to let her go, and the whole time, he wasn't telling you to. He was giving you permission to move on with your life."

Jack grabbed the sides of his head and leaned his elbows on his knees again. "No. I saw it in his eyes, Elise. I saw it. His hatred was so blatant."

"No, Jack."

The strength of her statement drew his eyes back to her. He felt his chest rise and fall as his breathing became fast and loud.

"That was you, Jack. You hated yourself. You blamed yourself. You scared us, Jack. Dad was afraid you'd do something horrible, think about suicide or something, and the more he tried to release you from your own self-imposed guilt, the angrier you became. He finally gave up and said, *Fine, Jack. Go wallow in your guilt. While away your life in some self-imposed prison. Is that what you want to hear?*" Elise stood and paced. "Think about it, Jack. You've always been so stubborn. You looked him in the eye and said, *Yes. It's the truth.*" She crouched before him and held his knees in her small hands, waiting until Jack was looking at her before continuing. "Jack, that's when he said it. That's when he told you that you were the reason she died. He said it to appease you, Jack, because every attempt to dissuade seemed to make you angrier and more belligerent. And do you remember what you did?"

Jack's chest hurt so badly that he couldn't tell if his tears were from the pain or the grief that constricted it.

"You thanked him, Jack, and then you walked out the door. And that was almost two years ago. My father has lived with the guilt of that conversation every second of his life. And you?" She leaned forward and ran her hand up his arm, finding the scar there. "You have lived with it, too."

Elise moved to the stone hearth and sat down across from Jack. She folded her hands in her lap and waited, respectfully shifting her eyes away from him as he wiped the tears from his cheek and weighing her words, allowing the truth of them to sink past the dam he'd built within him. The one that kept him upright during the day and anxious at night. They sat in silence for ten or fifteen minutes. It seemed like forever, but it wasn't uncomfortable. Jack didn't think of what to say next or how to act. He simply allowed himself to be present, to accept and feel the hurt of the reality she'd brought him—and that alone was a huge step forward.

"I got married, Jack, and I have a daughter."

Jack lifted his head again. This time a smile rose on his lips. "A daughter?" Linda had wanted a family so badly, and so had he. Seeing Aiden had reminded him just how much he wanted a family and how far away he'd pushed that desire.

Elise nodded. "Linda Marlene Rollins. She turned one last month."

"Linda." A small laugh escaped his lips. "Linda Rollins."

She nodded again. "I married Harry Rollins. I'm not sure if you remember him."

"I do. You had just started dating him a few months before…"

"Yes, that's him. He's a great father and a wonderful husband. You'd like him, Jack. At some point, if you'd like, I'd love for you to meet him." Elise came back to the couch and sat beside him again. "Do you mind that I named her Linda? I tried to contact you before she was born, but no one could reach you."

"I love that you named her Linda. Does she look like you? Like Linda?" *Elise has a child. Her father's dying.* Life was moving on for everyone, ending for others, and Jack remained in the same ugly, angry state that he'd been in two years before. His mind drifted back to Savannah, and he realized that over the last few days, he'd begun to see light at the end of the angry tunnel he'd been stuck in.

"No. She looks like Harry, but she has our eyes. Brown hair and blue eyes and louder than any child I've ever met. Totally not me or Linda." The pride in Elise's eyes was unmistakable.

Jack nodded. "I'm so happy for you. I'm sure you're a great mother."

"And someday, Jack, I hope you'll allow yourself to be the wonderful father Linda always knew you would be."

AN HOUR LATER, Jack loaded the bags of Linda's clothes and the unworn baby clothes into Elise's car.

"Promise me you're coming to see Dad tomorrow? No excuses? He's so fragile right now. I don't want to tell him and then have you not show up."

Elise looked at him with such hope that it tugged at Jack's heart. "I promise. I want this, Elise. I want to deal with all the stuff I've buried. I really, really want to move forward. I can't bring Linda back, and living in an angry state won't do it, either."

"You know that Linda wouldn't ever have let you remain in that state for more than—"

"Ten minutes. I haven't thought about that since before...." Sadness gripped him again, but somehow, the anger that usually came on the heels of it had been cleansed by their conversation. "Remember the ten-minute rule?" Jack said with a smile.

In unison, they said, "You have ten minutes to be angry, ten minutes to be sad, ten minutes to be anything other than thankful that you have an eleventh minute to look forward to."

"Do you think she always knew something might happen?" Elise asked as she started her car.

"No. I asked her about that once, and she said it was just a waste of energy to be anything but happy." He looked away, realizing how disappointed Linda would have been if she knew that not only had he broken her sacred rule, but he'd lived with his anger for two years.

"Speaking of angry, have you spoken to your family?"

"I'm working on it. I'm going to make this right, Elise. Thank you for coming out here and for not turning your back on me when you had every right to."

She turned smiling eyes up to him. "I'm Linda's sister. How

could you expect anything else? I love you, Jack. I can't tell you what it means to me to see you without your teeth clenched so tight that I feared they'd crack. I'm proud of you."

"Don't be. Besides marrying Linda, I haven't done anything to be proud of since my military years." He thought of how proud he'd been back then and how just putting on his uniform had made his chest swell. The man he'd been never would have cowered away behind a cold exterior and hundreds of acres of woods. *How have I fallen so far?*

"I forgot to ask. Where have you been living? I mean, everyone knows you haven't been here."

Jack thought about telling her the truth, but he just wasn't there yet. That cabin in the woods was still his security blanket, even if he was trying to outgrow it.

"Around." He leaned into the car and kissed her cheek. "I love you, too, Elise, and I'll see you tomorrow."

She nodded and pulled the car forward, then stopped and stuck her head out the window. "One more thing. Don't give up on Rush. He's as stubborn as you are—he learned from the best."

Jack watched her pull away and felt a little lighter as he crossed the driveway and headed back inside. He'd never cried so much in his life, and he felt as though he'd been drained of everything inside of him—his blood, his energy, and surprisingly, his anger. He closed the door behind him and waited for the ominous feeling that usually followed him into the house to return, but it didn't come. He glanced cautiously toward the kitchen, expecting Linda's image to be looking back at him, and when it wasn't, he felt a tiny shock of sadness and a larger pulse of relief. He closed his eyes and breathed deeply. He needed air.

He cranked open the casement windows in the living room,

and then he opened the glass doors in the dining room that led to the deck, and the brisk night air swept through the small house. The smell of autumn filled his senses and brought a smile to his lips. He closed his eyes again and recalled the feel of Savannah in his arms, all her softness pressed against him, her warm lips on his. He'd fought the urge to think about her since he'd left her the message earlier in the evening. He'd wrestled with guilt over what they'd done and where he was in his life, and since she hadn't returned his call, he worried that he'd blown the only chance he'd get at being with her. The world had passed him by hour by hour for months on end, and he hadn't even noticed, and now, every second he believed he'd never see Savannah again felt like a lifetime.

The cordless house phone rang, startling him out of his thoughts. Jack carried a cell phone, but he rarely used it, and he never gave out the number. As he listened to the house phone ringing for the third time, he wondered what Elise had forgotten to tell him, or if she was calling just to be sure he really was still there.

"Hello?"

"Jack?"

Before he could stop himself, he gasped a loud breath. "Savannah." Her voice was so sweet and tentative that he wanted to crawl through the phone and see her beautiful green eyes and wrap her in his arms.

"Hi. I got your message," she said.

Jack's eyes darted around the room. He didn't know what to say. He just knew that he needed to see her, to be with her. "Sorry I rambled."

"I like rambling. How are you?"

He heard the smile in her voice, and his heart soared.

"Good. A little better, even. Savannah, can I see you?" He didn't mean to be so blunt, or to say it so forcefully, but he had no control when it came to Savannah. Her allure was too strong.

"I thought you had to deal with your life."

Jack paced. "I am."

"In a day?"

He pictured her arching her perfectly manicured eyebrows, and it made him smile. "I didn't say I was healed. I said I was dealing with it. Savannah, I can't stop thinking about you."

She lowered her voice to a seductive cadence. "That's because we did all those dirty things, and it'd been so long since—"

"No, Savannah, it's not, so you can just stop right there. I've never been a guy who gets off on sleeping around, and that part of me hasn't suddenly changed. There have been plenty of women who tried to bed me. It doesn't take much to find a person to fool around with if you want to."

"To *bed* you?" She laughed, but Jack could tell she didn't think it was funny.

"You're so frustrating. You know what I mean. There have been opportunities, and if that's all I was looking for—if I'd been *looking* at all—I'd have hooked up with them, but I wasn't looking."

"Are you now, Jack?" Savannah asked.

The question threw him for a loop, and before he could configure an answer, honesty slipped from his lips. "No, I wasn't looking then and I'm not now. I swear, Savannah. I have no idea why or how you got to me, but you did, and that's something, isn't it?" *Isn't it?* Or was he so out of touch with his emotions that he didn't even know what was real anymore?

"I wasn't looking either, Jack."

He shook his head and covered his eyes as a different type of tears filled his eyes. *What on earth is wrong with me?* Jack's stone-faced facade cracked, and he didn't know how to handle it. He lowered himself onto a chair, and with a shaky voice, he said, "You weren't looking, and you called back. I couldn't stay away. Maybe we were fated to meet."

"Fated," Savannah whispered.

"I want to see you."

Her voice took a seductive turn. "I want to see you, too."

"Forgive me for being lame, but it's been a long time since I've done anything like this."

"Called a woman?"

"Well, yes, that too, but I was thinking more along the lines of even setting up a date." Jack sat up straighter. With Savannah, even the most uncomfortable things were easier to handle.

"A date? Like, a Friday-night-date type of thing?"

The idea of waiting that long to see her was torture. "It's only Tuesday."

"Where are you?" she asked.

"Home." The word resonated in a way that it hadn't in a very long time. "Bedford Corners." Jack rose to his feet, and four determined strides later, he had his keys in his hand. "An hour ten away if I go fast." He stood with his phone in one hand, the keys and the doorknob in the other, while he waited for her answer.

"Go fast."

Chapter Twenty-Two

SAVANNAH HAD NEVER been so nervous in her life. She pressed her palms against the window and stared into the darkness, watching the street below. There were so many butterflies in her stomach she was afraid they'd fly out of her mouth if she tried to speak. She'd showered and changed her clothes five times, finally deciding on a pair of designer jeans and a black, sleeveless V-neck blouse.

The roar of a motorcycle engine crawled down the street below, sending a thrill right through her. She watched as the driver maneuvered the bike into a parking spot, and she scanned the street for another open space for Jack. The driver's powerful arms clutched the handlebar, and as he turned to look behind him, Savannah caught a clear view of his broad, muscular back, and her eyes dropped to the familiar sexy vee of his waist. *Jack.* She gasped a breath. *A motorcycle? That's so hot.* His powerful thighs clenched the bike. The same powerful legs that had held her up in the stream and rubbed against her thighs at the boulder. She watched him climb from the bike and remove the helmet, then shake his thick hair free. She turned away from the window, her body humming with anticipation.

A few minutes later, Savannah opened the door. Jack's

broad shoulders filled the doorframe. His legs were planted hip distance apart, straining against his Levi's. In one hand, he held his black helmet, and the other arced out from his side, the veins in his biceps ripe from the ride over. On the mountain, there was nothing to give perspective to Jack's size. Now, with his head nearly hitting the doorframe, he seemed much taller. A smile lifted the edge of his lips as he took a step forward, and his free hand engulfed the curve of her hip.

"Hi," he whispered as he leaned down to kiss her.

One word from his smooth, rich voice was all it took to steal her breath and any chance she had at making small talk. The rough stubble of his cheek brushed against her face, and the combination of his soft kiss and the rough scratch sent her heart racing.

He closed the door behind him, and Savannah took a deep breath and blew it out slowly, trying to regain her composure. He smelled clean and earthy, a smell she'd come to think of as simply *Jack*.

"How was your ride over?" Savannah said, to stop herself from saying, *Kiss me again. Please kiss me again.*

"Too long." Jack didn't smile. He didn't move toward her or even look for a place to set his helmet.

He locked his eyes on her, and it was Savannah who took a step forward, placed one hand on the waist of his pants, and curled her fingers around his leather belt. She placed her other hand on his shoulder and stood on her tiptoes, but still the distance between them was too great. Jack met her halfway, settling his lips over hers. His lips were tender, his breath minty. Every swipe of his tongue was sensuous, erotic. He pulled back long enough to set his helmet on an end table, then pulled her to him once again in a long, delicious kiss. Savannah's knees weakened and, as if he'd felt the shift in her energy, Jack pressed her to him with one large hand on the center of her back, while the other found the back of her neck as he had the first time they'd kissed. Being enveloped by his strength while he loved her mouth was so sumptuous that a needy moan slipped from her lungs into his. He drew back, and Savannah gasped—not for air, but for him to return to her.

"I'm sorry. I can't seem to stop kissing you." He lowered his mouth to her neck, grazing her with his teeth before stroking the tender spot with his tongue, hard and continuous.

Savannah arched her neck back, and he dug his hands beneath her hair and cupped the back of her head, then brought his lips to hers again.

"Savannah." Her name was one long, hot breath.

No man had ever taken control of her body with nothing more than a kiss before. She could barely think, much less find the words to respond. Instead, she took his hand and led him down the narrow hallway to her bedroom. She took a step into the room, and he stopped on the other side of the threshold. She reached up and touched the cheek she'd been thinking about all afternoon and felt the tension beneath her palm.

"Jack?" she whispered.

His eyes caught hers with an ardent stare, but Savannah felt something else coming from him like a wave—nervousness, fear, sadness? She couldn't be sure.

"Your bedroom." He looked down at her and swallowed. "Savannah, I'm not sure I can go in there. I don't trust myself."

"Jack, I think we're past that. I know it's been a long time since you've been with a woman, but when a woman asks you into her bedroom, you don't need to trust yourself."

"That's not what I mean." He pulled her close and brushed

her hair from her shoulder. "I haven't even slept in a real bedroom for ages, much less been with a woman in one. I'm not sure if any weird stuff will go through my head. Savannah, I'm sorry. I know that this must sound strange coming from a man, but I'm just on the brink of dealing with everything, and I want to be close to you more than I want to breathe, but I don't want to risk my past sneaking in."

She wondered, briefly, if Linda's ghost would always be between them. Then guilt swooped in, trailed by Danica's advice. *If Jack turns out not to be ready—and there's a good chance that he's not—then what have you lost?* She knew the risks. Jack was still bathing her with his dark eyes. The worry and want in his eyes coalesced, drawing Savannah closer. She realized that she wanted any amount of time she could have with him. An hour, a day, a week. Self-preservation stopped her from thinking any further into the future.

"I probably shouldn't have come, but I couldn't imagine another second without seeing you," he said.

"Don't be silly." She led him back to the living room. "I have a glorious sleep sofa that has never been opened. It'll be new for you and me. We can make our own memories." There was no way she was going to wait another day to be next to him again, and from the way his eyes followed her as she crossed the floor and turned off the lights, then lit candles on the dining room table and on the windowsill, she could tell that he didn't want to wait either. Jack pulled out the couch, and Savannah dressed it with the decadent satin sheets Josh had given her the previous Christmas. At the time, she'd thought they were a ridiculously lavish purchase that she'd never use. Now she couldn't wait to feel the silky softness against her skin when she was beneath Jack's hard body.

MOONLIGHT STREAMED THROUGH the window and danced off of the flame, casting a romantic flicker of shadows across the luxurious sheets. Jack had never wanted any woman the way he wanted Savannah, and as he watched her come to his side, then felt her delicate fingers slip beneath his shirt and across his abs, he thought he might lose it from just her touch. He had to taste her again, had to feel those sweet lips on his, and he lowered his mouth to hers. He'd almost forgotten how good it felt to kiss a woman, and as he learned the contours of Savannah's mouth, it was as if no other woman had ever existed. His eyes blinked open at the thought, and he drew back. Savannah's lips were ripe from their kiss; her eyes filled with desire.

This is right. So very right.

Savannah reached for his belt buckle, and he grabbed her hand. "Not yet. I don't want to rush. I want to savor every second with you."

Her eyes widened, then narrowed as a smile lifted her lips. He ran his hands along her silky shoulders. "You feel so good."

He kissed the rosy blush on her cheek, then trailed kisses down her jaw to the spot just below her ear. He nibbled her earlobe, and she breathed heavier, held him tighter. When his lips found the gentle curve at the base of her neck, she arched her head back again. He freaking loved when she did that. She pressed against him, and he fought the urge to rip off her clothes and take her right there and then. But his interest in Savannah ran deeper than sex, and he planned on showing her just how much deeper.

He slipped his finger beneath the straps of her blouse and

slid them down her arms to the crook of her elbow, exposing her beautiful breasts. He lifted her chin and kissed away the new flush that had risen.

"You're beautiful, babe. Let me cherish you." The huskiness of his own voice surprised him, and he buried the surprise in another kiss. He could kiss her all night and never tire of it.

He took his time, touching her the way she deserved to be touched, pleasuring her time and time again until she was trembling all over.

"Jack," she pleaded, writhing beneath him.

He felt like the luckiest guy in the world to have been the one to bring her such pleasure, and he didn't stop there. A high-pitched needy sound escaped her lips, and he had to capture it. His mouth covered hers and she returned his efforts with such fervor it made his body shake. Every sensation with Savannah was heightened, more erotic. Jack wondered what he'd experienced before and realized that whatever it was, it had made him happy at the time. What he had before was good. What he had with Savannah was magnificent.

She grabbed his cheeks. Her eyes flashed open, dark and impassioned. "Take me, Jack. I want you."

He knew once he started he wouldn't be able to stop. He wanted every tender touch, every taste, and every moment to last forever. None of it was enough. He pushed himself from the bed and stripped from his clothes. As he moved toward the bed, Savannah reached for him, doing all sorts of naughty, unexpected things to his body. He tangled his hands in her thick hair and let her lead the dance. She was killing him, a slow, gloriously-torturous, pleasure-filled death. This was magnificent, but he wanted to be inside of her, to be gentle and loving. But every fiber of him ached for release.

"Savannah, no. Not like this."

She looked up at him and said, "I want to do everything with you, Jack."

Her eyes were wide, innocent, but in the next second, darkness stole the innocence and translated as pure, sexual lust. He wrestled with his next move. He wanted to be inside her, but how could he turn down such a desirous plea?

"Explore with me. I've never explored my sexuality like this with anyone, Jack." She rose to her feet. "I want you in ways I have never wanted anyone before."

"Neither have I." He took her in a rough kiss, their teeth clashing, their tongues digging deep.

All hope of restraint shattered. He lowered her to the bed, pressing her into the mattress.

"Yes, Jack," she urged. "Be rough with me. Let me feel *all* of you."

He'd do anything for her. With her. To her. Whatever she wanted, but this felt so good and so wrong at the same time. He wanted her to know how much he'd begun to care for her. He wasn't brought up to believe that you treated the person you cared for this roughly—even if it was what she wanted. Even if it spiked all the dirty thoughts he'd ever conjured up.

"I want more with you, Jack. I want to experience everything with you—sexually and otherwise," she pleaded. "I don't know why it's happened so fast and intense, but I do."

"So do I. But I want you to know how I feel about you. It's not just sex for me."

"For me either," she whispered. "Love me, Jack. I know it's crazy. We've only known each other a few days, but I can't pretend I don't feel it, and if you run the other way, you do. I want whatever I can have. A day, an hour."

She said everything he felt and had been hiding from. "A lifetime." The words came out before he could check them, and when he realized what he'd said, he knew he meant it. "I'm broken, Savannah, but I'm fixable. I know I am. You make me believe I am."

"I do believe it, Jack. I do."

His heart swelled with emotions he had ignored for so long that he'd wondered if he would ever feel them again. Instead of scaring him, it reassured him. He was going to be okay. His soul hadn't died with Linda after all.

Chapter Twenty-Three

SAVANNAH PROPPED HERSELF up on her elbow and watched Jack sleep. *If only every Wednesday morning could look this good.* She'd noticed when they were on the mountain that he hadn't slept much, and now his chest rose and fell in a peaceful cadence. His entire beautiful body was relaxed. There were no bulging veins or tense muscles, just six foot four inches of perfectly sculpted sleeping man. She thought about the scars she'd felt on his back and wondered how he'd gotten them. Jack was plowing through so many changes that she didn't feel pressure to know all of his secrets at once. She had a feeling that there were some things Jack had to reveal when he felt comfortable and safe. For him, she could be patient.

She had the urge to run her finger along the sexy tufts of hair on his chest, but it was only five thirty in the morning and they hadn't blown out the candles until three thirty. She lay back and stared at the ceiling, thinking about the hours they'd spent caressing every inch of each other's bodies. A shiver ran through her. She could practically feel him inside of her. A string of worry sifted through her mind. *Will he think I'm slutty because of the things we did? Was I too aggressive? He said I was not at all like Linda. What if he wants someone just like her?* She closed her eyes. *Will Linda always be with us?*

She felt the mattress move, and Jack's large hand covered her bare stomach. He pressed a soft kiss to her temple.

"Good morning, beautiful," he whispered.

Please don't think I'm a slut. She opened her eyes, and he smiled. Sleepiness hovered in his deep blue eyes, and just beyond, a spark flickered. A hungry spark.

"Morning."

"What time is it?" He ran his hand down her ribs, over the arc of her hip, and squeezed her thigh.

Jack's touch, his voice, his kisses—*Oh, his kisses!*—nourished her in ways she'd never known she was missing.

"Five thirty," she answered.

He sighed and lay back down. The comforter covered him from the hips down, and there was no mistaking what caused the tented fabric.

"I have to be somewhere at nine." He rolled onto his side again and pressed himself against her.

She wanted to climb right back on top of him and forget about work and whatever he had to do altogether. She put her hand on his cheek, and the rough stubble added another wanton thought to her already horny mind.

"I have to be at work at eight," she managed.

He kissed her lightly, then ran the pad of his thumb along her cheekbone, following the line of her jaw to her chin, and placed a kiss in the center of it. She loved when he touched her like that—like he was memorizing everything about her.

"About last night," he whispered.

Savannah closed her eyes. *Don't say it. If it was a mistake, please don't tell me. Send me a text. Leave me a message. Just let me live in this amazing fantasy for a few more minutes, please.* She opened her eyes, readying herself for the kick to her heart that she feared.

"I meant every word I said." Jack leaned his forehead against hers. "Every word, Savannah. I know it's fast and maybe even crazy."

She couldn't breathe.

He brushed her hair from her forehead and kissed her there. "But what I feel for you runs so deep. All those things we did together…"

Embarrassment clutched her.

Jack shook his head. His touch was so tender as he drew his hand up along her rib cage. Savannah gasped a quiet breath.

"I want to crawl beneath your skin and become one with you." His gaze was a sensual caress, his voice a tether to her heart.

She put her hand behind his neck and pulled him to her, and she kissed him as she had so many times the night before. She'd memorized the way he stroked her tongue with a rhythm that was all his own. His touch had already become familiar. She believed his words because every confession came with a touch of proof. Jack Remington was no longer hiding behind anger and guilt, and that was clear in his eyes, his words, his touch.

Savannah put her cheek against his and whispered, "Why did it take so long for us to find each other?"

His eyes narrowed. "Fate. I wouldn't have been ready before now."

When she was with Connor, she'd always felt pressure to perform, and with Jack it was just the opposite. She *wanted* to touch him, to please him, and she wanted to be loved by him— but there was no rush, no feeling of mandatory reciprocation.

Jack kissed her lips, and then he touched his forehead to hers and said, "I want you to know something."

"Sounds serious."

"I don't know if this is the time to talk, but I need you to hear this. I know I've got a long way to go in dealing with everything." His eyes played over hers. "And I'm sure you're wondering if I'll ever get over Linda. I spent two years wondering if I would. Last night I realized that I'll always love her, and I will probably always feel guilty about losing her the way I did. But the way you've touched my heart is one hundred and eighty degrees different from the way anyone ever has before. Everything about us—how we talk, how we touch, how we make love—it's all different. Deeper. There's no comparison between you and her, and I'll do my best to try to keep from mentioning her name."

She knew she could believe him, but she also knew the pressure that would put him under. She could already see the gears in his mind ticking away, worrying, preparing the guilt for when her name came up, and that's not what she wanted him to live with.

"Jack, Linda was a big part of your life, and I don't expect you to forget her or to pretend she didn't exist. She did exist, and that's okay. You are who you are because of everything you went through and everything you had together. I can't imagine that getting over the hurt and dealing with the grief is going to be easy."

"I can do it," he said. "I will do it."

"I know you can, and I believe you will. But please, you have to know that Linda is not a threat to me." As she said the words, she realized it was true. "You'll probably have times when you remember something about her and it makes you happy or sad, or when you just need to talk about her. I'm a big girl, Jack. I get that. I've watched my father grieve for my mother forever." *Not that I'd want you having conversations with your dead wife.* "You're not in this alone anymore. I'm here, and I'm not going anywhere." She brushed his hair from his forehead and cupped his cheek in her hand.

"I love you, Jack." The words came without effort or thought, and she didn't have any inclination to stop them. She didn't care if she'd known him an hour, a day, or a year. She knew she should worry about scaring him off, but after the things he'd said to her, she couldn't even hold on to that thought for a second. There were all sorts of things she should probably worry about, like if he'd ever get completely over Linda. If they'd ever be able to share a bedroom, or if the anger and guilt would come back and haunt him later that afternoon or the next day. But her father's words came back to her loud and clear. *The strength and ability to survive comes from within.* When Jack looked down at her, she knew he had everything he needed to survive. He was stronger than any man she knew. He had to be to survive what he already had.

And when Jack looked into her eyes with so much honesty she wanted to make love to him again and he said, "I love you, too. I really, truly do," she knew she could believe him.

Chapter Twenty-Four

THE MORNING SUN beat down on Jack's back as his motorcycle climbed the steep hill toward the Grays' colonial home. He felt stronger than he had in years and was certain he could deal with whatever lay ahead. The evening before played like a rerun in his mind, and he'd finally pinpointed the moment that he knew he was going to be okay. It wasn't when he and Savannah were making love or sharing secrets. It had nothing to do with the fact that he had an insatiable appetite for her and that she seemed to have the same for him. It was what Savannah had said and the look of love in her eyes when she'd said it. *I love you, Jack,* and then, *You're not in this alone anymore.*

He parked his motorcycle in the circular driveway and set his helmet on the back. Jack pulled his shoulders back and drew in a deep breath, trying to ignore the nervousness spinning in his stomach and the pinch to his heart from the bundle of memories—both happy and sad—that he'd gathered in the Grays' home over the last decade. He had to do this, and he was not going to chicken out. He walked to the front door, and as he reached for the doorbell, the door swung open.

"Jack." Elise opened her arms.

Jack embraced her, and the unique warm vanilla smell of the Grays' house sifted through the doorway.

"I'm so glad you made it," she said.

"I meant what I said, Elise. I'm ready to do this. It's time."

She led him into the expansive foyer, then across the ceramic-tiled floor to a grand living room decorated with velvet and ornately carved wooden couches covered in rich mulberry, greens, and blues. The walls were lined with cherry bookshelves, and a marble fireplace filled the space between two enormous bay windows. Everything looked just as Jack remembered. Everything except the addition of the hospital bed placed just beside the grand piano on the left side of the room. Jack swallowed past the sadness that pressed in on him. Ralph Gray's skin was ashen. His once virile body lay shrunken and diminished beneath white cotton sheets. The strength Jack had taken solace in on his way up the driveway fell away, and he felt another fissure form in his heart. He felt like he was in a sick game of tug-of-war. On one side was a life waiting to be lived. *And Savannah.* On the other side was the guilt not just of losing Linda, but of losing all the people he'd turned his back on. How was a man supposed to survive such heartache and enjoy the awaiting pleasure?

"Jack?" Ralph's voice was barely above a whisper, scratchy and painful.

"Yes. I'm here." He went to Ralph's side, and all the anger he'd felt for the last two years was replaced with sadness and regret. Ralph had welcomed him into his family, treated him like a son, and respected him, and Jack had thrown it away. Jack thought he'd cried all the tears he'd had in him over the past twenty-four hours, but as his tears returned, he knew the well had not been tapped dry.

He took Ralph's frail hand in his own.

"Jack." Ralph's eyes were already damp. "I'm glad you're here, you sorry bastard."

"Dad!" Elise chided him.

Jack's heart warmed, glad to see a remnant of his friend return. "I'm here, Ralph, and I'm sorry for all the time I missed."

Ralph drew his eyebrows together. "Cut the poppycock," Ralph said in a weak tone. "You listen to me. I don't have much breath left. This cancer crap really sucks. But you need to know that I never blamed you for Linda's death."

Jack's muscles tensed as a tear tumbled down his cheek. "Ralph—"

"You're the same old stubborn bastard as you've always been. I told you to listen." He sputtered a cough. "I'm still plenty of years your senior, so shut up and listen. You are a good man, Jack. You were a great husband, and I know Linda felt the same way. I couldn't have asked for a better son-in-law. She loved you, Jack. For all your stubbornness, for all the love you have in that gigantic heart of yours, and for all the things you had hoped to become."

Jack blinked away tears, but he could not ebb the flow of them. "Thank you," he managed.

"I'm not done yet." Ralph drew in a long, slow inhalation; then his body shook with another phlegmy cough. Elise came to his side with a box of tissues and helped him clean the gunk from his mouth.

Elise brushed her father's hair from his forehead. "You okay, Dad?"

Ralph nodded. "You're a good egg, Elise. Thank you." He turned to Jack. "Just like Linda, right?"

Jack nodded, afraid that if he spoke he wouldn't be able to keep himself from sobbing.

"There's one more thing that I want to say, and I know this is going to kick you in the gut, Jack, but you need to hear it. This baloney you've pulled of running away to a cabin in the woods and hiding from life, that's not who you are. You're a survivor, all right, but a survivor of a different kind, and I think you know that by now; otherwise you wouldn't be here."

"You know about my cabin?" *The cabin I haven't told a soul about?*

"Never underestimate people, Jack. You know that from your military career. Do you think I'd have let Linda down by letting you go from our lives forever? Of course not. Don't ever forget that there's nothing a man can't do if he really wants to do it. I had to know you were okay. Even if not emotionally. I needed to know where you were in case you really did need someone." He held up his palm to stop Jack from even thinking about refuting his words. "A good private investigator is worth every penny. I know where you've been, and I'm pretty certain I know where you're headed now."

"Headed?" Jack was blown away by the lengths Ralph had gone to after the way Jack had treated him.

"Remember Elizabeth and Lou?"

Jack narrowed his eyes. "Yes."

"They're my friends, Jack." Elise touched his arm.

Elise continued. "We didn't spy on you. She and Lou had registered for your course, and I found out about it after the fact but before she left. Dad really wanted to talk to you, and we weren't sure if you would be approachable. You were so angry for so long. I asked Elizabeth to let me know if you seemed okay enough for Dad to talk to you. I'm sorry, Jack. It was like fate stepped in."

"You went to that extent to make sure I was okay?"

She nodded. "And their son, Aiden, adores you."

Jack thought of how drawn he'd been to the little blond boy and how natural it had felt to teach him. Then the fear the day he went missing and how Jack had felt as if his world were crashing down upon him until he'd found Aiden, safe and sound in his makeshift shelter.

"Jack, Elizabeth told us about a woman. Savannah," Ralph said in a frail voice.

Ralph held his gaze, and Jack could not turn away. His chest constricted. "Yes."

"Elizabeth said she was quite fond of you, and that it appeared mutual." Ralph's eyes never left Jack's, and Jack didn't back down from the question.

He couldn't lie about Savannah, but he hated to hurt Ralph and Elise with the truth of his feelings. He settled on honesty. It was the least he could give back to them.

"Yes, sir. She was right." Jack addressed Ralph formally due to the importance of the subject they were addressing, and he hoped it conveyed the respect that he felt for him. He drew his shoulders back, ready to face whatever they might hand him. He knew he deserved it.

A weak smile spread across Ralph's face, gathering the loose skin around his mouth and multiplying the fine lines that surrounded his eyes. "That's good, Jack. That's good." Ralph motioned with his hand for Jack to come closer.

Jack leaned in close, catching a whiff of his medicinal breath.

"You deserve this, Jack. Be happy. Let love find you and have that family you always wanted. Linda would want you to."

Ralph reached up slowly and patted Jack's back.

Jack put his mouth beside Ralph's ear. "Thank you, Ralph. Thank you." He drew back, and Ralph grabbed his arm, his frail fingers pressing into Jack's skin.

"Jack, listen to me. You've got to let your guilt go. People die every day. We're all gonna go sometime. This woman, Savannah, she doesn't need to live with Linda's noose around your neck. Let yourself be happy. Linda would want that for you. You know she would." He released Jack's arm and settled back on the pillow, looking even more depleted than when Jack had arrived.

"Ralph, I'm so sorry for all that happened and for what you're going through now." Jack touched his arm.

Ralph's eyes met his. "I know you are. Let it go," he whispered.

"I love you, Ralph, and I'll always love Linda." Fresh tears pressed on Jack's eyelids.

Ralph nodded. "She knows, Jack. She knows."

An hour later, as Jack climbed back on his motorcycle and drove away, he finally felt as if he were moving forward instead of standing still.

Chapter Twenty-Five

AIDA BARGED THROUGH Savannah's office door and closed it behind her. She was practically bursting the buttons of her blouse with every heavy breath as she pressed her back against the door.

Savannah startled. "What the...? Is someone armed out there?"

"I ran from reception."

"Why would you do that?" Savannah came around her desk and eyed Aida's black pencil skirt and the four-inch heels on her Jimmy Choos. "*How* did you do that?"

"Are you kidding? I can run like a deer in these. I can pull my ankles behind my ears, too." She winked.

"You're so weird."

"Remember that creepy client of Ed's? He was out there when I was coming back from the ladies' room." Aida shivered. "He really creeps me out."

"You're so dramatic."

Aida grabbed Savannah's hand and dragged her to the chairs in front of her desk. She sat down and pulled Savannah down to the chair across from her. "Enough about the creeper. I had the hottest date last night with that attorney from Greenberg's office."

"The blond guy?"

Aida rolled her eyes. "Yes, the blond guy. The man has a body that should be tattooed with *too hot to touch.*"

"Yeah? Did you have a good time? Was he nice?" Aida wasn't known for a long track record of meaningful relationships. The other women in the office called her a man eater. She rarely went on a date with the same man more than three times.

She shrugged. "Eh. But he was incredibly talented in bed. Enough so that it might warrant a second time around. We'll see." Aida pursed her lips and ran her eyes up and down Savannah. "What's up with the after-sex glow?"

Savannah waved her hand in front of her face and made a *psht* sound.

"You think I didn't notice you humming in the meeting this morning? You might as well have worn a sign across your forehead that said, *I got laid, and no, I cannot stop smiling.*"

"You're such a pig," Savannah teased. "You always think you see something that has to do with sex."

"So? Tell, tell." Aida lifted her slim eyebrows in quick succession.

Savannah sat back and looked out the window, remembering the way her heart had stopped when she'd seen Jack in her doorway.

"Jack came over last night."

Aida arched a brow. Savannah hadn't thought twice about sharing all the dirty details of her affair with Connor. *The good, the bad, and the embarrassing.* But something about her relationship with Jack felt different. Private. More intimate.

"And?" Aida pushed.

"And we had a great night." She pushed to her feet and

circled the desk, then leaned over it and pretended to be looking for something.

"Yeah, that's going to work." Aida followed Savannah's path, shoved her body between the desk and Savannah and crossed her arms.

"Okay, fine." She felt her cheeks flush.

"Wait a second." She ran her eyes up and down Savannah. "Why all the deception? You're blushing. Give me your hand." She held her hand out.

Savannah put her hands behind her back.

"Mm-hmm. Clammy hands at the mention of him." She narrowed her baby blues, scrutinizing Savannah's every move. "Deception, embarrassment, humming. You like this guy. Like, really like this guy. Counselor, how do you plead?" She hiked herself up onto the desk and crossed her long legs.

"I hate you so much." Savannah took a step toward the door, and Aida grabbed her wrist.

"Hey, you okay?"

Savannah covered her face with her hands and groaned. "Yes, I'm fine." She lowered her hands and leaned in close to Aida. "You're going to think I'm crazy, but…" She slammed her eyes shut and whispered, "I think I love him."

"What?" Aida yelled.

Savannah jumped back. "I know, okay? It's way too soon and he's got stuff to deal with, and I'm on the rebound and a million other things that should send me running for the hills."

"Oh no, honey, that's what got you tangled up with him in the first place." Aida crossed her arms and tapped her cheek with her finger. "Good in bed?"

"Very."

"Treats you well?"

"Adoringly," Savannah answered.

"Kind?"

"Yes, but rough edges until he feels safe."

"Skeletons?" Aida narrowed her eyes again.

Aida's ability to cut through bull was one of the many traits Savannah loved about her. "Wife died in a car accident. He was the one who found her. He blames himself."

"Ouch."

"Mm-hmm."

"Priors?"

"No relationships or women for two years. Military background. He's also a pilot." She knew that would strike Aida's adoration for men in the fast lane.

"Wait, wait, wait. Hold up. Two years? You're kidding, right? Either that or this man is so good in bed that he's turned you into an idiot."

Savannah shook her head. "No women since his wife died."

"You sure he's not gay?"

"One hundred and fifty percent sure." Savannah leaned on the desk beside Aida. "What am I going to do? I can't keep my hands off of him, and I love his voice. His voice is like…it's like hot chocolate on a cold day."

Aida rolled her eyes. "Uh oh. Here we go down La-La Lane."

"I'm being serious. When he talks to me, I swoon like a teenager. And when he touches me, I turn into a sex-starved seductress."

"Hmm. Now, that could be interesting. Do you have anything in common? Besides sex, I mean."

Savannah shrugged.

"Wait. You think you love him and you know nothing real

about him? Savannah Braden, what would your father say? Or Treat? Treat would not be pleased."

"Actually, I told Treat that I really liked him and he was supportive." Savannah stood and pulled up Jack's website on the computer.

"Treat was supportive of a guy you're sleeping with and know nothing about?" Aida shook her head. "I don't believe you."

"He checked him out. You know my brother, always over-protective. He said he's a good guy. He just has a lot to deal with. Listen, I like him, okay? A lot. I think I…" She trailed off, then whispered, "Love him."

"Yeah, I got that. So when can I meet him? Let me see for myself." Aida pushed away from the desk and looked over Savannah's shoulder at his website. She squinted, moving closer to the screen, then backed away again. "The man is hung like a horse. Look at the bulge in his jeans."

Savannah clicked off the website. "Geez, Aida. Is that really all you saw?"

"No. I saw woods, dark hair, dangerous eyes, and a killer body with a huge schlong. No wonder you like him so much."

Savannah pointed to the door. "Out. I gotta get this document finished."

"Fine, I'll go, but I want a date and a time. If you really are falling for some mountain man, I gotta check him out myself." She pulled the door open and looked over her shoulder. "And I promise not to look at his package." Aida flashed a smile and walked out.

Aida had uncovered a new issue that Savannah hadn't yet contemplated. *The idea of being in the city with all those eyes on me makes my skin crawl.* Her life was in the city, and no matter how much she enjoyed a brief woodsy retreat, she'd worked too hard for too long to give up her career, and her career was in the city. She looked at her cell phone and wondered if she'd hear from Jack soon. He'd said he was going to see Linda's father. His emotions were already so raw, and Elizabeth had told her that Ralph was ill. She hoped the visit didn't prove to be too much for Jack.

What am I doing?

We aren't planning a future.

We're...falling in love.

I'm in big trouble.

Chapter Twenty-Six

JACK HAD FORGOTTEN how much he enjoyed driving his father's old Ford F-150. He'd given it to Jack when he and Linda had purchased the chalet. Jack was a motorcycle guy, not a truck guy, and at the time, he'd taken the truck as a way to hold on to the memories of riding shotgun with his father when he was just a boy. For all his father's gruff exterior, when he was in the old truck, that facade seemed to fall away. He'd ramble on about life, war stories, but not in the preaching way he usually did. When they were in the truck, it was almost as if his father forgot that Jack was his eldest son, and instead he spoke with the ease of a storyteller. Jack loved the old truck because of those memories. At first when he'd driven it, it had felt too confined, too slow, and too plain for Jack's taste, with the navy blue stripes above and below a wide silver band that ran around the body of the truck. Over the years, Jack had used it to haul lumber, move rocks, and pick up furniture, and such. Now, as the old truck ambled up the driveway on his way back from Home Depot, Jack took comfort in the vehicle. He liked knowing that his father had driven it before him, and he was coming to terms with the size and heft of it. *It only took twelve years.*

He parked the truck and unlocked the front door of the chalet, thinking about his visit with Ralph. He hadn't been prepared for the reality of Ralph's deteriorating condition or for his reaction to all that had transpired between them. Ralph's love for Jack, and his acceptance of the idea of another woman in Jack's life, should have been all Jack needed to move forward, but mending the fissure with his own family still loomed over him. He used the good that came from his visit with Ralph to spur himself into action. He couldn't change the past, but he could create a better future. First he had to gain control of his own life.

Jack carried the new door over his head as he mounted the stairs to the second floor. The sight of the splintered wood on the floor of the nursery turned his stomach. *What if Savannah had seen this?* Jack didn't work very hard at fooling himself. He knew that Savannah had seen that angry side of him. In fact, everyone had. But she didn't need to see the evidence of his broken shell. He didn't want to be that angry man anymore, and with Ralph's blessing and a plan in mind, he was determined to change.

With the new door installed and the old one in the back of the truck, he swept the last of the rubble into the dustpan, then vacuumed the small room and drew the curtains open. The afternoon sun had already disappeared, and evening was creeping in. He checked his watch and wondered what time Savannah got off work. *Savannah.* Even her name felt exotic. She'd blown his mind last night with her honesty, her openness, and her loving touch. It wasn't the physical act of being intimate. It was the way she put her heart into every stroke of her hand, every spoken word, and every kiss of her full, soft lips. She accepted his baggage. Instead of pushing him to move past

ADDISON COLE

it or ridiculing him for being weak, she'd simply led him away from the bedroom. Jack imagined that was not how most women would have reacted. Then again, Savannah wasn't like any woman he'd ever known. He'd been so nervous when he'd touched her, and she felt so good beneath him and on top of him. *So very good.* But there was more to a relationship than sex, and if anyone knew that, it was Jack. When he was in the military, he'd seen too many marriages fall apart while the men were on tour. A third of his team lost their wives to infidelity. He hadn't understood it then, and he didn't understand it now. Sex was a great release, but intimacy encompassed so much more, and it was the closeness of knowing each other that he missed most.

Jack went downstairs and pulled his cell phone from the drawer in the kitchen. He typed in Savannah's number, which had been running through his mind since the evening before, and created a contact for her. He scrolled through the few names in his address book. Elise, Kurt, Linda, Mom and Dad, Ralph, Rush, Sage, Dex and Siena. He scrolled back up to Linda's name and hovered over the edit icon. *I will always love you.* He clicked edit, took a deep breath and closed his eyes, steeling himself against whatever emotions might fight back, and then Jack opened his eyes and clicked delete. He released his breath and stood frozen in place, waiting for the emotional onslaught to hit. The house was silent, save for the fluttering of the curtains. Jack's pulse remained constant. His gut didn't take a nosedive. He carried the phone to the back deck and sat on a chair.

"I did it. That's a step." Jack looked up at the sky, contemplating his next move. He felt like he was in a giant chess game and the right move would bring him to the other side, but the wrong move might take him out of the game altogether—and he'd already been out of the game for way too long. He called Savannah, and she answered on the second ring.

"Hello?"

"Hey, beautiful." Her voice sent a thrill through his chest.

"Jack, hi. How'd it go?"

He pictured their kiss goodbye earlier that morning, the way her black slacks hugged her curves and drove a streak of jealousy through his heart. He'd had no competition when they were on the mountain, and the thought of her being ogled by men was unsettling.

"It went well. Ralph isn't doing well, but we talked and it was good."

"Yeah?" Savannah asked.

He could hear the restraint in her voice and knew she had a million questions. "Yeah. I'll share the details when we see each other." *Crap. I shouldn't assume you're free to see me.*

"Okay. I'm getting off work in about an hour. What's on your plate tonight?"

"I was hoping you were." *I sound like a cheesy movie.* "I mean—"

Savannah laughed. He loved her sense of humor.

"That sounds good to me, too. Want to come over? We could grab some dinner, talk?"

"I would like nothing more. I need to make a few calls, but I can leave here in half an hour or so. I should be there in less than two hours. Does that work?" It seemed like forever to him.

"Perfect. I'll pick up some wine on the way home," Savannah offered.

If I'm going to do this, I have to do it all the way. Jack hadn't spent any time in the city since Linda's death. There were too many people to avoid in the city, and he'd thought he'd seen accusations in everyone's eyes. As if they'd all known he'd let Linda leave the house the night of the accident. But after talking to Ralph and realizing how wrong he'd been and how he'd misinterpreted so many things, Jack wondered if he'd been projecting his guilt on to everything and everyone in his life. He was about to find out.

"Let's go out and have a nice dinner. Nothing fancy." *Another step in the right direction.* "Is that okay, or are you too tired from work?"

"I'm tired…but not from work."

Her seductive tone had him stifling a groan. "Savannah, if you only knew what you do to me with your innuendos."

"Oh, I have a good idea."

He heard her grin, and it only heightened his desires. "See you soon."

Jack ended the call and paced the deck, trying to calm his urges and debating whom he should call first. It took only a few minutes for him to decide.

"Hello?"

His sister's voice felt like coming home after a long trip: warm and inviting. "Siena?"

Silence stopped him in his tracks.

"Jack?" she asked in a hushed breath.

"Hi, honey."

"Jack. I can't believe it's you. Oh my gosh, Jack. Where are you? How are you?" Her words tumbled fast and hard.

"I'm back in Bedford Corners, and I'm pretty good, actually. I have a favor to ask—" Before he could finish his sentence, Siena interrupted him.

"Anything, Jack. Whatever you need."

Jack knew he didn't deserve her unconditional love, but he was thankful just the same. He cleared his throat in an effort to push away the lump that tried to suppress his voice.

"I want to see everyone, but I know Rush won't come willingly to meet me. Would you mind having a dinner or something at your place, or maybe Dad's? I...I have a few things I need to say. Actually, I have a lot to say, and I want to say it to everyone." Jack felt more like a favorite uncle than a brother to Siena, Dex, and Sage because of the age difference between them, whereas between Jack, Rush, and Kurt, there was a span of only seven years.

"I can't tell you how happy that makes me. Mom and Dad are going to be over the moon, and yes, of course I'll do it. I'll figure something out. Rush is pretty grizzly these days when we bring up your name, so I'm not sure what you should expect, but I'll do it." She paused, and Jack imagined her running her hand through her long brown hair. Siena had been modeling since she was eight. Although Jack hadn't seen his family more than a couple of times over the last two years, he'd made a point of keeping tabs on what they had going on in their lives, and he knew that Siena was more beautiful than ever, with his mother's tall, slim figure and his father's deep blue eyes.

"Thanks, honey. I really appreciate your help." When Linda died, Jack had secretly wished that his family didn't still reside so close together—all within an hour and a half of New York City. Now he was glad they did.

"Hey, Jack? Are you really going to try this time?"

The worry in her voice tugged at his heart. He hadn't meant to give her false hope before, but meaning to and doing were two very different things. Jack had no intention of failing her— or failing himself—again. And there was no way he was going to fail Savannah.

"Honey, you know how hard I tried to disappear?"

"All too well." Siena sighed.

"That's how hard I'm going to try to make this right. I have to run, but, Siena?"

"Yeah?"

"I love you. I hope you know that. And I love Dex, Sage, Kurt, and Rush, too. That's never changed. I just got lost for a little while." Jack felt like the trees had parted and a path appeared before him.

"I know, Jack. We all know that, even Rush. He's just being a jerk. I love you. I need to be able to reach you when I get it set up. Are you going to actually use your cell again, or are you going to carry it turned off forever? I never understood why you did that. It's so expensive to pay for if you're not going to use it."

Sometimes Jack forgot how careful Siena had always been with finances. She had more money than he ever would, and she still lived like she was always on her last dime.

"It was for emergencies, but I'm leaving it on now. Call me anytime, okay?"

After he ended the call with Siena, he took the stairs two at a time to the master bedroom. Hearing the smile in his sister's voice renewed his determination. He'd rued nightfall and dreaded the dawn of the coming day for way too long. He was going to fix this mess if it took everything he had. Being with Savannah woke him up and gave him hope for a future. Ralph had opened another door in his heart—the one that would allow him to heal the wounds that he'd caused to his relationship with his family.

Jack took a pair of jeans and a black button-down shirt from his closet and headed into the bathroom. Beneath the warm spray of the shower, he realized what he'd done without any thought at all. His heart had chosen the indoor shower, and his body hadn't hesitated. He stared at the two shampoo bottles—one lavender, the other dark blue—then he picked up the purple one, stepped from the shower, and crossed the floor buck naked and dripping wet. He tossed Linda's shampoo bottle in the trash, then glanced at her sink. He retrieved the trash can, whipped open the cabinet beneath the sink, and swept all of her belongings into it. Then he set it down and stepped back into the shower. *I turned off my emotions. It's time to turn them back on.*

Chapter Twenty-Seven

SAVANNAH FINISHED DRYING her hair and putting on her makeup, mentally ticking off her outfits and trying to decide what to wear for dinner with Jack. She tightened the towel around her body and walked across the hall to her bedroom, stopping to answer her cell phone.

"Hey, Aida. I'm in a hurry, sorry."

"Do we have a hot date?" she asked.

"I do, but you have to give me time to get to know him before I spring you on him. That would be like feeding him to the wolves on his first day in the forest. I can't even believe he wants to go to dinner. He said he doesn't really like cities." She dried off with the phone pressed between her ear and shoulder, then stepped into her sexiest lace thong.

"Dinner? That sounds nice. Where are you going?"

"I haven't even thought about it. Any suggestions? I think I'd like to eat outside, if I can eat at all. I have a feeling I won't be able to. Can you believe I've had butterflies in my stomach since he called?" She flipped through her closet and decided to dress a little sexier for Jack. He'd only seen her in jeans and her work clothes. *Time for a thrill.*

"Butterflies? What are you, twelve? I don't think I've ever

had butterflies in my life."

Aida was as confident and aggressive with men as she was in the courtroom, and Savannah couldn't imagine her being nervous about anything. "I know. It's stupid, right?"

"I don't know. Catherine believes in the whole fall-in-love, butterflies thing. But then again, I think all the assistants at our office do. That's so weird." She sighed. "What about that new little bistro on the corner by your place? You can eat outside, and it's not too stuffy. I can't imagine that a guy who doesn't like cities wants to be around an uptight crowd."

Savannah pulled a white minidress from her closet and held it against her in front of the mirror. "That sounds like a great idea. Now, help me pick out a dress. What about my scoop-necked white mini? He said casual, but he's only seen me in jeans."

"You know what that dress says, right? Remember how Connor reacted when he saw you in it?" Aida reminded her. "You ended up leaving the cocktail party to have sex in his car."

Savannah crinkled her nose at the memory. "Thanks for that. I'll burn the dress tomorrow." She flipped through a few more outfits. "Long-sleeved black mini?"

"Still says take me to bed, but you could probably get away with it. At least all your skin wouldn't be exposed. So, dinner, then your place?" Aida asked.

Savannah dropped her towel and slipped the dress over her head. "I guess. I don't know or care. I just want to spend time with him." She turned from side to side and smiled. "This looks hot."

"Of course. How could it look anything but? Boots, heels, or casual flats?"

"Well, boots say sexy, and heels just feel wrong. He's an

outdoorsman, not a dress-up guy. But he is like six four, so I'm not sure flats are the best choice, either." Savannah stared at the shoes in her closet, wishing she could just go barefoot. "You know what? Maybe I should just wear jeans. I feel like I look as if I'm trying too hard."

Aida sighed loudly. "You don't even have to try. He's into you, and you know that. You said you're falling in love with him. Why are you so nervous? Aren't you supposed to know true love by how comfortable you are?"

"That's all part of it, I think. I don't know. I haven't been in love before. I'm changing out of this." She glanced at the clock. "He's going to be here any minute. Can we catch up in the morning?"

"Of course. But I vote for the hot outfit."

A knock at the door sent a panic through her. "Uh oh. He's here. I gotta go."

She ended the call and debated tearing off her dress and putting on a pair of jeans. Another knock sent her hurrying down the hallway toward the front door, wishing she'd planned ahead like most women would have.

She pulled open the door with a ready smile, which fell flat the minute she saw Connor Dean. All six foot five, two hundred thirty pounds of him, complete with his Stetson and an armful of red roses. She shook her head. Blinked her eyes. *This has to be a bad joke.*

"Connor."

"Hello, darlin'." He swooped in and wrapped his arm around her waist, pulled her against him, then kissed her so hard their teeth knocked.

It took Savannah a minute to get her bearings and realize that his mouth was attached to hers in a very intimate and deep kiss that felt oh-so-good and was totally not what she wanted. She blinked away the confusion and tried to push him away as Jack's face came into focus over Connor's shoulder.

FROM THE THIRD-floor landing, Jack watched the tall, handsome man with a bunch of roses in his arms knock on Savannah's door. He lowered his chin and narrowed his eyes. The stab of jealousy he'd felt earlier that morning reappeared. He was ten feet away when Savannah opened the door. Five feet when the man took her in his arms and kissed her like he'd been there before, like the kiss was as familiar as the stinkin' cowboy hat he wore. He was inches from the man's back when Savannah opened her eyes and met his stare, then pushed at the man's stomach to try to disengage from the attack on her mouth.

Jack put one hand on the man's shoulder and yanked, knocking him off kilter. The man stumbled backward and spun around.

"Dude? Do you mind?" the man spat. He looked at Savannah again and managed a forced smile.

Jack fisted his hands. His chest rocked up and down as he closed the gap between them. He gritted his teeth and reminded himself that Savannah wasn't really his to protect, and he had no idea who this guy was. "Actually, I do." Jack's voice was cold as ice.

"Jack." Savannah touched his arm.

He kept his eyes trained on the man with the roses.

"Connor, what are you doing here?"

Connor?

She tried to pull Jack away from him, but Jack was rooted to the ground. He'd rather the guy had his back against the wall until he figured out what was going on.

"I came to apologize," Connor said. He shoved the flowers beneath Jack's arm toward Savannah.

"Apologize?" Jack shifted his gaze to Savannah.

Savannah blushed and looked away. "He's the reason I went on the survival weekend."

Jack's blood simmered. He drew his eyes back to Connor. "This is the lowlife who cheated on you?" Jack wanted to pick the bastard up by his collar and heave him down the stairs, then pummel him until he couldn't move. But the look on Savannah's face stopped him from moving a muscle. Embarrassment deepened the blush on her cheeks. He couldn't tell if she was embarrassed by his aggression or if she was embarrassed by the guy showing up. And he didn't trust himself enough to decipher the truth.

Connor held up his arms. "Whoa, listen. It was all a misunderstanding." He shot a worried look at Savannah from beneath Jack's hulking stare. "Tell him, Savannah."

Savannah narrowed her eyes at Connor. She crossed her arms and said in a harsh tone, "He's not worth it. Just let him go."

Jack stepped back, and as Connor moved around him, he grabbed his collar. His need to set the cheating jerk straight was too strong to ignore. He didn't want to have to worry that Connor would return and put his lips on Savannah again. Jack clenched his jaw, and with one arm, he lifted Connor two inches off the ground.

"You owe her a real apology."

"I'm sorry. I'm sorry, Savannah." Connor held his hands up in surrender.

"Jack," Savannah whispered.

The edge to Savannah's voice had him lowering Connor back down to his feet and pinning him to the landing with a hot stare. "I suggest you learn how to treat a lady."

Jack watched Connor disappear down the stairs. Then he wrapped his arms around Savannah. Only then did he realize she was trembling. "Are you okay?"

She nodded, snuggling against his chest.

"I'm sorry I was so aggressive, but I saw him kissing you, and the look in your eyes was—"

She looked up at him, and the fear in her eyes fell away. "Don't be. I'm glad you were here. He's the last person on earth I want to kiss."

Jack's boots added an inch to his height, and with Savannah in her bare feet, she was a good eight inches shorter than him. She looked vulnerable and small, and even though he knew she was anything but, the urge to protect her was strong no matter how fierce she might be in a courtroom—or when pulling herself away from him in the mountains. He leaned down and placed his hands along the curves of her cheeks and the sleek line of her jaw and pressed a gentle kiss to her lips.

"I don't think anyone has ever protected me like that other than my brothers."

Jack took her hand and led her into the apartment. "I can't lie to you, Savannah. There was a jealous streak that ran through me. I haven't been jealous in...*man*...ten years or more."

Savannah ran her finger down the center of his chest. "Jealous, huh?"

Jack scrubbed his face with his hand and breathed out a long sigh, allowing his muscles to unclench and his eyes to take in Savannah's minidress, which hugged every inch of her alluring figure.

"It's not nice to stare," she teased.

"Holy…*You*…Savannah, I don't think I've ever seen a woman look as beautiful as you do right now." He gathered her hair and held it in his hand, then leaned down and kissed her neck. "Mm, and you smell sinfully delicious."

She wrapped her arms around his neck and kissed him just below his earlobe.

Jack closed his eyes, enjoying the thrum of desire that coursed through him. He drew back from her and smiled. "We have dinner plans, remember?"

She looked up at the ceiling. "Ah, yes, dinner."

"Do you want to talk about that guy?" Jack couldn't even say his name.

"How about on the way to the restaurant? I was just going to throw on jeans, actually."

She started toward the hall, and Jack grabbed her wrist and spun her back to him. He put one hand on the small of her back, and with the other, he held her hand against his chest. "Don't," he whispered.

"Don't?"

Jack shook his head. He loved seeing the curves of her lithe figure, feeling the arc of her hip and the dip at the base of her spine beneath his hand with only the thin fabric between them. Most of all, he loved knowing that in a few hours they would be alone in her apartment again, and all that waiting would be worth every blessed second when he finally got to take that little dress off.

Chapter Twenty-Eight

USUALLY WHEN SAVANNAH walked down the street, she had a million things she had to do running through her head. She was always planning or strategizing, thinking several hours, days, or weeks ahead. Tonight, holding Jack's hand and walking beside him, she could not hold one clear thought in her mind other than how happy she felt. All her life, her brothers had stepped up to the plate for her, and in watching them, she'd learned to stand up for herself. Before meeting Jack, Savannah might have clocked Connor in the jaw when she'd finally been able to separate his lips from hers, but when Jack appeared and she'd seen the anger and jealousy in his eyes and how quickly it turned from venom to worry for Savannah's safety, she'd turned into a...girl. *A girl!* And it felt darn good to let her guard down and allow someone else to care for her for a little while.

"So, this guy, Connor. Is he someone I have to worry about bothering you in any other ways? Would he ever force himself on you...you know, in worse ways?" Jack's serious tone had returned.

"No. He's harmless. He's a playboy. Women don't tell him to bug off and I did. He came bearing roses, Jack, and all he did was kiss me. I don't mean to minimize it, but he wasn't trying to have his way with me. He wanted to woo me back just long enough to sleep with someone else again." She watched his eyebrows pull together. "What?"

He looked down at her and dropped her hand, then put his arm around her waist. "I was just thinking about the two of you. It was weird to see someone else kissing you, but it was even weirder to feel jealous. And that jealousy brought me back to the idea of you and him—"

Savannah cringed. "Jack."

"What? I just can't picture it. I know you've been with other guys, but when I try to put the picture together of you and other men, I can't hold on to it. I only see you in my arms." He smiled, and it lit up his entire face. "It's funny, isn't it? I can hold on to guilt and anger like a lifeline, but try to grasp an unpleasant thought about you and I haven't the slightest chance."

Savannah felt her heart open up a little more. She remembered what he'd said about being in the city, and as they strolled toward the restaurant, she hadn't felt any tension in his body or seen any in his face.

"Do you feel the eyes of the city on you?" she asked.

He laughed. "No, but I thought I would. I thought a lot of things that apparently were skewed by my guilt."

She tossed the worry that Aida had sparked earlier in the afternoon to the curb. They stopped at an intersection to wait for the light to change, and Jack pulled her against him. After she'd seen how her dress affected him, she'd decided to amp up the tease and she'd slipped on her four-inch heels, bringing her much closer to his lips, which she loved.

"Everything is better when I'm with you," he said before kissing her.

The lights from the nearby restaurants glistened in his dark eyes, and as his gaze fell upon hers, she felt warm all over. In all the years she'd lived in Manhattan, never once had the city felt so romantic. The lights, the sounds, the cool air against her warm skin, even the busy streets carried an aura of romance and love. How could she have missed it for so many years? Or was that what love did to a person?

"Savannah? Is that you?"

Savannah spun around at the sound of Aida's voice. She narrowed her eyes and shot Aida a harsh *I-cannot-believe-you-did-this* glare. "What are you doing here?" She knew exactly what Aida was doing, and as her friend scrutinized Jack from head to toe, lingering a little too long just below the belt, Savannah felt the claws of the green-eyed monster take hold. She narrowed her eyes at her well-meaning friend.

"I was just…out for a walk. You look gorgeous." She leaned in, kissed Savannah's cheek, and whispered, "Hot, hot, hot." Aida ran her hands down the hips of her black jeans. Her breasts pressed against the silky fabric of her low-cut, navy blouse in their usual look-at-me fashion.

Despite the fact that Jack didn't once lower his eyes past Aida's, Savannah had the urge to open her arms wide and stand in front of Aida, saying, *Don't look. Please don't look.*

"Hi, I'm Jack." Jack held out his hand.

Aida shook his hand. "Aida Strong." Her crimson lips lifted, and she put an arm around Savannah. "We work together."

Savannah couldn't stay upset with her. She knew Aida meant well, and if Aida had come home after one weekend claiming to be in love, Savannah would have probably done the same thing.

"Aida's also an attorney." She glared at Aida but topped it

off with a smile.

"Hey, let's grab a drink," Aida suggested.

Savannah tried to catch her eye, but Aida purposely avoided her gaze, looking at Jack, then at the restaurant, at the ground—anywhere but at Savannah. She watched Jack's jaw, waiting for it to clench, and again was surprised when he didn't show one ounce of discomfort. She wondered if seeing Ralph had anything to do with his more relaxed state. She was itching to ask, but first she had to deal with Aida. "Sure, *a* drink sounds good. If Jack doesn't mind."

"Of course not. I want to get to know your friends," Jack said.

"Great. That will give me time to get to know the man who's got Savannah's head up in the clouds," Aida said.

Jack raised his eyebrows, and Savannah shook her head and waved it off, as if to say, *That's just Aida.*

They were seated on a patio beside the restaurant. Savannah had been there a number of times before, but she'd never noticed the ivy climbing the iron gate or the yellow lights strung throughout, as if it were Christmas in September. Jack scooted his chair closer to hers so their legs touched, and he placed his arm around her shoulder. Aida sat across from them and folded her hands beneath her chin, watching Jack like a hawk.

"Aida, I assume you want the lowdown on me?" Jack's voice was dead serious again.

Savannah watched Aida slip seamlessly into interrogation mode. Her slim brows knitted together and she lowered her chin, looking at Jack with a defiant stare. Savannah cringed, though she knew both Aida and Jack could hold their own. She felt strangely like a seventh grader playing, *He said, she said.*

"Actually, I just came for the free drinks, but sure, I'll play along." Aida winked at Savannah. "What are your intentions toward my friend?"

"Aida," Savannah snapped.

Jack ran his hand through Savannah's hair, like he wasn't about to be drilled and prodded for intimate information. This was the most relaxed she'd ever seen him.

"I hope to make it through dinner and maybe a walk before taking her home and ravishing her for hours." Jack's voice was so serious that Savannah did a double take.

Aida cleared her throat, but just like in the courtroom, she didn't miss a beat. "What do you do for a living?"

"I'm a bush pilot and a survivalist. I've got eight years in the Special Forces, a degree in engineering, and enough money to live comfortably." Jack nodded, signaling her to fire away with more questions.

You do?

"Family?" Aida asked.

"I'm the eldest of six. Four brothers, one sister. My parents are both alive and well, and I'm in the process of reconciling with them after two years of…"

He drew his eyebrows together, and his jaw jumped in a nervous clench. Savannah hated seeing him put on the spot. She put her hand on his thigh, and when he answered, he looked at Savannah, not Aida.

"Two years of trying to regroup after the death of my wife."

Savannah couldn't stop herself from reaching up and touching his cheek. He kissed her palm, then turned his attention back to Aida.

"What else?" he asked.

Aida stole a look at Savannah. Savannah tilted her head and arched a brow, indicating to her to please ease up. True to

Aida's nature, she flashed a smile and dug a little deeper. "Do you live in the city?"

"Bedford Corners and in the Colorado Mountains."

"The mountains?" Aida asked.

"I have a cabin there." He squeezed Savannah's shoulder.

"You do?" Savannah asked. "I grew up in Weston, Colorado."

"I do. When you told me that, I remember thinking we might have been fated to meet," Jack said, touching her cheek.

Fated to meet. There goes another piece of my heart.

He returned his attention to Aida, and Savannah thought she was witnessing a flash of the confident, efficient, and intense man Jack probably had been in his Special Forces days. That much hadn't changed, but the guarded man she'd met in the woods seemed very far removed from the open book sitting beside her. She wondered what could have changed so quickly, and as she listened to Aida rattle off more questions and Jack fire back answers, her attorney brain clicked into gear and she realized why he'd spurred this interrogation forward. *The quicker you answer her questions, the quicker we'll be alone. Aren't you clever?*

"Favorite movie?"

"Aida, really?" Savannah asked.

The waitress brought a bottle of wine, and Jack filled their glasses while he answered. "I haven't watched a movie in years." He smiled at Savannah. "But I'm looking forward to doing it again."

Aida sat back and crossed her arms over her chest.

Jack grinned and lifted his chin. "Did I pass?" he asked.

Aida sighed. "You didn't crack, that's for sure. And you look at Savannah like every second you're looking away is a second too long, so yeah, you're doing okay." She picked up her drink and raised her glass. "That was so fun. I never get to interrogate people just for the heck of it. Thanks, Jack. You're a good sport."

Jack lifted his glass. "My turn?"

Aida downed her wine and rose to her feet. "I have to get back to my walk. Rain check?"

Savannah stood and hugged Aida. "You're such a pain," she whispered.

"I like him." Aida smiled at Jack. "Nice to meet you, Jack. Have fun ravishing."

JACK HAD NOTICED the way Savannah's body had tensed when Aida met them outside the restaurant, and now, as she settled into her seat beside him, the smile returned to her lips and she let out a relieved sigh. He leaned over and kissed her, glad to have her all to himself again.

"She seems nice," Jack said.

"I love her to death, but she's a little pushy." Savannah finished her wine, and the waitress refilled their glasses and took their dinner orders.

"She's watching out for you. I like knowing that you have friends like that. I hope you didn't mind that I sort of got things going."

Savannah shook her head, and as the light caught her eyes, she looked radiant and happy. "How could I mind? I knew you were just hurrying her along."

He slid his hand beneath her hair and put his cheek beside hers. "I meant what I said about ravishing you," he whispered.

Her eyes widened and her cheeks flushed. Jack was beginning to recognize the difference between Savannah's embarrassed blush and her wanting blush. When she was embarrassed, her eyes narrowed slightly, and when she was turned on, the green in her eyes darkened, she grazed her lower lip with her teeth, and she breathed a little harder. As her teeth slid over her lip, Jack suppressed the urge to run his tongue on the pink trail they left behind.

The waitress brought their meals, but Jack's mind was no longer on dinner. Savannah's leg had been pressed against his for the past hour, and he'd done well ignoring the desire that mounted in his body, but he knew there was no way he'd be able to put anything solid in his mouth—besides any number of Savannah's body parts. Savannah never looked down at her plate. Their eyes were locked on each other.

She licked her lower lip, and he could tell she was trying just as hard as he was to act appropriately. He wondered if the other patrons could see their secret intentions, too. He had to get control of his emotions. What kind of man couldn't make it through a meal with his girlfriend? *Girlfriend.* He felt a smile spread across his cheeks.

"What?" Savannah asked.

"Everything," was all he could think to say.

Savannah touched his cheek again. Everything she did turned him on. *Focus, Jack.* He needed a distraction to quell his desires.

"So, that was an interesting way to start our first real date."

"Connor or Aida?"

"Both." He took a sip of his wine. "I'm sorry he cheated on you. That must have been very hurtful."

Savannah lowered her eyes and shrugged. "It's kind of my

fault. I should have stopped seeing him. I don't know why I didn't. I didn't even really enjoy being with him for the last year or so, but..."

"You're a little competitive. Maybe you thought you could change him, or you wanted to prove you could." Jack didn't know where the thought came from. It had been years since he'd assessed other people's motives. He realized that parts of himself he hadn't even realized he'd lost were coming back to him. After Linda's death, he'd blocked out everything but the pain, anger, and guilt. As he relinquished those harsher feelings, it left space for his old self to fill itself in, and he was glad for the reminder. He felt like an old friend had stopped by to say hello, and he hoped that friend would bring more friends and stay longer. *One day I really might be whole again.* His response came naturally, and as he dissected it, he realized that Savannah was competitive, and he might be right on target. But when they were in the mountains, he'd also learned that she was sensitive and very, very feminine, and those traits would have left her hurt no matter what her motivation might have been. And he wanted to steal that hurt away forever.

"Maybe. I honestly don't know. But after being with you, I don't think that I've ever been in a relationship where I was this happy."

He turned in his chair so he was facing her. "I feel the same way. I've never felt so fulfilled or so alive."

"And you have a cabin in the mountains?" she asked.

Jack nodded. He'd been dead set on not revealing that fact, but when Aida asked him where he lived and he felt Savannah's eyes on him, he answered honestly. "I do. I'll take you there one day."

"I'd love that. You're so different than you were when I met you. Has something changed?" Her eyes searched his for the answers.

"Everything has changed," he said honestly. "You sparked something in me that made me want to live again, Savannah. We haven't really had the time to talk about what's been going on, and there's a lot I want to share with you." He looked at their uneaten food. "Do you want to eat?"

She shook her head.

"Want to take it home for later?" he asked.

She shook her head with a different kind of hungry look in her eyes.

Jack knew that the minute they got inside Savannah's apartment, there was no way he could stay away from her sweet lips, much less the rest of what was beneath that body-hugging fabric, and he'd never forgive himself if he didn't stop taking her every chance he got and treat her like she deserved to be treated.

"It's a beautiful night. Want to go on a carriage ride through the park?"

Her eyes lit up. "I haven't done that in years."

"It'll be a first for me." He put his hand on her lower back, and as they walked toward the park, Jack thought about how many firsts he'd already experienced with Savannah and about how many more were yet to come.

Chapter Twenty-Nine

SAVANNAH SNUGGLED AGAINST Jack's side. She loved being wrapped in his muscular arms, and as she watched Jack's sharp edges soften, she felt like the luckiest woman on earth.

"I can't believe you've never done this," Savannah said.

"There are a lot of things I haven't done, and I can't wait to do them with you." He kissed the top of her head.

The *clop-clop* of the horses provided a gentle cadence to their ride through the park. The last time she'd ridden in a carriage was with Matt, and they'd spent the whole time talking about kids—and how he never wanted to have any. The carriage ride with Jack was softer, more intimate than it had been before. She felt the gentle sway of the horses' gait, and if they did nothing else that night, just went home and went to sleep, she'd go to sleep happy and content.

"I emptied Linda's closet and gave her clothes to her sister, Elise," Jack said.

His confession came out of left field and his words were tentative, as if he were testing the waters for her reaction.

"Oh, Jack." She sat up so she could look into his eyes. "You kept them for all this time?"

He nodded. "I rarely went into the bedroom after her accident. It was too difficult to face. But after we came back from the mountains, I realized that I'd been hiding from it all, and I knew it was time."

"I'm sorry, Jack. I hope I didn't push you in that direction." *But I'm glad you're moving forward.*

"You have yet to push me to do anything, but being close to you was the catalyst. It was the nudge that I needed. I'd been feeling a little trapped within my own mind, and I didn't know how to break free. But that all changed when you and I came together. And as hard as it was to do, it was also freeing."

"That's good, then, right?"

Jack took her hand and brought it to his lips. "Yes, very good. At some point I would like to show you where I live, but I'm just not there yet."

"You're doing so much all at once, Jack. There's no rush." *You're the most honest man I know, and I love that.*

"Thank you for understanding."

The carriage slowed as they rounded a turn, and Savannah loved that Jack's attentive gaze never wavered.

"When I saw Ralph, we talked briefly about you, and he gave me his blessing." Jack laced his fingers into hers. "I never expected to want to be with another woman, and I certainly never thought about telling Linda's father and sister about caring for one. I'm glad we're together, Savannah, and I'm glad they know. I don't want to hide from anything ever again."

Savannah held her breath, contemplating telling him about Elizabeth's confession. He was pouring out his heart to her, and she owed him the same honesty. "Jack, Elizabeth knows Linda's family."

He narrowed his eyes. "You knew?"

"*You* knew?" she asked.

"No, but Ralph told me this morning."

"Elizabeth told me when we were up there. I'm sorry I didn't tell you, but I wasn't sure how, or even if, I should. You seemed so angry." She touched his chest.

He kissed her forehead. "So you planted that bobcat in the woods and took advantage of me?" he teased.

Just thinking of the bobcat sent thrill bumps up her arms. "That was the plan," she said.

His eyes darkened, and a serious look moved across his face. "I also called my sister." He shrugged. "It's a start."

"Jack," she whispered. She could only imagine how difficult this whole process would be for him, and he was trying to take it all on at once. "You're moving so fast. Doesn't that worry you at all?"

He nodded. "I moved fast when I cut them off, and I feel like I can't move fast enough to repair the damage."

Chapter Thirty

JACK FOLLOWED SAVANNAH up the stairs to her apartment, and when they reached the landing on her floor, his chest constricted with the memory of Connor taking her in his arms. He shook his head at how he'd reacted, though he knew that if it were to play out before him again, he would probably react in the same way.

He admired her figure from behind and had to run his hands along her hips as she dug in her purse for the keys. He followed the lines of her body to her shoulders and gathered her hair in one hand, exposing the curve of her neck. He lowered his lips to her skin and wrapped his other arm around her slim waist.

"Mmm." She arched her head back, and he kissed his way up the back of her neck, pressing his hips into her from behind. Feeling all of her luscious curves against him heightened his yearning.

"Jack," she whispered.

He turned her in his arms and kissed her, swallowing whatever words were falling from her lips. He pressed his body in to hers, her back against the door, and he deepened the kiss, knowing he would never tire of kissing her. She reached up and put her warm hands on his cheeks, and when they pulled apart, they were both breathing heavily.

"We should go in," she said, though she made no move to open the door.

"'Kay," was all he could manage. He could take her right there in the hall, and the look in her eyes told him that she wouldn't mind it at all. When she reached around his hips and grabbed his butt, he practically tore the keys from her hands and unlocked the door. They stumbled into the apartment, kissing between each hurried step. Jack reached back and pushed the door shut behind them. Savannah adeptly unbuttoned his shirt, slipping her fingers beneath the fabric in between each button.

He scanned the apartment, his eyes settling on the hall that led to Savannah's bedroom. Savannah followed his gaze.

"We don't have to go to the bedroom, Jack." She touched his cheek.

"Why are you so good to me? So patient?" Jack was used to being the alpha male in every aspect of his life, and as he looked down the hall, he realized that while he thought he'd been manly—running away to live a solitary life—he'd really been just the opposite. Men didn't hide from their fears. They faced them.

"You're a good person. Why shouldn't I be good to you? You just need time to heal."

"Savannah." He searched her eyes, wondering how he'd gotten lucky enough to have been the one she wanted. Savannah deserved more than making love on a pullout couch. *It's time to move on.* He took her hand and pulled her down the hall to the bedroom before he lost his nerve.

"Jack?"

He couldn't answer. It took all his concentration to walk

through the door. The first step caused his chest to constrict. In the next breath, her scent filled his lungs. He saw Savannah everywhere. In the colorful scarves that hung from her mirror, which he could think of several things to do with that had nothing to do with cold weather. Shoes lined up by the height of their heels. The black leather boots shot a new adrenaline rush through him. The open lingerie drawer revealing a hint of satin and lace. He nearly groaned aloud as he turned toward her, wondering what she had on beneath her sexy little dress. As he drew his eyes up, over her neck, and her lovely face, he saw the love he felt reflected back in her eyes. The constriction in his chest eased. This wasn't just a bedroom. This was Savannah's oasis. He took her hand, and as she took a step forward, their love filled the space where his anxiety had been. He slipped his arms from his shirt, and when her hands traveled up his abs and over his pecs, he wondered if she could feel his love for her in every beat of his heart, the way he could see the love she had for him in the way she looked at him.

Chapter Thirty-One

THE SMELL OF coffee greeted Savannah the next morning as she stumbled groggily out of the bathroom in her T-shirt and underwear. She found Jack leaning on the kitchen counter, freshly showered and wearing a clean pair of jeans and a long-sleeved shirt. He held the newspaper in one hand and a cup of coffee in the other. He turned as she entered, and his eyes lit up.

"Good morning, beautiful." He kissed her cheek and held up a cup of coffee. "I wasn't sure how you liked it. Cream? Sugar?"

Savannah glanced at the clock. *Five thirty.* "Both, please. Did you go home and come back already?" She blinked through her sleepy haze.

"Unfortunately, I didn't bring my Superman cape. That would be impossible with how late we stayed up." He winked, then fixed her coffee. "I had a backpack on my bike. I went down and got it this morning."

"You shouldn't leave stuff out like that in the city. I'm surprised it was still there this morning. Sorry I kept you up so late." She felt her cheeks flush.

"I'm not." He handed her the cup and kissed her cheek. "By the way, I'm not naive. I had the bag locked on the bike."

She couldn't concentrate on the words he'd just said; she was lost in his clean, fresh scent. Savannah touched his cheek as he drew back. "I love the feel of your whiskers."

"Then I'll be sure to skip a day between shaves. Your phone vibrated earlier." He nodded toward her cell phone on the dining room table.

"This early?" She picked it up and read the text. "It's my brother Hugh." She read the text. "Oh my gosh, he's coming into town. I can't wait to see him, but I thought his award ceremony was in Washington. I guess I messed that up. It's here this Saturday. It's a good thing he called, because I thought it was next weekend, and we've been so busy that I hadn't even made flight arrangements yet." She hurried across the kitchen and wrapped her arms around Jack's waist. "Come with me to the ceremony? Please?"

"Whatever you want, angel. What's he getting an award for? A particular race?"

"I don't know which race this is for, just that he's won another award." She wrinkled her nose. "Does that make me a bad sister? It does, right?"

He wrapped his arms around her. "You're not a bad sister. Does he know what cases you win?"

"Well, no, but those aren't awards."

"They're accomplishments, and they count just as much."

"Are you sure you're the same arrogant guy who flew me into the mountains? Because you're so sweet that I can't really see that other part of you anymore." She felt his body stiffen beside her.

"I'm still the same guy." He ran his hand through his hair. "Remember when I told you that I didn't used to be that guy?" He put down the newspaper and coffee and took her cup from her hands, then set it on the counter. He wrapped his arms around her waist and looked down at her. "The real me is starting to emerge, and it's all because of you." He kissed the top of her nose. "But don't be fooled. I worry that the angry bastard is still lingering and that we haven't seen the last of him yet."

"Well, if he comes back, we'll just have to tame him while we work through whatever gets his back up." She rested her head on his chest and closed her eyes, listening to the calm beat of his heart, so different from the racing pulses she'd felt only hours before.

"I love when you say *we*, angel." He rested his head on the top of hers.

"I love when you call me *angel*. Although my brothers will have a field day with that. I'm not really known for being angelic."

"No. Really?" Jack widened his eyes and covered his mouth, feigning surprise.

"Shut up." Savannah pushed away from him and laughed. "You can't grow up with five brothers and not be tough. Being girlie wasn't an option. My father made sure that I could do anything they could do, and I made sure I could do it just as well."

Jack pulled her close again. "You are still very feminine." He kissed her lips. "And very beautiful." He kissed her cheek. "And you're my angel because you saw through the smoke and mirrors I had hidden behind and you drew me out. So your brothers can take the name up with me. It's staying."

She loved that he'd stand up to anyone for her and that he saw something in her that she didn't think anyone else ever would. She felt more feminine around him than she ever had in her whole life. Actually, she felt different in too many ways to count when she was with him. She looked at the clock and groaned.

"I have to get ready for work." She furrowed her brow. "What does a bush pilot and survivalist do when he's not flying planes or teaching people woodsy stuff?"

"Woodsy stuff? You're so cute. Didn't I teach you anything out there?" He took a sip of his coffee.

"More than you'll ever know." She smiled. "In extreme conditions a man can live three minutes without air, three weeks without food, and three days without water."

"You did learn a little something." He set his coffee on the counter and took her in his arms. "Guess what I did?" He didn't give her a chance to answer. "You already know that I called Siena. Well, I asked her to try to get everyone together so we could talk. I'm going to try to fix what I've ruined."

"You did? Wow. When you say you're going to fix things, you don't waste any time, do you?"

"In case you haven't noticed, I'm not really a middle-of-the-road kind of guy." He smiled, but Savannah saw worry in his eyes. "I'm afraid this isn't going to be an easy road, but it's an important one."

Savannah went to his side and touched his arm. "Do you want to talk about it?"

"Yeah, actually, I do, but I don't want to make you late for work. It's almost six."

Savannah recognized the pain that swept over his face, leaving worry lines across his forehead. "I'm good. Let me just text Catherine and tell her I'll be in a little late." She texted Catherine; then the two of them went into the living room and sat on the couch. Savannah tucked her legs beneath her and faced Jack. He rested his elbows on his knees. His shoulders rode higher now, and Savannah scooted closer and rubbed the bundle of nerves at the base of his neck.

"You really are good to me, Savannah." He looked at her briefly, then focused on his hands.

She kissed the back of his neck. "That's because I like you at the moment," she teased. Savannah knew from working with people who were usually smack dab in the middle of a crisis that it was better to wait for them to bare their truths when they were good and ready than to push. She massaged the knot in his shoulders and waited.

Jack rubbed the back of his left arm with his right hand. Savannah could practically feel the scar on her palm. "I haven't shared this with you because I wasn't sure how, and every time I wanted to tell you, I worried about what you'd think of me." He drew in a long breath, then blew it out slowly and turned so he was facing Savannah. "The night of Linda's accident, there was a storm."

Savannah knew she should tell him that Treat had already filled her in, but she felt the weight of his confession between them and saw it in the rounding of his shoulders. She had to let him get this off his chest.

"It was only raining when she left, but the weather reports called for severe storm warnings. I never should have let her go." His eyes remained trained on hers. "The storm got worse while she was gone. Doubled in strength." He paused, swallowed hard, and his eyes welled with tears. "I can still smell the burning rubber and oil. I can see the flames. I never should have let her go. I had just come back from tour, and I was exhausted and so wrapped up in reports and data and still wound up in what we'd accomplished." He shook his head. "It was my fault.

I shouldn't have let her drive with the storm warning."

"Jack, you don't have to tell me everything. I know you blame yourself. My cousin Blake knows Rush, and I guess he told him about the accident, and Blake told my brother." Her stomach twisted at the depth of the pain she saw in his eyes.

"Does your whole family know?"

"Probably by now, but they don't blame you."

Jack shifted his eyes to the floor.

"She had a car accident. Anyone can have a car accident, any day and anytime. You couldn't have known that she'd get stuck in the storm." She took his hand in hers. "Look at me, Jack, please."

Jack looked at her, and she scooted even closer. "You didn't cause her accident."

"Did Rush tell them that I found her?" he asked.

She nodded. "I'm so sorry."

Tears hung in his eyes, and Savannah could see the tension in his face as he willed them not to fall. Seeing Jack so sad tore at her heart. She leaned forward and wrapped her arms around him.

"It's okay to be sad, but that sadness doesn't have to turn to guilt and anger and consume your every thought." She rubbed his back, and when he drew away from her with red-rimmed eyes, she wished she could take the day off and stay with him.

He wiped his eyes. "Thank you. Her father and sister forgave me, but, Savannah, I've driven away everyone who loved me because I felt so guilty. It took a long time, but I understand now that I projected my guilt on them when all they really wanted to do was help me through the pain of losing her."

"We all do things like that, Jack. You just did it to an extreme." She ran her hand along his arm.

He nodded. "Maybe. But Rush? Rush will never forgive me. We said things to each other that we never should have said, and if you think I hold on to anger…" He shook his head. "And he has my father pushing him to be a man, which means…oh, who knows what that even means anymore."

What he was going through sounded familiar to Savannah. Rex had held a silent grudge against Treat for years, and Treat had never known why until he finally confronted Rex. If brooding Rex could get over his anger, anyone could.

"If there's one thing I have learned, it's that the fiber that weaves a family together is stronger than anything we could ever imagine. I know it feels like you might never get through to him, but I don't believe it. You have to try, no matter how hard it is."

Jack sat up and rubbed his face with his hands. "I intend to try, but I'm a realist, and you don't know my father. Lately I feel like I don't know him, either. I might have dug a hole with Rush that's too deep for either of us to climb out of." He took her hand and rose to his feet, bringing Savannah along with him. "You need to go to work, and I need to get home and finish cleaning out the house. Can I call you later?"

Savannah smiled at the formality of his question. "I would be upset if you didn't." She started toward the hall, then turned back. "Jack, are you really okay with all of this? I can stay home with you if you need me to, to help you at your place or be there if you need to talk." She'd spent years nursing her career. It was time she gave her relationship—this relationship—the attention it deserved.

"See? You really are my angel. I'm a big boy, and you have a career to maintain. I'll be fine. And yes, I'm really okay with all of this. I never expected life to be easy, Savannah. I just expected it not to be quite so hard. But as far as I can see, the hardest part is over. Now I have to walk over the stones I've tossed along the way. Some will sting more than others, but in the end, it'll all be worth it. And, hopefully, Rush will find it in his heart to meet me halfway."

Chapter Thirty-Two

JACK WENT THROUGH every cabinet, every drawer, and every storage container in the house, boxing up Linda's mementos and separating the things he wanted to keep from the things he would give to Elise. He'd prepared himself for another bout of sadness, but Ralph's forgiveness had helped him put some much-needed distance between himself and the guilt that had ruled him for so long. As that distance became real in his mind and in his heart, he was able to enjoy the fond memories instead of ruing them. The phone rang, startling him out of his thoughts.

"Well, you're in luck," Siena began. "Sage just got back in town from a gallery opening in Washington State, and Dex, Mom and Dad, and Kurt and I can all make it."

"And Rush?" Jack clenched his jaw.

"He wasn't very receptive to seeing you. I'm sorry, Jack." Her voice faded as she said his name.

"It's not your fault. I appreciate you trying, and at least I can talk to everyone else. That's a start." Jack wasn't going to give up that easily. Maybe if he could bridge the gap with the others, Rush would feel pressure to at least see him.

"Sage leaves again on Saturday. Since it's already Thursday, do you want to do it tonight or tomorrow?"

The last thing he wanted to do was delay seeing his family. Throughout the afternoon, he'd been thinking about them, and not only was he anxious to clear the air, but ever since he'd started deconstructing the walls he'd built around his heart, the ache of missing his family had set in.

"Tonight. Your place or Mom and Dad's?"

"I can do it here at my loft if you want. Do you remember where it is? East Thirteenth, Greenwich Village."

"Yeah, I remember. Thanks, Siena. This means a lot to me."

"Me too, Jack. Does seven work for you?" she asked.

"Yes. Perfect. Want me to bring dinner?" Jack felt a surge of hope run through him. *It's my chance to start over.*

"Nah. I'll have something delivered. I gotta run, but I can't wait to see you."

"Me too, honey. See you soon."

After ending the call with Siena, Jack considered reaching out to Rush again, but if Siena couldn't get through to him, there was no way he would. Rush adored their sister. He'd just have to make it through dinner, and maybe one of his brothers or his parents would have an idea of how to deal with Rush. And if they didn't, then he'd find a way to make it happen.

He called Savannah, and when it went to voicemail, he felt a pang of disappointment.

"Hey, angel. Siena set up dinner with my family at her place for seven. As much as I would love to take you with me, I think I have to do this by myself. Rush isn't going, but the others are. Call me when you're free. Love you." The final two words sent a hum of happiness through him, and as he made his way up to the attic to put away the box he'd packed, he was still smiling.

SAVANNAH WAS AT her desk poring over a client's file when Aida came into her office and sat on the edge of the desk.

"How much do you hate me?"

Savannah suppressed a smile, her eyes still trained on the document she was reading. "I don't hate you."

"Okay," Aida said. "How annoyed are you?"

"Not at all. I learned a lot from your inquisition." Savannah looked up at her and couldn't help but chuckle at the worried expression in her eyes. "Why are you so worried? I'm not mad, but you could have told me you were coming by."

"And then you'd have warned him. I wanted to see what he was like with absolutely no prep."

"You're such a lawyer," Savannah teased, and turned her attention back to the document.

"I like him." Aida crossed her legs and put her hand over the document.

Savannah sighed and leaned back in her chair. "I do, too."

"I think he's pretty straight. I didn't get any evasive vibes from him."

"I could have told you that." Savannah leaned on the arm of her chair, thinking about the message he'd left while she was in a meeting. He was going to see his family tonight, and she was so nervous for him that it might as well have been her who was going.

"He's got it bad for you, by the way. I loved how attentive he was. And did you notice that he didn't check me out at all? I mean, really, how did he maintain *that*?"

Savannah laughed. "He's respectful. Not all men have no self-control."

"I've never met a guy who didn't at least check out the girls." She looked down at her cleavage. "I'd say he was gay, but by the insanely satisfied look you've been sporting lately, that's obviously not the case." She rose to her feet. "Anyway, he seems like a good guy. I'm happy for you." Aida began pacing.

"Have you heard from the magnificent lover from Greenberg's office?"

"Yes, but I'm not going to see him again. Once you've been there, why go back? You know what he has to offer."

Because it just keeps getting better and better. "How can you be like that? Don't you ever want to settle down?"

Aida shrugged. "I never thought I did, but watching you all googly-eyed and happy almost makes me want to."

"I almost forgot to tell you that Connor came by my apartment right as Jack was picking me up for dinner. He kissed me, and Jack basically pulled him off and scared the life out of him."

"What is up with him? First he cheats, then he shows up? Did he call? Did you know he was coming?"

"Nope. If he had called, I would have told him not to come. I don't want to see him, and when he kissed me, I wanted to sock him where it hurts. Who does he think he is?"

"So did Jack hurt him?" Aida asked with wide eyes.

Savannah saw the hope in her eyes and shook her head. "No, he just scared him. Connor brought roses with him when he showed up. He can be charming when he wants to be."

"Don't go down the Connor trail," Aida warned.

"No, I'm not. I mean that seeing his smile and the roses, and of course, feeling his kiss, I can totally see why I was so drawn to him. When he was with me, it was easy to believe his lies and buy into the whole apology thing. Don't get me wrong. I was definitely an idiot for buying into it for so long, but after seeing him again, I realized that probably most women would have done the same thing, so maybe I don't have big issues after all."

"Baby, if you think all of us don't have huge issues, you're wrong. We all have our own messes to deal with. Hey, want to grab dinner tonight, or are you going out with lover boy?"

"He's meeting his family, trying to make amends. Sure. Let's grab something."

The speaker on her phone beeped and Catherine's voice came through. "Savannah, Treat's on the line for you. Shall I put him through?"

"Talk about lover boys. That brother of yours is hot, hot, hot."

"And married," Savannah said as Aida walked out the door. "Grab me at the end of the day." She picked up the phone. "Sure, Catherine, put him through."

She waited for the click of the line, then said, "Hey, Treat, what's up?"

"Hi, Vanny. Max and I are coming into town for Hugh's award ceremony. It looks like everyone's coming now, even Rex. I'm trying to pull a family dinner together. Hugh's taking off Sunday, so we're thinking about right after the award ceremony. Sound okay?"

Savannah loved her brothers so much. She couldn't imagine not being on good terms with them any length of time. Once again her mind shifted to Jack, and she hoped his family would welcome him back without putting him through a guilt trip. That man put enough guilt on himself to keep him warm in the North Pole.

"Of course. Where and when? Do you mind if I bring Jack?" She held her breath while she waited for his answer. She and Jack had been moving so fast that she knew her brothers would be tougher on him than Aida had been, but he'd already become such a big part of her life that she couldn't imagine not including him in a family function.

"I'd love to meet him. I got the feeling last time we spoke that you weren't done with him. That's another reason I called instead of having Josh tell you about dinner. I wanted to make sure you were okay."

"You're such a good brother. I gave you a hard time for checking up on him, and you're still making sure *I'm* all right?" Of course he was. Savannah knew that no matter what she did, Treat would never turn his back on her. And she had a feeling that Jack wouldn't, either.

"You were all tangled in knots when I saw you. I knew you were struggling to figure things out, and I worry about you. Besides, Josh said you spent a lot of time with Danica at the concert, and I put two and two together. A little free therapy goes a long way."

She heard his smile. "I love her. She always makes me see things clearer."

"Good. I'm glad you're okay. Is he treating you well?"

"Of course. But you'll get a kick out of this. He calls me *angel*." She walked to the window and looked out over the busy streets, remembering how it felt to walk beside Jack the other evening and how she couldn't wait to do it again.

"I have no doubt that you are his angel, Savannah."

"Really? You're not going to tease me? I've never been particularly angelic." Her hand drifted to cover her heart. Why did Treat seem to understand so much more than most people when it came to love? She wondered if it was because he'd known their mother best. Maybe the rest of them had missed out on more than just having a mother around, but having learned life lessons from her, too.

"Savannah, you are angelic. You're tough and you're brilliant and competitive, but you've always put yourself out there for others, and you have the biggest heart of almost any woman I've ever met. With the exception of Max, of course. You're the girl who stayed up all night for a week with your college roommate to convince her that she wasn't anything like all those horrible things that idiot said she was. Remember? And still you aced your classes."

She imagined his thoughtful dark eyes and wished he were right there in the room with her so she could give him a hug. She wondered if Treat saw her more clearly than she saw herself.

"I had almost forgotten about that. I guess when I think of angelic, I think of purity and sweetness, and when I think of myself, I think of..." She hadn't really put words to her thoughts, and now, as she grasped for them, she could only reiterate Treat's. "Strong and stubborn."

"There's only one thing I can say to that. Thank goodness you've found a man who sees the real you, Savannah. Look at me. Look at Rex and Dane. Or walk down the street and look at Josh. It takes the right person—a special person—to see through our defenses. Just like you've seen through his. Don't you see why he calls you his angel?"

She leaned against the windowsill and smiled. "I guess I do. It has nothing to do with purity or sweetness and everything to do with seeing him for who he is on the inside. The man he's been protecting with the anger and guilt." She let out a loud breath. "Thanks, Treat. I didn't even know I needed to hear that, but I guess I did."

Chapter Thirty-Three

JACK LEANED AGAINST the side of Siena's building with his cell phone pressed to his ear, talking to Savannah. Music from the café where she and Aida were having dinner played in the background.

"I just wanted to hear your voice before I went upstairs. I'm a little more nervous than I expected to be," Jack admitted, though he downplayed just how nervous he was. Savannah didn't need to know that he'd spent the hour driving into the city contemplating every word he'd say that evening.

"I would be, too. But you'll be fine, Jack. They're your family. Just remember that. They might be hurt and angry and tell you exactly how they feel—at least my brothers would—but you can handle that. Besides, it's not like you haven't seen them in two years. You just haven't seen them *often*."

"Thanks, Savannah. Are you having a good time with Aida?" He looked up just as his brothers Dex and Sage walked past the connecting street. *Man, they look great.* They didn't see him, and he wasn't sure if he was relieved or disappointed. There was a time when walking into a room full of Remingtons meant slaps on the back and jokes about how things were hanging. Now he didn't know what to expect, but a jovial atmosphere was so far off the radar screen that he almost laughed. Lost in thought, he missed half of Savannah's answer.

"…I hope Aida means it. I'd like to see her date someone for more than a night or two."

He assumed he'd missed something about Aida's last date, so he answered in a way that he thought might be appropriate. "I'm sure she'll come around. Are you free later?" He hated giving up his evening with Savannah, but in a way the steps he was taking were for both of them and their future. *Our future.* If anyone had told him a year ago that he'd be in a relationship now, he'd have denied it until the cows came home. If they would have asked him six months ago, or even two months ago, he'd have done the same. Although in the weeks before meeting Savannah, he had begun to think about making his way back to the family he loved. Maybe fate did have a hand in their lives after all.

"Yes. Please come by," she said. "Do you have your bag, or do you need to go back home first?"

He smiled, knowing he'd been presumptuous when he'd packed his leather backpack before leaving home. "What do you think?"

"That's what I'd hoped."

JACK HEARD SIENA'S excited squeal from behind the closed door. The door swung open, and he didn't have time to say hello before she had her arms wrapped around his neck. Siena was Savannah's height and pencil thin, but when she plowed into him unexpectedly and lifted her feet off the ground, Jack had to take a step backward to keep from tumbling over.

"You're here! You're really, really here. I've missed you so much."

Jack embraced her with a laugh. He'd forgotten how enthusiastic she was. "Hi, honey. I've missed you, too."

She dropped back down to her feet and flipped her long dark hair out of her face with a quick snap of her chin. "Jack, you look great. Come on in." She took his hand and led him into her expansive loft. The track lighting on the high ceilings reflected off of the pristine light wood floors. Siena had never liked curtains, and Jack could see that nothing had changed. The four enormous windows set in the brick walls on either side of the loft were bare. Jack scanned the room for his brothers and spotted them behind the bar that separated the kitchen from the rest of the living room. He swallowed the pang of worry that would normally cause him to dip into his anger reserves and hide behind them. He wasn't going there again. *And certainly not now.* He rubbed a knot that had formed at the base of his neck and followed Siena to the kitchen.

"Look who's here." She flashed her bright white smile over her shoulder at Jack and waved her hands like she was presenting a gift.

Dex and Kurt came out of the kitchen with bottles of beer in their hands and wide smiles. Sage followed with a brooding stare and a bottle of beer in each hand.

"Dude." Dex embraced Jack. Even as a toddler he'd had a deep voice, and it had only gotten deeper. At six two, he was just a few inches shorter than Jack. His muscles strained beneath his tight gamer T-shirt. He and Siena were fraternal twins, and while Siena's hair was shiny and straight, Dex's was coarse and wavy and a shade or two darker. He wore it long, just touching his collar, and when he brushed the fringe from his forehead, he revealed eyes as dark blue as Jack's. "How long are you back for?"

"For good, pretty much," Jack answered.

"Righteous. It's about time." Dex took a swig of his beer. "Don't let me forget to tell you about this rad new game I developed."

Right after graduating from college with a degree in computer science and a minor in mathematics, Dex had created a video game that went viral. Now a millionaire and having developed several games since, he lived the life that many young people dreamed of. Jack, however, felt a world apart from the gaming community and its lingo, but he adored his brother and was happy that he'd found success doing something he loved.

"I can't wait to hear about it." Jack's heart raced with the warm welcome from Dex. Kurt had always been more reserved than the rest of his siblings, and now he stood with his beer in one hand and his other hand in his pocket. He smiled at Jack and took a slow drink of his beer.

"How's it going, Jack?" Kurt had written a number of bestsellers, and although he was very well off and fans knew him by sight, people seeing him on the street would never be able to tell that he was someone notable. Kurt was six three with electric blue eyes, short dark hair, and chiseled features, and tonight he looked comfortably casual in his khaki pants and polo shirt.

"Better. Much better. How's your writing?" Jack wondered if Kurt was as nervous as he was. Where Jack wore his emotions on his sleeve, Kurt kept his close to his chest.

Kurt lifted his bottle. "Good. You know, bringing life to the voices in my head." He grinned.

Jack took a step forward and opened his arms. Kurt stepped in, patting Jack on the back. "Good to see you, Kurt."

"You too, bro. You too." As they drew apart, Kurt touched Jack's arm. "Are you doing okay? I mean, really okay?"

Jack took a deep breath. "Yeah. For the first time in what seems like forever, I really am. I wanted to get from here…" He fanned the space in front of him. "To there." He looked around the room at his siblings. "But I couldn't figure out how. Are you pissed at me?"

"Pissed?" Kurt opened his eyes a little wider. "Do I ever get pissed at anything?"

Jack laughed. Kurt had always been the most evenly keeled of his siblings.

"You didn't abandon us, Jack. You just couldn't take it. I get it. Besides, it made great fodder for my upcoming novel, *Bonds of Steel*."

"*Bonds of Steel*? Really? Sounds like a bad bondage porno." Jack glanced at Sage, his most complex brother. Sage was the epitome of an artist, from his contemplative eyes that were so dark blue they appeared almost black, to his wavy dark hair that usually hung in front of his eyes and always looked windblown. Tattoos climbed his arms, and one could never tell if his brooding stare was meditative, calculating, or ruminating. When he was young, Jack worried that he lived in a constant state of unhappiness, but as he aged and began to share his thoughts, Jack realized that he simply saw life in a completely different way than Jack ever had. To Sage, everything in life, whether it was living or inanimate, held some deeper meaning than what met the eye.

"I hear you had a gallery opening in Washington," Jack said as he approached Sage. He and Sage had spent many hours together out in the woods around their parents' house. Sage liked to hike and chill, while Jack was always looking for an adventure. They'd made a great exploration team with Jack pointing out the larger discoveries like animal tracks and paths made by other hikers and Sage teaching Jack to appreciate the sound of the creek or the flight patterns of the hawks. Jack wondered if at twenty-eight Sage still found beauty in all things living, or if life had kicked his butt. He hoped for the former.

Sage nodded. "Good to see you, too, Jack." He handed him a beer, and when Jack took it, Sage pulled him into a hug and held him longer than the others had. "What took you so long?"

"Lost my compass."

"You should have called me. I would have brought you one." Sage embraced him again. "I'm glad you're here."

Jack's heart was so full, he felt as if his chest might explode. Could he possibly get this lucky? He'd been so worried about finding his way back and being turned away. Could it really be this easy?

Siena sailed out of the kitchen with a tray of cheese, crackers, and fruit in her hands and an unopened bottle of wine under her arm. Jack took the tray and set it on the long barn wood table. The loft was spacious and bright, with one bar separating the kitchen and just beyond and down a short hallway, a comfortable master bedroom and bathroom. Siena had been modeling for years, and while she'd graduated with a degree in biology, they all knew that was just to appease their father. *Every woman needs a career to fall back on.* Siena was one of the most sought after models in New York, and as Jack watched her teasing their brothers and gracefully moving from the kitchen to the table as she set out plates and silverware, he could see why. She had a natural beauty that radiated through to her eyes. A sparkle that most women didn't possess— although he'd seen the same beauty in Savannah, who he wished was by his side at that very moment.

"Mom and Dad are on their way," Siena said. "They had to stop and pick something up."

"What can I do to help, sis?" Dex asked. "Napkins? Condiments?"

"I'll open the wine," Kurt offered. "Although we all have beer. Do we need the wine?"

"Mom and Dad prefer it," Siena answered.

"Right, of course." Kurt retrieved the corkscrew.

Sage sidled up to Jack. "You sure you're ready for this?"

Jack lifted the right side of his mouth in a half smile. "Who knows, but I want to be." He felt Sage's hand on his back.

"I envied you, you know. As much as I hated not seeing you, I was envious of all that time alone, just you and nature. Man, what I wouldn't give to escape the rat race for a while."

His voice was so serious that Jack had to turn and look at him. "You okay, Sage?" He searched his eyes for hidden trouble, but they hadn't changed. They held the same unreadable look as they always had.

"Yeah. Sure. Anyway, I'm glad you're back. We've all missed you."

Jack leaned in close and said, "Not all of you."

"Right. Well, you know Rush can be a bonehead. Give him time. He's just pissed that you took off. He'll get over it." Sage patted him on the back and went to answer a knock at the door.

It can't be this easy. Jack watched his siblings talking and joking with one another as if one of the biggest defining moments of his life hadn't just taken place. Was it even possible that his siblings could accept him back that easily without any angst over his not keeping in touch? Could Savannah have been right about family ties?

"Jackson."

His father's serious tone sent a jab of reality to his gut. There wasn't the slightest chance this was going to be an easy night. *What was I thinking?* He turned to meet his father's somber stare. His military-style haircut was now more gray than brown, though his thick, furrowed brows were still dark as ever. The skin on James Remington's once chiseled features now hung a little looser from his cheekbones and jowls, but his imposing nature was just as strong as it had always been. Jack looked into the midnight-blue eyes—which were so much like his own—of the man who was his mentor, his hero, and his harshest critic. He pulled his shoulders back, knowing that even though he was younger and stronger, he couldn't quite pull off the same commanding dignity that his four-star-general father always had.

"Dad. Mom." Jack had the urge to run into his mother's arms, as he had when he was a boy. He wanted to settle into the comfort and surety of her unconditional love and forget so much time had passed. But that wasn't an option. Instead, he took in his mother's beauty, his heart warming as she crossed the floor toward him.

Joanie Remington was the polar opposite of Jack's father. She dressed in loose bohemian clothing and wore her gray hair long, while James looked as though he'd walked out of a military photo shoot: pristine navy jacket with perfectly pressed slacks and white dress shirt. Joanie opened her arms and embraced him.

She touched his cheek and looked up at him with the same bright blue eyes that she'd passed down to Kurt and Rush, and the love he saw pulled at his heart.

"Jackie, I'm so glad to see you," she said.

She was nearly the same height as Siena—and Savannah, Jack realized. Her hand on his cheek reminded him of the endearing way Savannah had touched him earlier that morning. He'd turned his mom away so often, and once he moved to the cabin, he didn't even have a phone line. He'd kept his cell phone but never left it on. When messages rolled in, he ignored them. Things between him and his father had gotten so tense after Linda's death that it had been easier to block his mother out of his life, too, than to try and volley between the two. He realized now how much that must have hurt his family, especially his mother, who had been nothing but supportive his whole life.

"Me too, Mom. I'm sorry it's taken me so long to come around." He kissed his mother's cheek and tried to suppress the tears that welled in his eyes. He blinked until his eyes dried, then shifted his gaze back to his father. Sage remained by the open door, and Jack had a fleeting thought that maybe he should just walk out that door. Escape his father's torment. *There is no escape. I deserve whatever he doles out.*

"Dad." He felt like he was sixteen years old again, telling his father that he wasn't going to join the military right after high school—and he wasn't sure if he ever would. His heart had hammered in his chest then just as it did now.

"Son." He shot a look at Joanie, who lifted her brows and her chin in the silent urge Jack had come to know as a child. His father had ruled their house with an iron fist. No one dared go up against him, but every so often, his mother would take a quiet, though meaningful and determined stance, and in those times, Joanie headed the charge. There was no mistake in Jack's mind that his father had a diatribe ready to push his disgruntled agenda—or that his mother would not allow that to happen.

His father continued. "You look good, Jack. Different."

"I am," was all he could manage.

Sage shot a look at Jack. His eyes widened, and in that flash, Jack knew that Sage had seen something unnerving. A second later, Rush walked through the door with the same stern look as his father and took his place beside him.

Jack clenched his jaw, wondering why his brothers and sister hadn't warned him that Rush would be there after all. He felt Siena's gentle touch on his shoulder, her breath in his ear.

"They didn't tell me," she said; then she crossed the tense space between the three men and embraced her father. "Hi, Daddy." She hugged Rush, though it was more of a fast grab than a hug.

"Sweetheart, thank you for having us all here today," his mother said, as Siena kissed her cheek and took her place beside her. Jack knew that by standing on the side of the room with him, they were supporting him, too.

The lines drawn in the Remington family weren't like other families, where lines were faded and the families were unsure if they were imagined or really existed. James Remington made no bones about the lines he'd drawn through the years. He expected high achievements and ethical conduct—and military careers. As the eldest, Jack had forged the path for the others to follow. When he'd chosen not to attend West Point, his father had been livid, but after a few tough months, their relationship survived, and Jack assumed it was yet another one of his mother's determined battles that had kept him from having the same struggle with each of his other kids.

The decision to join the military had less to do with his father than with something inside Jack—a need to do more for his country than engineering—and it had pleased his father, which was why Jack was so confused now. He didn't understand why his father had been so angry with him when he moved to the mountains. He thought, of all people, his father would understand, but, then, he hadn't been thinking straight at that time. His father probably felt that Jack had shamed him on some level, embarrassed the family.

"Isn't it wonderful that Jack's really coming back to New York?" Siena's cheerful voice reverberated against the tension in the room like she'd thrown it at a brick wall. "Daddy, would you like some wine?"

"Yes, please, honey. Thank you."

Always the gentleman. During his formative years, Jack had tried to emulate his father with his gruff nature and arrogance, but by the time he hit puberty, he'd seen his harsh exterior as unattractive, and he'd done everything he could to avoid becoming the same man. As he looked at his brother and father, two strong-willed opponents, he realized that he was more like his father than he cared to admit. The last two years, he'd hidden behind the stone wall he'd learned from James Remington. Now Jack took a deep breath and did the only thing he could under the circumstances. He opened his arms as the man he hoped to be and embraced first his father, who stood rigid against him, then Rush, whose muscles were so tense they jumped against Jack's chest.

"Good to see you both," Jack said. It had been a long time since Jack was the one reaching out. Heck, it seemed like forever since he'd been palatable on any level.

Sage answered another knock at the door, and they turned their attention to the deliveryman as he handed several bags of food to Sage.

"I've got this," Dex said. He pulled out his wallet and paid for the food, then helped Sage carry the bags to the table.

"This looks great, Siena," Kurt said as he lifted several cartons of Italian food from one of the bags.

His mother put her hand on the small of Jack's back. "Jack, Rush, why don't you join us at the table."

Jack noticed that she hadn't invited his father, and while he was thankful for the support, he was sick of the ominous stares and the lines that determined sides within their family. Lines caused pain, and Jack had experienced enough pain for one lifetime.

"Thanks, Mom. I'll join you in a moment," Jack said.

Rush's face flushed. His eyes darted between Jack and their father. "Dad?"

Jack watched the exchange and wondered why his thirty-two-year-old brother was asking for his father's permission to sit at the dinner table.

His father narrowed his eyes at Jack and said, "Go on, son," to Rush.

While the rest of the family dished food onto their plates and talked among themselves, Jack and his father had a silent battle of wills. Jack gathered his courage like a shield before speaking.

"Want to take this up to the roof?" Siena's loft was on the top floor of her building, and she had access to a narrow set of stairs that led to a sitting area and garden on the roof of the building. The idea of having it out with his father in front of everyone else twisted his gut and made every nerve in his body burn, but if he'd have it no other way, Jack was determined not to walk away without a resolution.

His father nodded, and Jack led the way.

"James," his mother called.

They both turned toward her.

"Why don't you take Rush with you?" she suggested.

As Rush rose to join them, all eyes shifted to Jack.

Jack wondered why his mother was putting him up against the firing squad.

"Jack?" Sage said with a lift of his hand, a silent offer to come along.

"I'm good." Jack led them out of the apartment and up to the roof. The cool night air did little to clear the mounting tension. He had to hold it together no matter what they said, and he knew that falling right back into anger wouldn't solve a thing. He felt more like his old self than the angry man he'd become, and he wasn't going back.

Jack folded his arms across his chest and planted his feet hip width apart, then watched Rush do the same. Jack knew from his military training that he and Rush were using their arms like protective shields that would deflect the pain of whatever was to come. But his father had mastered deflection without any props. He stood with his shoulders back, legs strong, and his arms by his sides.

Jack opened his mouth to speak, and his father's words silenced him.

"Why now?" his father asked.

The question took Jack by surprise. He wasn't sure what he'd expected—a lecture about how everything he'd done for the past two years was crap or how he'd shamed the family. But, *Why now?* He blinked away his confusion and tried to form an answer that his father would find acceptable, but he couldn't string together any coherent thoughts. His answer came all on its own. Honest and simple.

"It was time, Dad."

Rush shot a look at their father. Jack knew he was weighing the narrowing of their father's eyes and the repetitive clench of his jaw and trying to figure out his next move. A sense of empathy washed through Jack. Rush was a major competitive skier, a celebrity in his own right. Six two, strappingly handsome, well educated, and he had the world at his fingertips. Yet he was still hamstrung by their father's rule—it was the reasons why that Jack couldn't figure out.

His father nodded. "And what changed? What brought you to this realization that your family finally meant something to you?"

Jack took a deep breath, feeling anger swell in his chest at the jab. "My family has always been important to me. You know that. I lost someone I loved." He fought against his raising voice but was powerless to stop it. "That's not a glitch in a strategy or a failed mission. It was a life-changing event." He took another deep breath and ran his hand through his hair, buying himself time while he calmed down.

"No, Jack," his father began. "What has changed *in you?*"

Rush's brows drew together, and he looked between Jack and his father. Jack rubbed the scar on the back of his arm, feeling pinned between them as Rush struggled with some internal battle.

"Everything," Jack said through gritted teeth. He began pacing, an act that he knew his father saw as a weakness. *Always face your enemies head-on.* He didn't care. He wasn't a puppet, and he wished he could show his father that Rush wasn't a puppet, either. Jack was there to make amends, not have his spirit crushed by his father.

"Look, I'm not you, Dad, and I'm not Rush." He stared at his brother until he saw a shadow of something he hoped was understanding pass through Rush's eyes. "I might be weaker than you both, but that's who I am. My wife died. I didn't know how to deal with it, and I blamed myself." He took a step forward, standing only inches from Rush. "You blamed me. You said if I hadn't been so wrapped up in myself, I wouldn't have let her go out that night." He held his stare for a beat longer, seeing the nervous twitch in the left side of Rush's mouth that he'd forgotten about until that moment. Then he faced his father. "You fought in battles. You led men and you led your family. You protected the citizens of this country, and you continue to protect your family every single day of your life." He felt his nostrils flare and took a moment to get a grip on his emotions again, channeling his anger to the flexed muscles in his legs and back.

"Everyone except me, Dad. Because you couldn't protect me from Linda's death. No one could. You were so busy demanding strong work ethics and achievements that you didn't prepare me for tragedy within my own family." Anger caused his voice to rise again. "When I joined the military, you said, *Be proud of those you take down, Jack. You're a good man. Always put your country first.* Be proud? Do you see the irony?" He stomped a few feet away, then paced back and looked his father in the eye. "Well, guess what? My wife's dead because I was so wrapped up in putting my country first and preparing strategies for the next mission that I couldn't drag my butt away long enough to go out and pick up the things she needed from the store. And guess what else, Dad? I'm not proud. And why are you so mad anyway? Because you couldn't protect me from the guilt and hate I harbored? Well, guess what? No one could protect me from myself."

The truth of his words hit him like a punch to the gut. Did

he really blame his father? He took two stumbling steps back, his arms hanging at his sides. The fight drained from his muscles like lumber turned to sawdust. When he spoke again, his voice was barely a whisper. "No one could."

Rush took one step toward Jack before his father touched his arm, stopping him in his tracks. Jack saw the motion and was past caring. The realization that he'd turned away from everyone because he felt alone in his torment was still kicking his butt and twisting his brain into a repetitive cycle of reality slaps. No one could have protected him. His dad had prepared him for school, for the military, heck, he'd prepared him for killing human beings and getting past it.

Jack's eyes welled with angry tears. "You never sat me down and said, *Jack, sometimes life will kick your legs right out from under you and hurt the people you love most, and when you can't help them, the guilt will eat you alive.*" He swiped at his eyes with the crook of his elbow and stalked away to the brick wall beside the door to the stairway.

"Jack," Rush said.

Jack looked up just in time to see Rush break free from his father's grasp and cross the roof to him. Rush's eyes shifted between his father and Jack several times, before Rush said, "Aw, hell," and wrapped Jack in his arms. "I'm sorry, man. I'm so sorry. I was so pissed at you for not being a man and carrying on with your life. You left the Grays high and dry—at least that's what I thought."

Jack embraced him, and Rush put one hand on the back of Jack's head, the other on his back, and held him against his massive chest. Their hearts beat in a frantic, angry rhythm against each other.

"I couldn't help the Grays. I could barely help myself," Jack said through his tears.

"I know. I get that now. I messed up, Jack. I'm so sorry."

The lump in Jack's throat practically stopped his breath from passing through. It took all his focus to choke out the last of his words. "I love you, man."

Jack caught sight of his father, stone faced and standing in the same stoic position as he had been the entire time. Jack couldn't fix whatever his father was holding against him, but he couldn't carry any more anger in his own heart, either. He'd overdosed on anger and felt as though one more ounce would be too much. He drew back from Rush, nodding a silent acceptance of his apology, and crossed the roof back to his father.

"I don't really blame you, Dad, and I no longer blame myself. I made a poor decision by letting her leave the house that night and by not going myself. But that decision cannot define me for the rest of my life. I'm a good man, and I have to believe that Linda knew that." He looked down, took another deep breath, then met his father's eyes again. "And I think that you know it, too. Even if you can't allow yourself to admit it."

Rush motioned Jack over with his hand. When Rush put his arm over Jack's shoulder, he had no regrets. He'd told his father the truth. *Almost.* He hadn't told him about Savannah, and he wanted a clean slate. He faced his father again and forced his shoulders back, forced his spine to straighten, and in an uneasy voice, he said, "I met someone, Dad. And she knows I'm a good man, too."

Rush opened the door, and he and Jack descended the stairs.

While Rush filled one of the missing pieces in Jack's heart, there was another piece of his heart still on that roof—and he felt the gaping hole it left behind. He'd given all he had to give, and knowing it wasn't enough made him sick to his stomach.

AT THE BOTTOM of the stairs, Rush said, "So you met someone?"

Jack knew Rush was just trying to turn the tides between them, but Jack couldn't stop thinking of his father. He wished he understood what he'd done. If only his father had said something. Anything to clue him in. How could a father and son become so lost to each other? He turned back to Rush, surprised at how quickly Rush had become his buddy again. *Maybe the ties that bind families together really are stronger than anything else.*

"Yeah. Savannah Braden. She lives on the Upper East Side." *Savannah Braden. The woman who changed my life.* "You know her cousin Blake—"

"No way. Blake Carter's cousin? No wonder he was asking about you. Is she cute?" Rush asked.

"Beautiful. And smart. She's a lawyer."

"What's she doing with you?" Rush teased.

Jack feigned punching his arm, and Rush pretended to punch Jack in his stomach. They were laughing as they approached the door to Siena's loft, but Jack's laugh was forced. Rush touched his arm.

"Jack. I was a real jerk to you, and I'm sorry. I know I said some horrible things. It's just...you were the guy I always looked up to, and when you fell apart..." He shrugged. "My hero had fallen. You disappeared and I got pissed. And then I saw how mad Dad was, and I jumped on that train, I guess. I'm sorry."

"It's all right, Rush. We all messed up. I just wish I knew why Dad was so mad."

"Got me. He's never said anything. He was real supportive of you until you disappeared, and then it was like a switch turned and he was like he is now."

"Well, maybe he'll find a way to tell me what he's thinking. And, Rush, I wasn't exactly kind in the way I handled things with you, either. Let's just say we were both jerks and move past it." Jack patted him on the back, and when Rush flashed the smile Jack hadn't seen in two years and he heard laughter coming from inside Siena's loft, he knew they were on the right path.

"Okay. Maybe you can forget that I said you were my hero. I'll deny it if you ever say it in front of them." He nodded toward the door.

"Jackass," Jack teased.

The second they stepped into Siena's loft, the room silenced. He could have heard a pin drop. Instead they heard their father's loud footsteps descending the stairs right before the door swung shut.

"Where's your father?" Their mother rushed to Jack's side and touched his arm. "Are you okay?"

Jack placed his hand over hers. "Yeah, actually. I am."

The door swung open, and his father stepped inside. He made a wide arc around Jack and his mother and joined the others at the table. Without a word, he laid a napkin in his lap and reached across the table for a dish of lasagna.

Jack's mother pursed her lips and shook her head. She patted Jack's chest, then took his hand, as she'd done so often when he was a boy, and they sat at the table. Siena and Dex exchanged a roll of their eyes at their father's behavior, and

Kurt, too passive to get involved, was probably taking mental notes to use in one of his thrillers. Sage lifted his beer bottle and smiled at Jack and Rush.

"To family," he said with a wink.

Everyone except his father toasted, and it broke Jack's heart to see his father alone on the opposite side of the Remington line.

Chapter Thirty-Four

SAVANNAH CLIMBED THE steps to her apartment, thinking about Aida and Jack. Now that she had Jack in her life, she felt transformed. It struck her that she was finally in a relationship where she wasn't the only one doing the giving. *It feels good.* She shook her head at the thought. *No, it feels great!* She was less on edge. Their lovemaking wasn't one-sided, and she felt herself changing as much as Jack was. She'd always thought she needed to be a man's only true love, and what she discovered with Jack was that love came in different levels. She knew Jack loved Linda, but she saw the way he looked at her and felt the way he touched her, and she knew in her heart that regardless of what he'd felt for anyone before her, he loved her in a completely different way than he'd loved anyone else.

She hoped that Aida would find the same kind of true love one day and that at some point the right person would see Aida's boisterous, flirtatious nature as a layer that they just needed to delve beyond and love her for it as much as for what lay beneath. Just as she'd seen Jack's anger as a mask of pain and she'd known that below that pain could only be a passionate, loving man with a heart so big it just about strangled him.

She flipped through her keys on her way up the stairs.

"There's my angel."

She looked up and met Jack's smile with her own.

"Jack. How did it go?" She rushed up the stairs and stood on her toes to kiss him. She'd been trying to push away the question that Aida had planted in her mind over dinner, and now that she was looking at Jack, the thought moved to the forefront of her mind. *How did you get that scar and the ones on your back?* Aida had wondered if it was something that happened in the military, but Savannah had noticed that he rubbed it when he spoke of Linda, and she'd have to be blind not to see the connection—and that's what had kept her from asking him all along.

"Better than I'd expected. Let's go inside and we'll talk."

Inside the apartment, Savannah poured them each a glass of wine, and they settled onto the couch.

"So it went well? Your family was receptive?"

"For the most part. Siena, Dex, and Kurt were very open and welcoming. Sometimes I forget that while I've been angry for two years, that's my own little circle of life. For everyone else, life goes on as normal. They work, they hang out with friends, and I'm sure they have passing thoughts about me as their brother, but really, it was my life that was messed up, not theirs."

"It's hard to keep that perspective. I know that sometimes I get really wrapped up in a case and I can't understand why everyone else isn't feeling as conflicted or overwhelmed as I am." *And since I've fallen for you, I wonder why everyone else isn't on cloud nine like I am.* "What about Rush? I know how worried you were about him."

Jack sipped his wine. "Rush…Rush was good. He's in a tough place. He's always tried to be the man our father wanted us all to be—and I don't even know who that man he wants us to be is anymore. I've been thinking about it. We're all good men, and we've always worked hard and done our best, and I always thought it was enough, but after tonight, I have to wonder…" Jack took Savannah's hand and looked deeply into her eyes. "You've changed me, Savannah. You've given me strength to do what I needed to, and you've taught me to look beyond the hurt and anger. Tonight, when I looked at Rush, I saw his anger as something other than an attack on me, or hatred for what I'd done. Because of you, I understood where it came from."

"What do you mean?" She saw a smile form on his lips, then fade, as if he didn't want to believe that whatever he was thinking could be true.

"I realized that Rush was doing what he thought my father needed or wanted him to do. He was stuck. My whole life, he idolized me. I can't even imagine anyone idolizing me."

"Jack." The pain in his eyes drew her hand to his cheek. He covered it with his own hand and smiled.

"My mom does that same thing, touches my cheek like that. You'd like her." He kissed her palm, then held her hand within his own. "Anyway, Rush said he felt like I let him down by giving up. He actually said his hero had fallen and that he was pissed that I took off, but beyond that, I could see that it was his own messed up need for our father's approval that pushed him to act the way he did toward me. And I get that, you know? We all want our father's approval."

"I'm sorry, Jack. I'm missing something. What happened with your parents?"

"My mom was just glad to have me back in her life again. She's very earthy. You know, the love-thy-neighbor and to-forgive-is-divine type." He smiled. "To this day, I have no idea how she ended up with my father. He didn't say much to me tonight. He and Rush and I went outside to talk, and I was very open with him about everything, and he didn't soften once."

"I'm so sorry. I'm sure he'll come around. He's your father, and really, what does he have to be mad at? Because his son needed time away to deal with the death of his wife?"

Jack placed his hands on her cheeks. "You're an amazing person, Savannah. You see the good in everything and everyone." He kissed her softly. "In my father's defense, I said something to him tonight that I never realized I felt, but somewhere in the back of my mind, I must have. He'd prepared me for war, and he'd prepared me to act ethically and work hard and for all the things he deemed important for a man. But no one ever prepares you for the death of a spouse, and I guess I wish he had."

"Jack, how could he have done that? That's not something parents do."

"No, but talking about death in a manner other than being proud about snuffing out the enemy is, and that's what was missing. I do remember my mom talking us through when our pet bunny died when I was probably eight or nine, but what I remember most about that summer was my father's belligerent attitude and his blatant disregard for what she was trying to teach us. I can only recall his words, not hers. *Stop crying. Sissies cry. You're a man. That rabbit's life is over. Time to move on.*"

"As horrible as that sounds, he was probably trying to get you to, you know, man up, or whatever guys think. I can't imagine that any father would say that if he thought it would have long-term negative effects. Do you know how long you mourned that rabbit? You know how kids are. Is there a chance you were milking it for weeks like kids do?" There had to be another explanation. Jack was too good in his heart to have been raised by someone so cold.

"I honestly don't remember."

"Maybe your father has a hard time with the line between manliness and sensitivity. It's okay to be a virile man and have feelings."

Jack shrugged and shook his head. "My father's not always like that. Maybe I am overreacting. I don't know. But I know that I didn't overreact tonight. I kept my cool, and other than that one burst of blame, which I'll retract the next time I see him, I was pretty calm."

Savannah sat back and sipped her wine. "So you'll try again?" Savannah's family was such a big part of her life. She couldn't imagine trying to navigate a situation where one parent was not welcoming of their child. She'd deal with anything for Jack, but in her heart she had to believe that he and his father could move past whatever was blocking their path to a happier relationship.

"Yes, but not tonight. Tonight I want to hold you in my arms and just know you're there."

Savannah wanted that, too. She rested her cheek on his shoulder, and as her hands slid up the back of his arms, she felt his scar, and she knew that, like everything else with Jack, when he was ready, he'd tell her how it got there.

Chapter Thirty-Five

JACK WOKE UP to an odd ringing noise. He reached for Savannah, and his arm fell on empty sheets. Jack sat up and looked at the clock. *Six fifty-eight?* It took him a minute to realize that he'd actually slept right through the night. He loved going to sleep next to Savannah just as much as he'd loved being there when she arrived home the night before.

He climbed from the bed and located the ringing as he dug his cell phone from the pocket of the jeans he'd worn the night before. By the time he'd retrieved it, the call had gone to voicemail. He wandered through the apartment looking for Savannah and found a note from her on the counter.

Dear Jack,

You were sleeping so soundly that I didn't want to wake you. Make yourself at home. I'm leaving you my extra key, so come and go as you please. I'm tied up most of the day in meetings, but call my cell and I'll pick up if I can. Good luck with whatever you have planned today.

Love,
S

PS: Happy Friday. I can't believe we met a week ago today!

Xox

Jack picked up the key from the counter and rubbed it between his thumb and index finger. They'd moved so fast and so seamlessly into a relationship that it seemed like the most natural thing in the world to be holding a key to Savannah's apartment while standing alone in her kitchen wearing nothing but his boxers. He hadn't thought about how things might flesh out with their living arrangements. He'd never ask Savannah to leave the convenience of her apartment and move out to Bedford Corners, and now that Savannah was in his life, he wondered how often he'd make the drive there himself. Or if he'd ever want to again.

He looked at the missed call registered on his cell and recognized his parents' number. Although he wasn't awake enough to deal with his father, he didn't want the call looming over him for the next twenty minutes, inducing anxiety while he drank coffee and showered. He punched in their number while the coffee brewed.

"Hello?"

His mother's cheerful voice greeted him. "Hi, Mom. It's Jack."

"Oh, honey. Do you really think I wouldn't recognize my own son's voice? How are you? You sound tired."

Jack poured himself a cup of coffee and sat down at the table. "I'm good. Actually, I slept better last night than I have in forever." He and Savannah had gone to bed shortly after their talk the evening before, and true to his word, Jack had curled his body around her luscious curves, and instead of making love to her, as his body had craved, he'd held her until she fell asleep. The cadence of her peaceful breathing and the comfort and warmth of her body against his had eased him into a deep sleep.

"I called your house phone," his mother said.

He knew she was fishing for information, and he also knew his father would have told her what Jack had said the evening before. "I'm not there, Mom."

"You're not?"

Her feigned surprise brought a smile to his lips. "Mom. Who told you, Dad or Rush?"

"Your father. I didn't have a chance to talk to you last night, Jack, and I would like to."

"I'm happy to talk, Mom. Things were a little uncomfortable last night. I have to do some clothes shopping. Why don't you come along, maybe have some lunch afterward?" Jack hadn't spent time with his mother in so long that he missed spending time with her and he hoped she'd agree to meet him. "It might be fun."

"Your father is out for the day. He had an early meeting in New Haven, so why not? Where are you now?"

She would spend all day fishing for details rather than asking. Jack ran his finger over the edges of the key and decided to ease her mind. "I'm at my girlfriend's apartment in the city." *Girlfriend.* He'd played the word over in his mind only a few times since he'd been with Savannah, and even though it rolled off his tongue smooth and secure, it felt much too light for the emotions he had toward her.

"Oh, Jack. I'm happy for you. You'll have to tell me all about her. Are you shopping in the city? Other than coming into the city for dinner at Siena's, I haven't been there in weeks. This will be an adventure."

He pictured his mother rising to her feet from her favorite reading chair in the sunroom. The room they both loved most.

It was filled with plants and flowers that she tended to daily. He could almost feel the cold tiles beneath his feet and the warm transition to the colorful throw rug that had been there since he was a boy.

"Yes, it will, Mom. Want to meet me at Savannah's or at the store?" Jack glanced at the clock. He had plenty of time to shower and dress before the stores opened.

"Savannah? Is that your girlfriend's name? That's just beautiful. Is she Southern?"

He loved hearing the tenderness in his mother's voice as she tamped down her excitement. If she were Siena, she'd have *whooped* into the phone at the thought of a girlfriend.

"She's from Colorado. She grew up on a ranch. I'll tell you all about her when I see you. Ten o'clock?" He thought about his cabin in the mountains, and he wondered if Savannah would enjoy it as much as he had. Jack took a drink of his coffee and noticed a picture frame on the bookshelves that he never noticed before. He rose as he gave his mother Savannah's address and picked up the photograph.

"I'll see you at ten, Jack."

"Okay. Love you, Mom. Thanks for calling." He was distracted by the photograph, and even after his mother hung up the phone, he still held his against his ear. His hand slid down his face, and he held the frame in both hands, then ran his index finger over the image of Savannah's face. She was nestled between her brothers, who were all big, strikingly handsome men. But it wasn't the beauty of her family that struck him. His own family was quite attractive. It was the natural closeness between them that had him mesmerized. They weren't posed. Their smiles did not appear feigned or forced, as evident in the way Savannah was looking at the tallest brother, her head thrown back midlaugh, his eyes laughing right along with her. He imagined the sound of her laughter. The brother to her left was Hugh. Now that she'd told him who he was, he recognized him. He looked rather playful, with one arm around Savannah and the other around another brother who wore his hair much shorter than the rest and who was looking over Savannah's head at the two brothers on her other side.

Jack remembered when pictures like that were annual events for his own family. His father would pester them to stand up straight and look at the camera, and inevitably they'd have thirty photographs of them laughing and teasing and one photograph with stoic faces caused by a final threat to behave. He could still hear his mother trying to calm his father down during the process. She'd say, *Aren't they cute? Leave them be, James. They're happy.* And his father would clench his jaw and wait another five minutes before trying to regain control.

He set the frame back on the bookshelf and thought about his father. Jack's grandfather had raised his father with an iron hand. That was old news in the Remington household, but even his grandfather wouldn't turn away his own son for reacting the way Jack had. Not for the first time, Jack wished he understood his father better.

He called Savannah and was surprised when she answered on the second ring.

"Hey there," he said.

"Hi, sleepyhead. I was so happy to see you sleeping this morning. I couldn't wake you." Her consideration of him was just another thing he could add to the growing list of things he loved about her.

"I haven't slept this late for years. Thank you for letting me sleep, but I don't want you to feel like I'm taking over your space or becoming an imposition." He looked at the key in the center of the table.

"Jack, I loved coming home to you last night and waking up to you this morning. You're anything but an imposition. Did you get the key I left you?" she asked.

"Yes, that was really thoughtful. I promise not to abuse the privilege." He wanted to tell her that he'd like to be there every day when she came home from work and every morning when she woke up, but Jack knew that they were moving at the speed of light and he had a feeling that the men in the picture he'd just looked at might not take too kindly to his moving in with their sister so quickly.

"Please, abuse it," she teased. "What's on your plate today?"

"I'm meeting my mother in a little while. We're going to shop for clothes for your brother's award ceremony and then have lunch."

"Oh, Jack. That's wonderful. But please don't buy new clothes on account of my family."

"I'm not. I'm revamping so much of my life that the idea of putting on dress clothes from two years ago just doesn't sit well with me." He didn't need to tell her that the last time he'd worn dress clothes was to Linda's funeral, or that he'd burned those particular clothes the minute he'd gotten back home. The past was slowly being pushed to where it rightfully belonged— behind him. And he was excited to move forward. If only he could resolve the issues with his father. He was determined to heal that relationship. He rubbed his scar and realized that he still hadn't told Savannah about what else had happened the night of Linda's accident, and he had to face that, too. As soon as he felt strong enough, he would do it, and then he hoped he'd be able to bring Savannah fully into his life, which meant welcoming her into the home he had shared with Linda and to the cabin. Once he was secure enough to do those things, their biggest hurdles would be behind him.

"Well, have fun. I can't wait to see you tonight. Will you be at the apartment, or are you heading back to your house?"

He heard the hope in her voice that he'd come to love, and he knew the answer to the question he'd asked himself earlier. He had no interest in driving back to Bedford Corners when Savannah was right here in the city.

"I'll be here when you get home for as many days as you'd like me to be." He walked into her bedroom and began taking his clothes from his backpack.

"I'm a needy girl, Jack. I never used to be. In fact, I've never wanted any man to stay overnight at all. But with you, I want nothing more. So let me know if I smother you."

"Impossible." The word flew from his lips.

Chapter Thirty-Six

JACK LOVED SHOWERING in Savannah's bathroom. Her sweet scent was everywhere. The steam in the shower held the coconut aroma of her shampoo, and when he stepped from the shower, the clean towels smelled like her linens and clothing. As he brushed his teeth, he picked up her perfume bottle and was reminded of their first kiss. The night everything about her became ingrained in his senses.

He rinsed and dried his toothbrush, and as he was putting it back in his toiletry bag, he stopped and instead put it in the toothbrush holder beside hers. For a moment he stood and stared at the plastic handles. *How could two three-dollar toothbrushes hold so much meaning?* He didn't want Savannah to feel as though he'd overstepped his bounds, though he assumed she wouldn't feel that way after the things she'd said to him and having given him a key. Just in case, he tucked the rest of his toiletries in the bag and zipped it up, then put it back in his backpack.

Ten minutes later, there was a knock at the door, and Jack felt a rush of happiness. He opened the door and found his mother and Siena on the other side.

"Two beautiful women? I am a lucky guy." He hugged

them both as they came into the apartment.

"You didn't think I'd let you guys go shopping without me, did you?" Siena breezed past him in her jeans, T-shirt, and very fashionable cropped jacket. She scanned every inch of the living room. "Or that I'd pass up the opportunity to see who's rocked my big brother's world?" In the next breath, she zeroed in on the photograph that Jack had only just discovered.

"She called when I was on my way over. I hope you don't mind." His mother's hair was pulled off her face with a large leather clip. She wore dangling green earrings and a flowing white blouse atop a pair of linen pants and looked as stylishly casual as she always had. In each of Jack's memories of his mother, she was smiling. Siena got her natural beauty from their mother, though their mother put more effort into her children and her art than she did her looks. Sage was blessed with their mother's artistic talent. As Jack looked at his mother, who was trying hard not to nose around Savannah's apartment, he was thankful for the loving and stable home she'd given them, and while his father may have been too harsh at times, his mother had probably been too soft. His parents complemented each other well. Even with the trouble he and his father were currently experiencing, Jack had to admit that his father's strength was what made him a strong man to begin with—and his mother's gentleness was what allowed him to love so deeply.

"Jack, is this Savannah?" Siena held up the picture frame. "She is gorgeous."

"That's her and her brothers," he said.

"Do you mind if I take a look?" his mother asked before reaching for the picture.

She was always so considerate, and it struck Jack how she and Savannah were alike in that way. "Not at all, Mom. Go ahead."

"What a lovely family. Look, Siena, she has a big family like ours."

"They're really close," he said.

His mother set the picture down on the shelves and patted his hand. "We will be again, too."

"I'M NOT SURE why I'm even here," Jack teased. They'd gone to three different clothing stores, and Siena and his mother wouldn't let him buy anything he picked out. Jack held up a white dress shirt.

Siena scrunched her face. "You're not an old man, Jack."

"I'm thirty-seven. That's pretty old," he said.

"When you get to sixty-seven, then you can say you're old. Until then, you're approaching middle age." His mother winked.

Siena pulled out a black dress shirt with white embellishments. Something Jack could see Dex wearing. Her eyes lit up as she showed it to him. "Now, this is cool, Jack. You'd look so hot in it. Try it on."

Jack shook his head. "I'm not twenty-five, Siena. I'd look ridiculous."

"He's right. That'd be good for Dexy but not Jack." His mother sifted through the fitted shirts and came away with one that was light blue and another that was dark blue. She held them against Jack's chest. "Siena?"

Siena turned around and her eyes grew wide. "Oh, perfect. Either one. He has those magnificent dark blue eyes, so he could wear the dark one with a light tie, or go light and spruce that one up with a dark tie, or a Jerry Garcia tie. Those are always fun."

Jack shook his head, enjoying every second of his mother's and sister's smothering and realizing how much he'd missed it.

With shirts, slacks, belts, and even boxers purchased, because his mother insisted, *When you turn over a new leaf in life, you should have new things to solidify the path,* they headed back out to find a restaurant for lunch.

Jack was enjoying spending time with Siena again. Her energy was contagious, and she appeared oblivious to the gawks from men they passed on the street. Jack found himself walking closer to her just to keep the ogling to a minimum.

"Why are you practically on top of me?" she asked as they entered a little café and waited to be seated.

"I'm trying to dissuade the oglers," Jack said.

His mother laughed. "You haven't changed one bit."

"Jack, I'm a big girl. I can manage my own safety." She looked around the café. "Besides, no one here is ogling besides that woman over there, and she's not ogling me."

Jack shook his head. He'd built so many walls around himself that he'd grown immune to glances from women. He looked over, and Siena was right; the pretty brunette in the corner of the café was definitely undressing him with her eyes. Jack turned away. He had eyes only for Savannah.

The waitress sat them on the other side of the café, and after they ordered lunch, his mother folded her hands on the table and narrowed her eyes at Jack. She had fine lines around her lips, which were pressed tightly together, but her eyes held the bright light Jack had always admired.

"So, do you want to talk about your father?" she asked.

"Mom, don't ruin his day," Siena said.

"It's okay, honey," he said to Siena. "Actually, I would, Mom. I've been racking my brain over this, and for the life of me, I cannot figure out why he's still so angry with me. I apologized. I told him I handled things poorly. I took responsibility. What am I missing?"

His mother reached across the table and put her hand on his. "Jack, have you ever heard of Esther Loone?"

Jack shook his head.

"Who's that?" Siena asked.

"We've never told any of you about this because it really had nothing to do with our family. But then again, nothing ever does...until it does." She smiled. "What I'm going to tell you cannot go to your brothers." She looked at Siena and narrowed her eyes. "Not even Dex, Siena."

"I won't tell him."

"You've never been able to keep a secret from him," she said.

"If it's that important, maybe you shouldn't tell either of us," Jack pointed out.

"No. I've covered for your father for a very long time, and it's time he deals with what he couldn't so many years ago. I can't sit back and watch our family divided any longer, Jack. I know how much courage it took for you to find your way back to us, and I'm sure much of that has to do with the new woman in your life."

"Savannah," Jack said, missing her more than ever.

"Yes, Savannah. She must have sparked something in you that reminded you of how beautiful love could be, and I'm thrilled by that, Jack. She must be very special."

"And very patient to have gotten through all that anger you had," Siena pointed out. She picked up her water and sipped it through a straw, ignoring the harsh glare her mother cast her way. She rested her head on Jack's shoulder. "I love you whether you're angry or not, but I can't imagine falling for someone who was as angry as you."

"Thanks, sis," he said.

"You know what I mean." Siena righted her head as the waitress brought their meals.

"Anyway, Esther and your father dated before we met. They were best friends for years, and it turned romantic. Esther got very sick and, well, she never made it past her eighteenth year. That was the year your father was to join the military. Well, you know your grandfather. There wasn't much wiggle room with where your father's future lay. He was never given the opportunity to mourn the loss of his best friend, and he could never do what you did, Jack. You took things into your own hands and threw caution to the wind. You took care of you instead of appeasing everyone else, and I admire you for that—even if it was the hardest thing a mother could watch her son go through."

Guilt squeezed his heart again, but not so much that he lost sight of what his mother had just unveiled. "Do you think Dad is upset because I went away and he couldn't or didn't?"

"I think that might have something to do with it, yes. I don't think he's upset with you, necessarily. He just doesn't know what to do with his own grief." His mother reached across the table and touched his hand again. Her eyes softened.

Jack felt as if he were stuck. He had no idea how to fix things between him and his father, and it didn't sound like his mother had the answers, either.

"I've missed you, Jack."

"I've missed you, too, Mom. I'm sorry. I just didn't know

how to move forward. I thought everyone blamed me as much as I blamed myself."

"I never blamed you, Jack," Siena said.

"I know." He put his arm around her and pulled her close. "Savannah has helped me to deal with a lot of that garbage. Mom, you're right. She is a big part of why I'm finally taking the steps I should have taken a long time ago. She's helped me break down the barriers I've put up between me and the rest of the world. But if what you're saying is that Dad is upset because I did what he couldn't, then I'm not sure how I can fix that."

"Your father is stubborn, but he's a loving man. I know you don't always see the softer side of him, but it exists. Remember when you came back from your last tour and you were up for days on end worrying about the guys who were still over there?"

"I forgot about that. He stayed up on the phone with me almost all night for several nights in a row." The memories were filtering back, like pieces of a puzzle falling into place. He'd known his father was exhausted. He'd heard it in his voice, and yet he remained steadfast in his support of Jack, telling him how proud he was of him and how well he'd done for his country.

"Do you remember when he gave you his old truck? He didn't want to. Did you know that?" she asked.

"I thought it was to haul things, as he said." Jack took a drink of his iced tea.

"He knew you needed something to haul things with all that acreage, but more important, he knew how much it meant to you. You used to ride in it just to be close to him. He wanted you to have those memories. He's a good man, Jack, just like you."

She sat back, and Jack felt her watching him as he mulled over what she'd just said.

"How is Jack supposed to navigate this, Mom? It sounds like it's Dad's issue, not Jack's."

"Correct. It's your father's issue. Jack just needs to be patient and try to remember who your father really is at his heart, so when he's ready to forgive and apologize, Jack is receptive to it."

Jack wondered why he'd buried the more positive memories of his father, and he wondered if he'd repressed them before or after Linda's accident. He wished he knew.

"Do you remember the rabbit we had when I was about eight?" he asked.

"Of course. Wubbles." She smiled.

"Right."

"Wubbles? I don't remember a Wubbles," Siena said.

"You weren't born yet," their mother said. "Jack had a rabbit that he adored. Heaven knows why he had to have that rabbit, but he did, and he loved the darn thing so much. One day when he went out to feed him, he found that Wubbles had gone to the great rabbit hutch in the sky."

"Aw. That must have been so sad," Siena said.

"It tore him up, and your father wasn't very patient with him." She pointed her index finger at Jack. "But you were a little pill. You refused to eat or sleep for days, and while I don't agree with how your father pushed you to get you back into life, I do think you needed to be pushed."

Jack rubbed his hand over his face. *Savannah was right.* "I guess perspective is everything. I have a kid's-eye-view with that one. I just remember him telling me to basically get over it. I don't remember anything that I did around that time. You know, Mom, I wonder if I should just talk to him again, now that I know about Esther. Maybe if he knows I understand what he went through…"

"Don't you dare. You promised me you'd keep it a secret, and I trust that you will, Jack."

She said it so forcefully that Jack put his hands up in surrender. "I will. I'm sorry."

"It could be a year before he comes around, or he could come around tomorrow. I don't have any idea, and I can't talk with him about it. This is too close to his heart. All I can tell you, Jack, is that he's your father and he loves you. When he's finally ready, I hope you'll treat him with the same unconditional love that your sister and brothers have treated you."

"I want nothing more than to be a family again, Mom. I promise you that I'm done with the anger. I'm feeling a lot like my old self again, and it feels too good to ever go back."

Chapter Thirty-Seven

SAVANNAH WAS ON the phone with Josh when her apartment door opened and Jack walked in. He held up the key and mouthed, *It worked.* He set a number of packages on the floor and joined Savannah on the couch. She held up one finger and blew him a kiss while listening to Josh.

"Okay, so we'll see you and Riley tomorrow night. Yeah. I can't wait. Love you, too." She ended the call and was surprised to see how many shopping bags Jack had. "Wow, you guys really did go shopping. How fun."

"Fun? You've never shopped with Siena and my mother. Siena wants to dress me like I'm a twentysomething skater, and my mother has strong opinions of her own. I did enjoy spending the day with them, though." He leaned over and kissed her. "Sorry I'm so late. I spent a little time getting reacquainted with the city."

"You did? With all those eyes on you?" she teased.

He kissed her again, and Savannah deepened the kiss. She'd been thinking about him all afternoon, and just the thought that he now had a key to her apartment kicked up her excitement. She'd never left a man alone in her apartment before, much less given one a key, and with Jack she didn't have one second of unease about either.

"I'm so glad you were able to spend time with them." The way he looked at her, the way he moved, even the way he spoke was more at ease. Savannah had a feeling that she was finally seeing the real Jack Remington—and she loved him even more than she did the day before.

"Actually, I got you a few things, too." He retrieved the packages and brought them to the couch.

"You didn't need to get me anything." Savannah loved gifts as much as any woman, and her stomach jumped with anticipation to see what he'd picked out for her.

"I noticed that you had on cowgirl boots when we were in the mountains, and while they were extremely sexy, I thought you might want something a little more sturdy. That is, assuming you'll want to spend any time at all at my cabin." He handed her a beautiful pair of leather hiking boots.

"Oh, Jack. That was so thoughtful. How did you know my size?" She ran her fingers over the soft leather.

"I might have peeked in your closet, but I promise I didn't snoop at anything personal."

She wrapped him in a tight hug. "I love these, and I would love to spend time at your cabin. I'd spend time anywhere with you."

"Well, that's good, because I have a few more things for you. They're not as exciting, but I think you'll appreciate them." He handed her a bag, and Savannah withdrew the contents.

"Toilet paper? Body wipes? Flannel pajamas? A bathrobe. Indoor-outdoor slippers? Are you trying to tell me something?"

Jack smiled. "Only that I love you. I know how you hate going to the bathroom in the woods, and you can't always shower in the stream. If you're going to come on any survival weekends with me, I want you to be comfortable. The toilet paper and wipes are biodegradable, and the bathrobe is in case you do decide to take a dip in the stream. It'll keep you warm afterward. And these..." He held up the pajamas and slippers. "Are for when you get cold at night. Although you'll be in my tent, and I plan on keeping you very, very warm."

The seduction in his voice and the hungry look in his eyes drew her lips to his.

"You're so thoughtful. I love everything. Thank you."

Jack kissed her again. "After Siena and my mother left, I had time to do some thinking."

Savannah's pulse sped up at the mix of sensuality in his eyes and the seriousness in his voice. Before she could decipher what it might mean, there was a knock at the door.

"Are you expecting someone?" Jack asked.

Savannah went to answer it. "No." She looked through the peephole. "I don't know who it is. A man."

In a few quick steps, Jack was between Savannah and the door. He pulled it open, and Savannah saw his body stiffen. She peered around him, and the resemblance between the two men was undeniable. The same dark eyes, the same high cheekbones, the same broad chest.

"HELLO, JACK."

His father stood before him in a gray suit and tie, and for a breath, Jack's world stood still. "Dad," was all he could say. *How did you find me? Why are you here?* He felt Savannah's hand on his lower back, and he stood between the two of them. His father could hurt him with his harsh stares and whatever else he had in store, but he wouldn't allow any of that nonsense toward Savannah. He put his arm around her and, feeling torn between pride for his strong, war-hero father and remembering how much it had hurt the evening before when he hadn't accepted his apology, Jack raised his chin and did the only thing he could—he showed Savannah that despite what might happen in the next ten minutes, he was proud of her and proud of himself.

"This is my girlfriend, Savannah. Savannah, this is my father, James Remington."

Savannah's trusting eyes smiled at his father. James shook her hand and smiled, and Jack felt a pang of hope—and tried not to let it carry him away. After what his mother had told him, he knew this was not going to be an easy fence to mend.

"Nice to meet you, Savannah. Please excuse the interruption into your evening. My daughter gave me your address, and while I should have called first, I wasn't thinking as clearly as I should have been."

His father had always exhibited good manners, which, Jack realized, was one reason he was so struck by the way he'd treated him the previous night.

"Don't be silly. You're welcome here anytime. Come in, please." She stepped back and allowed him to pass.

Savannah touched Jack's hand, but he was busy trying to figure out how to politely take whatever conversation was about to happen out of earshot from Savannah to respond. She slid her hand up his arm and squeezed his forearm.

"I'll just take my things back to the bedroom and give you some privacy," she said.

Jack watched her gather her things. He couldn't find his voice to say thank you, but as Savannah touched his cheek on the way to the bedroom and her green eyes reassured him, he knew he didn't have to.

"Would you like to sit down?" he asked his father. Jack's nerves were tangled in knots. He'd promised his mother not to reveal what she'd shared with him, and he knew his father never would. Which left him wondering what could possibly be done to bridge the gap between them—something he wanted more than almost anything else at that moment. The thing he wanted most was to move forward with Savannah, but no matter how contentious things had become between them, his father owned a hunk of his heart that would never belong to anyone else, and Jack wanted to move forward with his new life with a whole, fulfilled heart.

He followed his father to the couch, then opted for a chair instead so he could look him in the eye.

"Your mother doesn't know I'm here, so before we talk, I'd like to ask that you don't tell her I came." His father rubbed his hands together, then settled them in his lap.

Jack had never seen his father act any other way than in complete control, and now, watching his hands unclasp and rub the thighs of his slacks and his eyes dart around the room, he saw a different man emerging, and Jack wasn't sure what to make of it.

"Okay." *Breathe. Just breathe.*

"Son, I'm not here to berate you, so you can put your shoulders back down where they belong."

Despite his nerves, Jack breathed a sigh of relief.

"Ever since you were a boy, you wore your emotions on your sleeve. I recognize the tension in your body and the worry in your eyes, and I'm sorry that seeing me instills such a reaction. But I think maybe it always has."

"No, Dad—"

His father raised his hand. "Please. If there's one thing I know, it's truth. And I'm well aware of the choices I've made in life. Jack, when you were born, my entire life changed. The minute I held you in my arms, the responsibility that pressed in on me was all-consuming." His stare softened as he continued. "Your mother handled it differently, though she was equally, if not more, enamored by you and amazed by the magnitude of responsibility that comes along with having a child. She believed that we needed to love and support everything you did, even if it was, for lack of a better word, stupid."

Jack looked away. That crack cut him to the bone. *I wasn't stupid for missing Linda.*

"You know how hard your mother works on her sculptures and paintings, and I know you remember her toiling in the garden for hours so our family could eat organic vegetables, of all things. But you may not remember the day you thought you'd make your own sculpture while she was off taking a shower or something. You gathered all of the vegetables—every last one of them—and you brought them into her studio and used pounds and pounds of clay to create a garden sculpture. It was one big gloppy mess of clay with vegetables stuck haphazardly throughout. Your mother had a gallery deadline to meet at the time, and of course it was a Sunday evening, so getting her hands on more clay before the next morning wasn't even an option. Being the resourceful kid that you were, you washed up and never said a word until she was putting you to bed hours later. Do you remember how she used to say good night and then she'd toil away in her studio for hours while I was on kid duty?"

Jack vaguely remembered something about her garden and

clay, but he couldn't reconcile the story—or his father taking over their care—to any concrete memory. He shook his head.

"No. I guess you wouldn't. When your mother came back inside, she didn't say a word. She didn't have to. The light in her eyes was gone. When I saw what you had done, I was livid. I knew your mother was devastated to have lost the clay she relied on, and I knew the idea of her hard work in the garden being for naught was even worse, because she'd grown them for us. For you kids. I laid into you, Jack. As I believed I should. I told you how irresponsible you were being, and I made you work for the next month doing anything your mother asked—in the garden and in her studio."

Jack shook his head. "Dad, I don't even remember that."

"Maybe not, but I remember every second of it. You said you hated me, and I thought"—he raised his eyebrows and smiled—"that's okay, because you'll learn from it and it'll make you a better, more responsible man."

"Dad, how does this have anything to do with what's going on now?" Jack leaned forward, trying to understand.

"Because I remember that like it was yesterday. And I did more of that, pushing, instilling harshness upon you, trying to strengthen your resolve and make you understand the importance of being a responsible man. Jack, you were my first child. I had no experiences to fall back on or learn from. I know now that kids do silly things all the time, and I know you didn't make that sculpture out of anything other than a child's curiosity or wanting to do something you thought your mother might be proud of, and I'm sorry for pushing you so hard." He looked away and clenched his jaw, and when he looked back, his eyes were damp. He blinked away the dampness, and Jack lowered his eyes, ashamed to see his father as a weaker man. *No.*

He raised his eyes and met his father's gaze. *You're not weak at all. You're human.*

"Jack, when you turned your back on your family and on everyone, I took that as a personal affront. I saw it as my fault, because I taught you how to be a man. And the only way I could diffuse my own guilt was to thrust that guilt back on you."

Jack swallowed past the growing lump in his throat. He sat back and clutched the armrests of the chair, not out of anger, but as a way to gain control of the emotions that were seeping out of his heart and swelling his chest, working their way out of every pore of his body and threatening to tear him apart.

"You're more of a man than I could ever be, Jackson, and I'm here to tell you that I'm sorry for how I treated you and for how I raised you. I'm ashamed of the way I thrust on you the things my father thrust on me."

All the air in the room dissipated. Jack could only stare at the man he'd looked up to and disliked all at once. He couldn't think about the words he'd said or the way his eyes reached for forgiveness. He could only rise to his feet, cross the floor, and embrace him. His father's large hand pressed against his back, and at that very second, Jack was sure he heard his mother's voice whispering, *He's a good man, Jack. Just like you.*

Chapter Thirty-Eight

SAVANNAH PACED THE bedroom floor, dying to know what was going on out in the living room. She hadn't heard any yelling and assumed that had to be a good sign. She jumped to her feet when the bedroom door cracked open.

"Hi, angel," Jack whispered.

The concerned look on Jack's face and the way every muscle in his body tightened had her thinking the worst. She ran into his arms. "Are you okay? You're shaking. What happened?"

"I'll explain it all tonight, but first, there's something I want to do. Would you be okay if we stayed at my house tonight?"

"Your house? What about—" Her mind spun in fifteen directions, and she couldn't hold on to any coherent thoughts.

He pressed his finger to her lips. "Please?"

"Yes, yes, of course. Jack, I'm happy to do anything you need or want." She pulled a bag from her closet and began packing clothes for the night.

"There's something I need to do, and I want you and my father there."

Savannah stilled. "Is your dad still here?"

Jack nodded. "He's going to follow us out."

"Jack, you're worrying me. What's going on?" She tried to

read his expression, but it hovered someplace between happy and scared, and again, she felt lost.

"We're moving forward."

Chapter Thirty-Nine

THEY'D BEEN DRIVING for more than an hour, and Savannah had been a good sport about riding on his motorcycle, though he'd have liked to have had a safer vehicle to share with her. *Just another thing on my "New Life List."* He was thankful for the motorcycle on one level, though. He'd had enough time to think on the way over to know he was doing the right thing, and he hoped that Savannah would think so, too.

He glanced in his rearview mirror and spied his father's Lincoln a safe distance behind. He patted the zipped pocket of his jacket and felt the package he'd purchased earlier in the afternoon. He finally felt almost whole again—almost.

Jack drove in the back way to his house, descending the steep hill toward his driveway. He pulled the motorcycle over where the pavement dipped to the left, exactly eighty-seven paces from his property line, and he parked in the grass. His father parked behind him, and while Jack helped Savannah off of the bike and set their helmets down, Jack tried not to concentrate on the blood rushing through his ears or the adrenaline pumping through his veins, causing his pulse to race.

"Jack, where are we?"

Savannah looked around, and Jack knew she couldn't see

the hidden driveway, and she wouldn't think anything of the gaping emptiness in the otherwise overgrown woods across from them. She couldn't see the flashing lights or feel the burn of the flames as he'd rushed over the edge two years earlier. Savannah couldn't smell the pungent smell of burning oil and rubber, and—as Jack rubbed the back of his arm—he knew her heart wasn't racing as his was, just as it had been the night of the accident, when he'd sped down the driveway after hearing an earth-shattering crash amid the thunder of the raging storm. She wouldn't have to squint to see through the driving rain, as he had, and she wouldn't feel the thick metal carving a path through his arm—almost to the bone—as he tried to free Linda's lifeless body from the car. Savannah would never know that less than sixty seconds after he dragged her away from the burning car, he covered her body with his own, shielding her from the explosion. He rubbed the thick, rough scar, feeling the pain anew. She would not feel the searing heat as debris blew into his back, and she would never know the torture of the exact moment Jack realized that even with his body pressed against Linda's, he couldn't feel her heartbeat. And there was absolutely no way that she'd ever put the pieces together and realize that in that blink of an eye, his heart had stopped beating too—until he'd met Savannah.

He looked at Savannah's trusting eyes and folded her into his arms. Her heart beat strong and true against his. Hopefully, what Savannah would know tonight was that Jack said goodbye to Linda—and his past—for good. He hoped she'd remember that tonight he promised his future to her and her alone, and that all the anger and all the guilt she'd helped him heal from and all the energy that he'd poured into holding on to the hurt would now be redirected. And every moment of every day he'd show her the man he was always meant to be. *Her man.*

"Son?"

Jack held Savannah's hand as he turned to face his father, and for the first time in two years, there was no fight left in his father's eyes, either. The guilt that had once swallowed Jack was now a shadow, fading a little more with each passing breath.

"Thanks for coming, Dad." Flanked by Savannah and his father, he led them across the street. Jack reached for his father's hand and felt it stiffen, then relax and, finally, embrace his large hand. Savannah held tight to his other hand. A million unanswered questions hung in her eyes.

"Savannah, this is where the accident occurred. The break in the woods is where Linda's car spun out of control and flipped, landing upside down atop a number of trees that crumbled against the crushing impact of her car."

Savannah wrapped her arms around his left arm and kissed his muscle, then rested her cheek against him. Jack drew strength from her love.

She slid her hand up the back of his shirt and over his scars, and when she looked up at him, he saw the question in her eyes.

He nodded, and knew she understood where his scars had come from, or at least that they happened that night, and that was enough. He loved that she didn't push him for more. He would have told her whatever she wanted to know, but he would rather spare her the pain of knowing what he'd gone through.

"Dad, I thought you might need this final goodbye as much as I did." He had no reason to believe that his father would know that he was giving him an open invitation to leave *his* past behind, too. All he could do was hope that he would take the opportunity to let it go.

Jack took a deep breath and closed his eyes, recalling every image of the night of the accident as if it were unfolding before him anew. He knew that he would never forget what had happened or the agony that followed, and he wasn't trying to. He needed to see it one last time before releasing the hold it had over him and leaving it behind for good, so that when he walked away with the man who raised him and the woman he adored, he would be whole, without the weight of a ghost around his shoulders.

He opened his eyes and squeezed Savannah's hand. "It's time to say goodbye once and for all. It took me a long time to believe this, and with Savannah's help, I can now see clearly what you, Dad, and everyone else who loves me, was trying to tell me all along. Linda's death was not my fault."

He felt his father's large hand on his shoulder.

"That's right, son. Leave it all behind."

Jack nodded, hoping his father was doing the same. He turned and stood eye to eye, man to man, and for the first time in his life, truly felt like his father's equal. "Dad, I think you can leave the guilt of your past here, too." He knew his father would interpret his words to be related to the conversation they'd had at the apartment, and that was good enough for him. His father had carried more burdens than any man he knew, for too many years, and just because he didn't wear his emotions on his sleeve didn't mean they didn't exist. He hugged his father and whispered against his rough cheek, "Let it go, Dad. I love you."

Savannah was as selfless as ever, offering him support and strength while giving him the grace of silence to say his goodbyes. When the air around them lightened and Jack felt the oppression of the past ease, he said, "Dad, I needed you here with me." He covered his heart with his hand. "Thank you. I think I'm okay now."

His father nodded.

"Please go see Mom and tell her that we're okay. She's been so worried."

His father didn't utter a word. He pulled Jack into another hug, tighter than before; then he put his hands on Jack's cheeks and kissed his forehead. His paternal touch infused Jack with so much love that he could not hold back the tears that streamed from his eyes, and he didn't want to. Jack was finally ready to feel everything life had to offer.

He watched his father embrace Savannah, then kiss her forehead in the same sweet manner.

"Thank you for helping us both," his father said.

Jack watched his father drive away, and then he and Savannah mounted his motorcycle. Savannah's body pressed against Jack's back as they rode up the steep driveway. Jack swore he could feel the remaining claws of the past ripping from his body and mind and freeing him from its confines.

Chapter Forty

SAVANNAH STEPPED FROM the bike, finally understanding why Jack had hidden away in the mountains for so long. Not only had he lost someone he loved, but he had the added stab of a daily reminder just down the road. How many times had he driven by before he snapped and decided he never wanted to go back? She didn't quite understand everything that had transpired with his father, but she trusted that Jack would fill her in when he was ready. She trusted everything about Jack, from his understanding of what he needed to make it through his days to the safe and real love he felt for her.

He came to her side and looked up at the house. "This is where I live."

The way he said it was not convincing, as if he'd said, "The earth is square." Savannah knew what he was really saying. *This is where I lived when it happened.* It was obvious that Jack hadn't really lived anywhere after the accident...until these past few days when he'd begun living again.

Savannah stood on her tiptoes and kissed him. "I'm right here, Jack, and no matter what happens, I'm not going anywhere."

He looked down at her and furrowed his brow; then he

placed his warm hands on her cheeks and pressed a soft kiss to her lips. "I know you're not, and neither am I."

Jack opened the door and they stepped inside. The house smelled woodsy and masculine with a hint of cedar. *Kinda like Jack.* He motioned to the open living space.

She took another step inside and looked at the warm furniture, the expansive fireplace, the mix of textures: woods, stone, granite. "This is very nice," she said. "It looks like a place I could envision you spending time in, reading in front of the fireplace, sitting on the deck." Her eyes caught on a photograph on the bookshelf next to the fireplace. She moved closer, and recognized Jack in his cap and gown. "Your college graduation?"

"Yes. That's my family."

She realized that the blond woman beside him was probably Linda. She was very pretty and was looking up at Jack adoringly. *Who wouldn't? He is worth adoring.*

"And Linda," he added. "If it upsets you, I can put it away."

"No need. I feel like I know where her life ended, and I know she had a life with you, so it's nice to put a face to the woman who loved you. I'm glad you kept it."

Jack went to her side and pulled her against him. He kissed the top of her head. "I really don't need to keep it out. It was just a happy time with my family."

She looked up at him and smiled. "Jack, I'm not threatened by her. If it doesn't make you sad, then to me, it's just another family member who's no longer here but who doesn't deserve to be forgotten."

"How can you be so good, Savannah?"

"When you love someone, you want them to be happy, and repressing ten years of your life can't make anyone happy. I didn't know her, but I assume she was a good person, or you wouldn't have been with her. And now you have me. There's no issue. If you compared me to her all the time or complained that I should be more like her, that would be cause for some different action to be taken, but I can't see that happening." She put her hands on his waist. "I do like your house. It's very you."

"I'm selling it," he said. "I needed you to see where everything happened so you would understand what I'm going to do next."

"Why?" The minute she asked, she knew why. It was one thing to say goodbye to his past, but another to be reminded of it every day.

"My life is no longer here, Savannah."

A powerful and unexpected thought came into her mind, and she furrowed her brow, thinking it was too impetuous and she should tuck it away, but when she looked into Jack's eyes and saw the love there, the desire to squelch the thought disappeared.

"Move in with me." The words tumbled out. Her heart raced at the thought, and the faster it beat, the more she was sure it was the right thing to do.

He looked down at her, and behind the shock of his gaping mouth and wide eyes, she saw—and felt—the same excitement that sent her up on her toes to steal a kiss from him.

"Jack, no one knows what tomorrow will bring. No one knows that better than you."

He searched her eyes, and she wished he would say something, anything. She knew in her heart this was the right thing to do. She didn't want to come home one single night and know Jack wasn't there. She thought of him all the time, and the more time they spent together, the more she loved him.

Jack stuffed his hands in his pockets and looked around the

room, blinking so much that she was sure he was trying to figure out how to let her down easily.

"It's okay," she said quickly. "I was just excited. I…I don't know what I was thinking." She looked away, her heart shattering into smithereens. *What have I done?*

Jack lifted her chin with his index finger, and when she drew her eyes to him, he was smiling.

"Savannah, after my mother and sister left today, I spent two hours walking around the city, making sure that none of those dark thoughts would find their way back to me and thinking about us."

"And?" Her stomach twisted into a knot. Hadn't he just said goodbye to his past? Was he now going to tell her it was still there? She held her breath as he continued.

"You have taught me that life is about living, and you've loved me through the scars that my past left behind. Do you remember the rules of three? In extreme conditions a man can live three minutes without air, three weeks without food, and—"

"Three days without water," Savannah added.

"Yes. Three days without water. Angel, my rules are now three plus one. I don't want to live three seconds without you in my life. If you'll have me, I want an eternity with you. I want to fall asleep with you in my arms and wake up to your warmth beside me. I want to be there when you laugh and I want to share your sadness so you know you're never alone. Savannah, you are my future, and I hope that I can be yours."

Her chest constricted. She could barely breathe. "Jack?" she whispered. "Are you asking me…"

"Marry me, Savannah. I don't care when. Tonight, next year, five years from now. Promise me an eternity and I'll promise you the same. I've never wanted anything so much in my entire life."

Now she knew why he'd been blinking so much, because as her eyes filled with tears, she couldn't stop her lashes from trying to blink them away so his handsome face could come back into focus again.

"Yes, Jack! *Yes,* I promise you forever and a day."

He reached into his pocket and pulled out a sparkling diamond ring. As he put the ring on her finger, he said, "Diamonds, so you know how much I value our love, and the infinity symbol because my love for you is endless."

"Oh, Jack…" she said softly.

Savannah reached for him as he lifted her into his arms. It was the most natural thing in the world for her to wrap her legs around his waist and lower her lips to his, then deepen the kiss with thoughts of spending forever with Jack spinning in her head and filling her heart.

"I want to take you upstairs," Jack said, then kissed her again.

"Take me." Savannah was lost in their next kiss, and only when they drew apart again and she looked into his eyes did she understand the significance of what he'd said. *Upstairs. In the bedroom he couldn't sleep in.* "Are you sure?"

"As certain as I am that I want forever and a day with you," he said.

He lowered her to the floor and they went upstairs hand in hand. "I want to take you to my cabin in the mountains. Think you can break free next weekend?"

"I would love nothing more. I feel like the mountains are our place, Jack."

He stopped at the landing and eyed the second door.

"The nursery?" Savannah asked.

He nodded, and she touched his cheek. "It's okay, Jack. One day you'll have a family. One day we'll have a family."

"Do you want children?" he asked.

"Many," she said with a smile.

"Me too, angel. Me too." He took her face in his hands and pressed another kiss to her lips. "Are you okay?"

She placed her palms against his chest. "As long as I'm with you, I'll always be okay."

Chapter Forty-One

THE NEXT NIGHT, after Hugh accepted his award, Savannah and Jack went to meet her family at Josh's Manhattan apartment. The blue shirt and Jerry Garcia tie Jack had picked out with Siena and his mother was perfect for the fun evening, and Savannah wore her favorite blue minidress, which complemented Jack's outfit nicely.

"Hugh looked so handsome accepting his award," Savannah said.

"He looked happy, that's for sure," Jack said.

Savannah hung up their coats as they moved toward the voices coming from the living room. She felt like a bundle of nerves. She found herself having flashbacks of dates she'd brought home in high school and her five brothers hunkering over them with threats and harsh stares.

"Are you okay, angel?" Jack touched her cheek as they entered the hall, and she stopped walking to look up at him.

"I'm just nervous. I know they'll love you, but I never really know what to expect."

Jack kissed her forehead. "I'm a big boy. I can handle anything. Don't you worry."

She remembered her father's words, and as she looked at the

man who had made her the happiest woman in the world, she realized how true they were. "*You can learn all the fancy skills you feel you need, but the strength and ability to survive comes from within.*"

He lowered his lips to hers, and Savannah melted into his arms.

"Don't let your brothers catch you making out before you even say hello."

Savannah pulled back from Jack and laughed. "Riley, wow. You look radiant." Josh's fiancée hugged her; then she took Jack's hand. "This is Jack."

"So you're the man who rocked Savannah's world. It's nice to meet you."

"I think it's the other way around. She rocked my world. I was just a bump in the road for her," Jack teased.

Riley led them into the living room. "Look who's here," she called out.

Her brothers turned, and she cringed as each one of them ran their eyes up and down Jack, then across their linked hands. The ten seconds of once-overs felt like an hour.

"Jack Remington, survivor man." Hugh extended his hand and patted Jack on the back. "Man, you have one cool job."

"Thanks, but it doesn't compare to yours. Congratulations on your award." Jack didn't seem nervous at all, and for that, Savannah was thankful.

Josh hugged Savannah and whispered, "You look happy. So I take it dating Jack is a good thing?"

"A great thing."

Josh held out a hand to Jack as Riley snuggled against his side. "I'm Josh, Savannah's younger brother. It's a pleasure to meet you."

"Thank you, Josh. I recognize you from the picture in Savannah's living room. I appreciate you having us over tonight, and I hope we'll see more of each other since we'll be neighbors."

Savannah cringed and noticed that Treat and Dane were eavesdropping. She hadn't had a chance to mention to her family that they were moving in together.

"Neighbors? Do you live nearby?" Josh asked.

Savannah was about to jump in when she felt a heavy hand grip her shoulder. She turned toward her father, glad for the break in the conversation. His deep tan set off his dark eyes, and Savannah noticed a little more gray in his five-o'clock shadow. He was as handsome as ever. Even at his age, he still had a commanding presence.

"Hi, Dad."

He hugged her tight. "I've missed you, darlin'."

"Me too. Dad, this is Jack. Jack, this is my father, Hal Braden." Savannah had called her father and told him about Jack moving in. She wanted to give him a chance to say whatever he felt he needed to in private instead of springing it on him. She'd also told him about Jack's wife and how difficult her death had been for him. Her father's response was more than she could have hoped for—and then some. *You mother always knew that you were destined to change someone's life, and that day you told me about Jack was the day I knew that she'd been right.* She wished she'd known her mother better. She and Jack had talked that morning about families, and Jack wanted to have children as much as she did—only she hadn't even realized how badly she'd wanted them until she'd seen Jack with Aiden.

She watched Jack offer his hand to her father, and her father opened his arms. "Son, in this family we hug." He patted Jack on the back and then pulled him out of earshot of her brothers, though Savannah took a step closer to hear what her father had to say.

"That's my little girl, Jack Remington. She's stubborn and smart and she's the light of my life. If you hurt her, I will have no qualms setting those men on you, you hear?"

Savannah froze. She'd never heard her father speak like that to any man she'd dated.

Jack drew his shoulders back and looked right at Savannah as he spoke. "Sir, if I ever hurt her, I'll sic them on me myself." Then he looked at her father and said, "I adore Savannah, and I will make you proud that I'm with her."

Her legs grew weak, and she was thankful for Treat's arm as it wrapped around her.

"He's a keeper, huh?" Treat kissed her cheek.

"Definitely," she said.

Dane appeared by Jack's side. As the founder of the Brave Foundation, a nonprofit organization whose mission was to educate and advocate on behalf of sharks, Dane and his girlfriend, Lacy, traveled often and sported year-round tans. Dane spent time researching and tagging sharks, and Lacy worked remotely for World Geographic as an account manager developing marketing plans for nonprofit organizations.

Dane put his arm around Jack's shoulder, and Savannah loved to see him embracing Jack into the fold of their family.

"I know a secret," Max said as she sidled up to Savannah's other side with Lacy in tow. Max's dark hair had grown just past her shoulders, and it looked much fuller than it had the last time Savannah had seen her.

Lacy handed Max a glass of water and whispered to Savannah, "I know what it is, too." Lacy's blond corkscrew curls hung thick and heavy over her sun-kissed, lean shoulder.

"That's not fair," Savannah said. She moved in close to Lacy. "Tell me," she whispered in Lacy's ear.

Lacy whispered, "No way."

Max grabbed Savannah's hand and squealed. "Oh my gosh. You have an infinity ring? Lacy, look. Riley, you've got to see this."

Savannah felt a flush run up her neck and spread over her cheeks, still thinking about Max and Lacy's secret. Jack wrapped his arms around Savannah's waist and kissed her cheek.

"I feel like I'm on display with all of you looking at me." She put her hands on top of Jack's, took a deep breath, and said, "I asked Jack to move in with me, and he asked me to marry him." She couldn't stop her smile from lifting her cheeks as she added, "And I said yes." Her brothers' dark eyes locked on her. Each one more serious than the next.

Max, Riley, and Lacy rushed in and hugged her, laughing and *ooh*ing and *aah*ing over her ring. Savannah gushed while sharing the meaning behind the ring, "Jack said, *Diamonds, so you know how much I value our love, and the infinity symbol because my love for you is endless.*"

The girls squealed, while her brothers turned hot stares at Jack.

Jack rose to his full height. "I know it seems sudden. I have a little sister, too. Siena, she's twenty-six."

"Is she hot?" Hugh asked.

Savannah punched him in the arm.

"Yes, actually. She's one of New York's top models," Jack said with a proud smile.

Savannah rolled her eyes at Hugh. "You're such a pig."

"What? Just because you're biting the marriage bullet

doesn't mean that I have to," Hugh said.

Jack continued. "I know it's impetuous, and I would worry about any man who moved in with my sister and claimed to love her after such a short time, too. I understand if you're concerned, and all I can do is tell you the truth." He took Savannah's hands in his. "I adore your sister. She's the most loving woman I've ever met, and—"

"We don't need those juicy details," Dane said.

Lacy poked him in the side as he put his arm around her.

"Caring—that's probably a better word. Generous, empathetic, funny. You all know who she is, and I love her for all the same reasons you do." He shrugged. "That's all I've got."

Savannah couldn't believe her brothers weren't congratulating them and welcoming him into the family as they'd welcomed Riley, Max, and Lacy. She felt her heart deflate, and as she turned to make sure Jack was okay, she wondered why he had a stupid grin on his lips. "Why do you look so happy?" she asked in a harsh whisper.

"Savannah, I'm an older brother, too. Do you really think I'd ask you to marry me without first speaking to each of your brothers?"

She spun around and saw cocky grins on her brothers' faces.

"And your father?" Jack added.

"You...I don't understand." Savannah looked at her brothers' guilty faces. "Treat?"

Treat threw an arm around Jack's shoulder. "He's telling you the truth, Vanny. He called Dad; then Dad gave him our numbers. You have all of our blessings."

"But? What about those stares you guys gave him? And, Josh, what was that ruse asking about where he lived?"

"We didn't want to expose his secret. We left that up to him to decide, and we had to play the part," Josh answered.

She shot a look at her father. "When? How?"

"He called me yesterday afternoon," her father said. "I'm sorry I didn't let on when you called earlier, darlin', but you were so excited. I didn't want to ruin that for you."

She turned back to Jack. "You did that?"

He nodded. "After I had lunch with my mom and sister—who, by the way, also gave us their blessing—I knew I wanted to marry you. I think I even knew it when we said goodbye at the plane, but before I went to Tiffany's, I called your father. I know how much he means to you, and I know how much your brothers do, too. I didn't want to take a chance that I would come between you and your family." He ran his finger down her cheek. "So I told each of them about my past, and we talked about my relationship with my family and my career. I have to say, your family is very protective of you. I think they know everything about me, including what year I went through puberty."

"That was me." Hugh held up his hand.

"You did that for me?" She couldn't believe the depth of his consideration of her feelings, and the feelings of her family members.

"There's nothing in this world I wouldn't do for you, angel."

She smiled up at him and touched his cheek, knowing she'd love him even on the days that his hurt returned, because now that she knew the real Jack Remington, she understood the love that her father so desperately held on to, and she, too, was never letting go.

Ready for More Bradens?
Fall in love with Brianna and Hugh in
AND THEN THERE WAS US

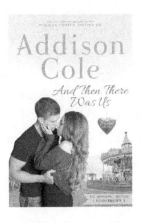

Chapter One

KAT BURST THROUGH the stockroom doors of Old Town Tavern, nearly plowing into Brianna.

"Jeez, Kat. What the heck?" Brianna Heart had been working since noon, and she had another two hours to go before her ten-hour shift was over. She didn't have the energy for Kat's drama. Not tonight, when she still had to muster the energy to pick up Layla, her five-year-old daughter, from her mother's house, get her to bed, and then make invitations for Layla's birthday party.

"Patrick Dempsey is here. I saw him. He's sitting at a table in the bar. Oh my gosh—he is even hotter in person." Kat flipped her long blond hair over her shoulder and tapped her finger on her lip. "I wonder if he's looking for a date."

"Kat." Brianna shook her head. "You're crazy. You always think you see famous people. Not a lot of famous people are clamoring to get into Richmond, Virginia."

"Bree, I'm telling you. I think I need to change my underwear." She looked at Brianna and furrowed her perfectly manicured brows. "Oh, honey. Here. Let me help you with your hair. You could be the prettiest bartender slash waitress out there and you know it. Well, besides me, of course." She began fluffing Bree's straight, shoulder-length brown hair.

Brianna shook her head. "Please. If it is Patrick Dempsey, I'll be the last person he's looking at." She wiped her hands on the little towel she kept looped over her belt at all times—because she didn't have time to breathe, much less go searching for something to dry her hands on.

"Oh, come on, Bree. Don't you want to get out of this place? What better way than with a famous sugar daddy?" Kat looked at her reflection in the glass and flipped her long blond hair over her shoulder.

"*Ugh*. No, thank you. The last thing Layla needs is that kind of lifestyle, and the last thing I need is to stand in the stockroom talking about fictitious people. I love you, Kat, but I gotta get out there." She patted her back pocket. "I need the tips. Layla's birthday is coming up."

"I can't believe she's going to be six. Gosh, that went quick. What does she want?"

"A puppy, a kitten, a bigger bedroom." Brianna sighed. "But I think I'm going to get her a winter jacket. Kill two birds with one stone." She winked as she headed out of the stockroom and up to the bar. A quick scan told her that Patrick Dempsey was definitely not there. She snagged the empty glasses from the bar and wiped it down.

Mack Greenley, the manager of the bar, sidled up to Brianna. She'd worked for Mack for the past five and a half years, and though she was twenty-eight and he was only thirty-eight, he'd taken her under his wing as if she were his daughter.

"Booth." Mack was a big man with a mass of brown hair and a thick, powerful neck.

"Got it." Bree wiped her hands on the towel, grabbed an order pad, and went to the only occupied booth in the small bar. It was Thursday night at seven o'clock. Another half hour and the bar would be packed for Major League Baseball playoffs. Brianna focused on her order pad, thinking about Layla's birthday and wishing she could afford the time or money to get her a pet, like she wanted. But as a single mother, she couldn't balance working fifty hours each week with taking care of Layla *and* a pet. It was just too much. She pushed the thought away and feigned a smile.

"Hi, I'm Brianna…Bree. What can I get you?"

The guy in the booth lifted his head in her direction, and Brianna's breath caught in her throat. She felt her jaw go slack. The man's thick, windblown dark hair looked as if someone had just run their hands through it. *While kissing his glorious lips and feeling that sexy five-o'clock shadow on her cheek. Wow, he does look like Patrick Dempsey…on steroids.*

"A sidecar and a glass of water, please," he said.

Brianna couldn't move. She couldn't breathe. She couldn't even close her mouth. *Shoot. Shoot. Shoot.*

He cocked his head. "Are you okay?"

Are you kidding me? Does your voice have to be so darn smooth and rich? That's so unfair. She cleared her throat. "Yeah, sorry. Long day. One sidecar coming up." She cursed at herself all the way back to the bar.

Kat grabbed her arm and pulled her toward the sink, their backs to way-sexier-than-Patrick-Dempsey steroid guy. "I told you," she whispered. "You're so lucky. What are you going to do?"

Brianna looked over her shoulder at the handsome man. *Trouble.* That's what she saw. She'd known men like him before. That's how she ended up with Layla.

"Nothing. He wants a sidecar. You take it to him." Brianna handed her the pad and went to help the woman she and Kat called Red—a slutty redhead who spent every Thursday night trolling the bar for men.

Brianna focused on making Red her cosmo. The din of the customers fell away. Her mind circled back to the Patrick Dempsey look-alike's voice. It was so…so…different from any other man's voice. He didn't speak as if he were rushed, and he looked at her eyes instead of her chest, which was also different from most of the male customers at the tavern. She started when Kat touched her shoulder.

"Bree, come on. You do it. I can't take him from you. He's probably a big tipper. Look at that jacket."

Brianna glanced at the brown leather jacket hanging on the end of the booth. "It's okay. You go. I'm good." She handed Red a cosmo.

"Do you know who that is?" Red lifted her glass toward the handsome man.

Bree shrugged. "No idea." *But I'm sure he'll take you home.*

"I think that's my date," Red said.

Isn't every man? Brianna watched Kat bring him his drink.

Her crimson lips spread with a flash of her sexiest smile. Brianna knew Kat's next move. The hair flip. Then she'd touch his shoulder and...She watched Kat throw her head back in an exaggerated laugh. Brianna sighed and turned away. *He's probably a jackass.* She'd made it this long without a man dragging her through emotional torture; she wasn't going to cave now. She pulled her shoulders back and rotated just in time to see Red sliding into the seat across from him.

ALL HUGH BRADEN wanted to do was disappear in the fog of a few drinks, then go back to his house and chill. Instead he was stuck waiting for a blind date, and with a race around the corner, there'd be no drinking for him. A beautiful woman with the most contemplative eyes and the sweetest face he'd ever seen had taken his drink order. At least he could look forward to seeing her when she brought it to him. He had planned on ordering seltzer water, but one look at her and he was unable to remember what he wanted. *Sidecar* came off his lips like he ordered it all the time, and he'd had a sidecar only once—and that was several years ago. Now he'd have to stare at the stupid drink all night.

It had been a grueling day. Hugh didn't know why he'd let his agent talk him into the stupid photo shoot, and just as he'd anticipated, it had been a painful few hours. They'd taken the photos at the track and had scheduled another shoot for Saturday morning. The photographer was cool enough, but fake smiling and posing in positions he'd never stand or sit in made his already sore body ache. Ever since he won the last three Capital Series Grand Prix races, he'd been hounded by the media. *Annoying sponsor obligations.* As much as he was thankful for the sponsors, he rued the attention, and he needed another racing magazine cover like he needed another expensive car or another house.

A blond waitress set his drink on the table. "Hi. I'm Kat. Enjoy your sidecar."

Really? This is definitely not my night. "Thank you." He peered around Kat, looking for the dark-haired beauty who had taken his order. *Bree.* He spotted her taking a drink order from a stocky blond man in a flannel shirt. The first thing Hugh had noticed when she'd taken his order was that she looked as if she was thinking about a hundred things and taking his order was white noise to her internal thoughts. In the space of a breath, she'd struck him as interesting, beautiful, and intense in a way that had nothing to do with sexuality—which in and of itself struck him as strange that he'd notice something like that. But he had. And now he was unable to look away as she moved from one customer to the next, focused and efficient and completely oblivious to him.

Hugh had picked the Old Town Tavern to meet the blind date because it was out of the way. A little bar with a smaller restaurant. The last thing he wanted to deal with was another group of sex-craved or money-hungry women eyeing him like they hadn't eaten in a month and he was a big juicy steak. He'd hoped he could go unnoticed. When Brianna had finally lifted her eyes to his and her jaw dropped open, he'd worried that she'd recognized him. But she'd ditched him and sent Kat as a replacement. She hadn't even taken a second look. He might not want to be recognized for who he was, but being noticed as a man rather than a race car driver and then rejected by Brianna was a whole different story. This was definitely not his night.

He'd accepted the blind date only because his buddy and crew chief, Art Cullen, had claimed he had the perfect woman for him—smart and beautiful, and best of all, she had no clue who he was. Now, as an overdeveloped redhead slid into the booth across from him, he questioned that decision.

"Hey, sugar. Are you Art's friend?" The redhead put her glass on the table between them and ran her red fingernail around the rim of the glass. "I'm Tracie. That's with an *I E*, not a *Y*."

I'm going to kill Art. Tracie looked like a dime-store hooker with overprocessed hair and a tight red dress that was three sizes too small across her rounded hips and breasts. Hugh pressed his lips together and forced himself to lift his cheeks into a smile. "Hugh. Nice to meet you."

"Art said you were handsome, but I never expected you to look like that guy on television. McDreamy? McSteamy?"

She laughed, and Hugh sighed. At least Art had promised not to tell her what he did for a living. *No more fan girls.* Based on the other patrons' eyes locked on the pre-playoff show on the large-screen televisions, and the lack of attention from any of the guys in the now-packed bar, Hugh assumed he was safe from being identified. *Might as well make the best of it.*

"Yeah, I've heard that. Patrick Dempsey," he answered. He was already bored. He glanced at the group of guys coming into the bar, each one louder than the next as they approached the bar. The blond waitress, Kat, picked up a tip from a table, then headed back in his direction, seating two more people on her way across the floor.

Kat appeared by his side and scowled at Tracie, then flashed a smile at Hugh. "What can I get you, darlin'? Another sidecar?"

If looks could kill. One more drink. Then I'm out of here.

"Get us both another one. On me," Tracie said, fluttering her false eyelashes.

On you? Right. Women like Tracie were made of hollow offers and a boatload of needs. Not that Hugh needed anyone to buy his drinks. He eyed his untouched beverage. *Not very observant, are you?* "No. I'm good." He nodded at his full drink, wishing he could escape the booth and sit by himself—or maybe at a table where the cute brunette would take another order he wouldn't drink.

"My pleasure," Tracie said.

There's that sex-hungry stare again. *No way. Not gonna happen.*

"Thank you," Hugh said, showing the manners his father, Hal Braden, an affluent thoroughbred horse breeder from Weston, Colorado, had instilled in him. With a bigger trust fund than he could ever spend, Hugh didn't need women buying him drinks, but dealing with the wrath of a woman who felt put off would be worse. He could spare another half hour, have a drink, then politely excuse himself.

He watched Kat return to the bar and whisper to Bree. Even her name was appealing. She wiped the counter with a serious look in her eyes, served up drink after drink, and dodged a guy putting his hand on hers—"Behave, Chip," she said with a shake of her head—all in a matter of seconds. She didn't look at any of the men at the bar. In fact, she seemed to be purposely shifting her eyes to the counter every time a guy spoke to her. She was the only person in the bar not smiling—besides him— and Hugh wondered why.

He turned his attention back to Tracie, who was rattling on about *Grey's Anatomy*. Hugh didn't watch television, and after Tracie finished her next drink, he looked at his watch with a loud and purposeful groan.

"Well, Tracie, this has been nice, but I'm afraid I have to run. I've got an early meeting tomorrow." He stood and extended his hand. "Thanks for coming out to meet me. I appreciate it."

She climbed from the booth. "I don't have my car here. A friend dropped me off. Can you drive me home?"

Are you freaking kidding me?

Kat appeared by his side again. "Leaving already?" She glanced at the fifty-dollar bill he'd left on the table.

"I'm afraid so. It's getting late," he said. "Thanks for everything."

Red wrapped her arm around his, and Hugh noticed Kat's eyes narrow.

"Right," Kat said. She snagged the money from the table and stalked back to the bar.

As Hugh pushed the door open for Tracie to pass through, he noticed Kat and Bree watching them leave. He smiled—and this time it wasn't forced. Kat waved. Bree turned away.

To continue reading, be sure to pick up the next
Weston Braden love story,
AND THEN THERE WAS US

Have you met the Seaside Summers crew?

Fall in love with Kurt and Leanna in

Read, Write, Love at Seaside

(Offered **free** in digital format at the time of this printing.
Price subject to change without notice.)

Chapter One

THE TIDE LAPPED at the sandy shore beyond the deck of the cedar-shingled bungalow where Kurt Remington sat on the deck of his cottage, fingers to keyboard, working on his latest manuscript. *Dark Times* was due to his agent at the end of the month, and Kurt came to his cottage in Wellfleet, Massachusetts, to hunker down for the summer and complete the project. He lived just outside of New York City and he wrote daily, sometimes for ten or twelve hours straight. In the summers, he liked the change of scenery the Cape offered and was inspired by the Cape's fresh air and the sounds of the sea.

He'd bought the estate of a local painter a few years earlier with the intent of renovating the artist's studio that sat nestled among a grouping of trees on the far side of the property. Initially, Kurt thought he might use the studio as a writing retreat separate from where he lived, with the idea that leaving the cottage to work might give him a chance to actually have a life and not feel pressure to write twenty-four-seven. What he found was that the studio was too far removed from the sights and sounds that inspired him, and it made him feel like even more of a recluse than he already was. He realized that it wasn't the location of his computer that pressured him. It was his internal drive and his love of writing that propelled his fingers to the keyboard every waking second. The idea of making the studio into a guest cottage crossed his mind, but that would indicate his desire to have guests, which would mean giving up his coveted writing time to entertain. So there it sat, awaiting...something. Though he had no idea what.

The cottage was built down a private road at the top of a dune, with a private beach below. A curtain of dense air settled around him. Kurt lifted his eyes long enough to scan the graying clouds and ponder the imminence of rain. It was seven twenty in the evening, and he'd been writing since nine o'clock that morning, as was his daily habit, right after his three-mile run, two cups of coffee, and a quick breeze through the newspaper and email. Once Kurt got into his writing zone each day, other than getting up to eat, he rarely changed his surroundings. The idea of moving inside and breaking his train of thought was unsettling.

He set his hands back on the keyboard and reread the last

few sentences of what would become his thirteenth thriller novel. A dog barked in the distance, and Kurt drew his thick, dark brows together without breaking the stride of his keystrokes. Kurt hadn't risen to the ranks of Patterson, King, and Grisham by being easily distracted.

"Pepper! Come on, boy!" A female voice sliced through his concentration. "Come on, Pepper. Where are you?"

Kurt's fingers hesitated for only a moment as she hollered; then he went right back to the killer lurking outside the window in his story.

"Pepper!" the woman yelled again. "Oh geez, Pepper, really?"

Kurt closed his eyes for a beat as the wind picked up. The woman's voice *was* distracting him. She was too close to ignore. *Get your mutt and move on.* He let out a breath and went back to work. Kurt craved silence. The quieter things were, the better he could hear his characters and think through their issues. He tried to ignore the sounds of splashing and continued writing.

"Pepper! No, Pepper!"

Great. He was hoping to squeeze in a few more hours of writing on the deck before taking a walk on the beach, but if that woman kept up her racket, he'd be forced to work inside— and if there was one thing Kurt hated, it was changing his surroundings while he was in the zone. Writing was an art that took total focus. He'd honed his craft with the efficiency of a drill sergeant, which was only fitting since his father was a four-star general.

More splashing.

"Oh no! Pepper? Pepper!"

The woman's panicked voice split his focus right down the center. He thought of his sister, Siena, and for a second he considered getting up to see if the woman's concern was valid. Then he remembered that his sister often overreacted. Women often overreacted.

"Pepper! Oh no!"

Being an older brother came with responsibilities that Kurt took seriously, as had been ingrained in him at a young age. That loud woman was someone's daughter. His conscience won over the battle for focus, and with a sigh, he pushed away from the table and went to the railing. He caught sight of the woman wading waist deep in the rough ocean waves.

"Pepper! Pepper, please come back!" she cried.

Kurt followed her gaze into deeper water, which was becoming rougher by the second as the clouds darkened and the wind picked up a notch. He didn't see a dog anywhere in the water. He scanned the empty beach—no dog there, either.

"Pepper! Please, Pep! Come on, boy!" She tumbled back with the next wave and fell on her butt, then struggled to find her footing.

Come on. Really? This, he didn't need. He watched her push through the crashing waves. She was shoulder deep. Kurt knew about the dangers of riptides and storms and wondered why she didn't. She had no business being out in the water with a storm brewing.

Drops of water dampened Kurt's arms. He swatted them away with a grimace, still watching the woman.

"Please come back, Pepper!"

The rain came in a heavy drizzle now. *For the love of...* Kurt spun around, gathered his computer and notes and took them inside. He checked to see that he'd saved his file before pushing the laptop safely back from the edge of the counter, then turned back to the French doors. *I could close the doors and go right back to work.* He eyed his laptop.

"Pepper!"

She sounded farther away now. Maybe she'd moved on. He went back out on the deck to see if she'd come to her senses.

"Pep—" Another wave toppled her over. She was deeper now and seemed to be pulled by the current.

"Hey!" Kurt hollered in an effort to dissuade her from going out any deeper. She must not have heard him. He scanned the water again and saw a flash of something about thirty feet away from her. *Your stupid dog.* Dogs were smelly, they shed, and they needed time and attention. All reasons why Kurt was not a fan of the creatures.

The rain picked up with the gusty wind. *Good grief.* He grabbed a towel from inside and stomped down the steps, *Dark Times* begrudgingly pushed aside.

LEANNA BRAY WAS wet, cold, and floundering. Literally. She'd been floundering for twenty-eight years, so this was nothing new, but being pummeled by rain, wind, and waves, chasing a dog that never listened? That was new.

"Pepp—" A wave knocked her off her feet and she went under the water, taking a mouthful of saltwater along with her. She tumbled head down beneath the surface.

Now Pepper and I will both drown. Freaking perfect.

Something grabbed her arm, and she reflexively fought against it, sucking in another mouthful of salty water as she broke through the surface, arms flailing, choking, and pushing against the powerful hand that yanked her to her feet.

"You okay?" A deep, annoyed voice carried over the din of

the crashing waves.

Cough. Cough. "Yeah. I—" *Cough. Cough.* "My dog." She blinked and blinked, trying to clear the saltwater and rain from her eyes. The man's mop of wet, dark hair came into focus. He held tightly to her arm while scanning the water in the direction of where she'd last seen Pepper. His clothes stuck to his body like a second skin, riding the ripples of his impressive chest and arms as he held her above the surface with one arm around her ribs.

"Come on." She coughed as he plowed through the pounding surf with her clutched against his side. She slid down his body, and he lifted her easily into his arms, carrying her like he might carry a child, pressing her to his chest as he fought against the waves.

She pushed against his chest, feeling ridiculous and helpless...and maybe a little thankful, but she was ignoring that emotion in order to save Pepper.

"My dog! I need to get my dog!" she hollered.

Mr. Big, Tall, and Stoic didn't say a word. He set her on the wet sand and tossed her a rain-soaked towel. "It was dry." He pointed behind her to a wooden staircase. "Go up to the deck."

She dropped the towel and plowed past him toward the water. "I gotta get my dog."

He snagged her by the arm and glared at her with the brightest blue eyes she'd ever seen—and a stare so dark she swallowed her voice.

"Go." He pointed to the stairs again. "I'll get your dog." He took a step toward the water, and she pushed past him again.

"You don't have t—"

He scooped her into his arms again and carried her to the stairs. "If you fight me, your dog will drown. He won't last in

321

this much longer."

She pushed at his chest again. "Let me go!"

He set her down on the stairs. "The waves will pull you under. I'll get your dog. Please stay here."

Her heart thundered against her ribs as she watched him stalk off and plow through the waves as if he were indestructible. She stood in the rain on the bottom stair, huddled beneath the wet towel, squinting to see him through the driving rain. She finally spotted him deep in the sea, wrapping his arms around Pepper—the dog who never let anyone carry him. He rounded his shoulders, shielding Pepper as he made his way back through the wild waves.

She ran to the edge of the water, shivering, tears in her eyes. "Thank you!" She reached for Pepper and the dog whined, pressing his trembling body closer to the guy.

"You have a leash?"

She shook her head. Her wet hair whipped across her cheek, and she turned her back to the wind. "He doesn't like them."

He took her by the arm again. "Come on." He led her up the stairs to a wooden deck, opened a French door, and leaned in close, talking over the sheeting rain.

"Go on in."

She stepped onto pristine hardwood. The warm cottage smelled of coffee and something sweet and masculine, like a campfire. She reached for Pepper. Pepper whined again and pressed against the man's chest.

"He…" Her teeth chattered from the cold. "He must be scared."

"I'll get you a towel." He eyed the dog in his arms and shook his head before disappearing up a stairwell.

Leanna scoped out the open floor plan of the cozy cottage,

looking for signs of *crazy*. How crazy could he be? He'd just rescued her and Pepper, and Pepper already seemed to be quite attached to him. *He went into the water in a storm without an ounce of fear. The man was crazy.* It dawned on her that she'd done the same thing, but she knew *she* wasn't crazy. She'd had no choice. To her right was a small kitchen with expensive-looking light wood cabinets and fancy molding. A laptop sat open beside two neatly stacked notebooks on the shiny marble countertop. The screen was dark, and she had an urge to touch a button and bring the laptop to life, but she didn't really want to know if there was something awful on there. He could have been watching porn, for all she knew, although he hadn't checked her out once, even with her wet T-shirt and shorter-than-short cut offs. She couldn't decide if that was gentlemanly or creepy.

She shifted her thoughts away from the computer to the quaint breakfast nook to her left. Her eyes traveled past a little alcove with two closed doors and a set of stairs by the kitchen to the white-walled living room. There was not a speck of clutter anywhere. A pair of flip-flops sat by the front door, perfectly lined up against the wall beside a pair of running shoes. She located the source of the campfire smell. A gorgeous two-story stone fireplace covered most of the wall adjacent to an oversized brown couch. There was a small stack of firewood in a metal holder beside the hearth. The cottage was surprisingly warm considering there wasn't a fire in the fireplace. Dark wood bookshelves ran the length of the far wall, from floor to ceiling, complete with a rolling ladder. The room was full of textures—a chenille blanket was folded neatly across the back of the couch, a thick, brown shag rug sat before the stone fireplace, and an intricately carved wooden table was placed before the couch.

Leanna had a thing for textures, and right now she was texturing the beautiful hardwood with drops of water. She snagged a dishtowel from the kitchen counter as the man came back downstairs with Pepper cradled in his arms like a baby and wrapped in a big fluffy towel.

The possibility of him being crazy went out the door. *Crazy people don't carry dogs like babies.*

He shifted Pepper to one arm and handed her a fresh towel. "Here. I'm Kurt, by the way."

Pepper sat up in his arms, panting happily. *Show-off.*

"Thank you. I'm Leanna. That's Pepper." She tried to mop up the floor around her. Every swipe of the towel brought more drips from her sopping-wet clothing. "I'm sorry about this. For the mess. And my dog. And..." She frantically wiped the floor with the dishrag in one hand, using the fisted towel in the other to scrub her clothes, trying desperately to stop the river that ran from her clothes to his no-longer-pristine floor. She lifted her gaze. He had a slightly amused smile on his very handsome face. She rose to her feet with a defeated sigh.

"I'm so sorry, and thank you for rescuing Pepper."

He glanced at his laptop, and that amused look quickly turned to pinched annoyance. His lips pressed into a tight line, and when he glanced at her again, it was with a brooding look, before stepping forward and closing his laptop.

"You should have"—Pepper barked in his ear; he closed his eyes and exhaled—"had the dog on a leash."

The dog.

"He hates it. He hates listening, leashes, lots of things." Pepper licked Kurt's cheek. "Except you, I guess."

Kurt winced and set Pepper on the floor. "Sit," he said in a deep, stern voice.

Pepper sat at his feet.

"How did you do that? He never listens."

He dried Pepper's feet with the towel, apparently ignoring the question.

"Labradoodle?"

You know dogs? She was intrigued by the dichotomy of him. He was sharp, brooding, and maybe even a little cold, yet Pepper followed him to the fireplace as if he were handing out doggy biscuits. Leanna couldn't help but notice the way Kurt's wet jeans hugged his body. *His very hot body.* He crouched before the fireplace, his shirt clinging tightly to his broad back, his sleeves hitched up above his bulging biceps, and she made out the outline of a tattoo on his upper arm.

"Yeah, Labradoodle. How'd you know? He looks like a wet mutt right now."

He shrugged, expertly fashioning a teepee of kindling, then starting a small fire. "Where's your place?" He slid an annoyed look at Pepper and shook his head.

"Um, my place?" she said, distracted as much by Pepper's obedience as by Kurt's tattoo. *What is that? A snake? Dragon?*

He looked at her with that amused glint in his eyes again. "House? Cottage? Campsite?"

"Oh, cottage. Sorry." She felt her cheeks flush. "It's about a mile and a half from here. Seaside. Do you know it? My parents own it. I'm just staying for the summer. I've known the other people in the community forever, and Pepper likes it there."

He looked back at the fireplace, the amusement in his expression replaced with seriousness. "Come over by the fire. Warm up."

She tossed the towels on the counter and joined him by the fire, shivering as she warmed her hands.

He kept his eyes trained on the fire.

"Did you drive here?" He picked up a log in one big hand and settled it on the fire.

"No. I biked."

"Biked?"

"I bike here a couple times each week with Pepper, but we usually go the other way down the beach. Pepper just took off this time. I left my bike by the public beach entrance."

His eyes slid to Pepper, then back to the fire. "I don't know Seaside, but let me change and I'll drive you home." He headed toward the stairs with Pepper on his heels. Kurt stopped and stared at the dog. Pepper panted for all he was worth. Kurt looked at Leanna, as if she could control the dog.

Fat chance. "He's not really an obedient pet." She shrugged.

Kurt picked up Pepper and brought him to Leanna. "Hold his collar."

Okay, then. She looped her finger in Pepper's collar and watched Kurt go into the kitchen and wipe the floor with the towel he'd given her. Then he wiped the counter with a sponge before disappearing into the alcove by the kitchen. He returned with a laundry basket, tossed the dirty towels in, and then returned the basket to where he'd found it and climbed the stairs.

"Guess he doesn't really like dirt...or dogs after all," she said to Pepper.

Pepper broke free and ran up the stairs after Kurt.

Leanna closed her eyes with a loud sigh.

Just shoot me now.

To continue reading, please buy
Read, Write, Love at Seaside

More Books By Addison Cole

Sweet with Heat Big-Family Romance Collection

Sweet with Heat: Weston Bradens

A Love So Sweet
Our Sweet Destiny
Unraveling the Truth About Love
The Art of Loving Lacy
Promise of a New Beginning
And Then There Was Us

Sweet with Heat: Seaside Summers

Read, Write, Love at Seaside
Dreaming at Seaside
Hearts at Seaside
Sunsets at Seaside
Secrets at Seaside
Nights at Seaside
Embraced at Seaside
Seized by Love at Seaside
Lovers at Seaside
Whispers at Seaside

Sweet with Heat: Bayside Summers

Sweet Love at Bayside
Sweet Passions at Bayside
Sweet Heat at Bayside
Sweet Escape at Bayside

Stand-Alone Women's Fiction Novels
by Melissa Foster (Addison Cole's steamy alter ego)

Chasing Amanda (mystery/suspense)
Come Back to Me (mystery/suspense)
Have No Shame (historical fiction/romance)
Megan's Way (literary fiction)
Traces of Kara (psychological thriller)
Where Petals Fall (suspense)

Acknowledgments

There are so many people to thank for their support, energy, enthusiasm, and inspiration, not the least of which are my readers. It's difficult to convey how much your messages inspire me. I hope you continue to enjoy my stories, and please keep your letters and emails coming.

I am indebted to my team of editors and proofreaders: Kristen Weber, Penina Lopez, Juliette Hill, Elaini Caruso, and Justinn Harrison. I'm under no ill-conceived impressions that I could complete this process without each of you. Thank you for allowing me to work with you.

To my girlfriends—far and near—you have pulled me through intimate scenes, forehead-slapping frustrations, and days when I've been too tired to think straight, and you've done it with levity and grace. Thank you for always being there. You know who you are, and I appreciate you.

To my mother and my children, you are so kind to put up with my crazy schedule. Thank you for your support. Last but never least, thank you to my hunky husband, Les, who may or may not be my inspiration for my hunky heroes. He always wants to know, and I'll never tell.

Meet Addison

Addison Cole is the sweet alter ego of *New York Times* and *USA Today* bestselling and award-winning author Melissa Foster. She enjoys writing humorous and deeply emotional contemporary romance without explicit sex scenes or harsh language. Addison spends her summers on Cape Cod, where she dreams up wonderful love stories in her house overlooking Cape Cod Bay.

Visit Addison on her website or chat with her on social media. Addison enjoys discussing her books with book clubs and reader groups and welcomes an invitation to your event.

www.AddisonCole.com
www.facebook.com/AddisonColeAuthor

CPSIA information can be obtained
at www.ICGtesting.com
Printed in the USA
LVHW110838070819
626805LV00002BA/206/P

9 781948 868198